MW00780340

ROAD KILL:
TEXAS HORROR BY TEXAS WRITERS VOL 3

Edited by
E. R. Bills

Associate Editor
Misty Contreras

A HellBound Books Publishing LLC Book
Houston TX

A HellBound Books LLC
Publication

www.hellboundbookspublishing.com

Printed in the United States of America

Acknowledgments

Special thanks to our family and friends for nurturing and putting up with the more acute symptoms and actual manifestations of our wayward and unconventional spirits.

Cover photo of automobile by Andrew Smith of Seattle, Washington, USA.

Foreword

This, the third volume of ***Road Kill: Texas Horror by Texas Writers***, features a goodly number of Lone Star authors that you're going to be seeing big things from in the future. Some, like Jeremy Hepler, are already turning (and decapitating) heads. Others, like Madison Estes and Shawna Borman, are brand new and look to be crafting a haunting brand of their own soon. Then, of course, there are the established, creepy hands, like former indie horror director and producer Bret McCormick, *Forgotten Horrors* creator Michael H. Price and *HellBound Books Publishing LLC* progenitor himself, James H. Longmore. Well established, or brand new, the voices recorded in these pages will be drawing blood at a bookstand near you in the days to come, so tread carefully. Here there be monsters.

Enjoy this collection.
And keep reading.

E. R. Bills
September 29, 2018

CONTENTS

A Real Haunting
by Madison Estes

*T**he following story is inspired by real life reports regarding paranormal activity on Bowden Road. All other hauntings mentioned in this story are also based on true reported sightings. The characters appearing in this work are fictitious. Any resemblance to real persons, living or dead, is purely coincidental.*

Tall weeds around leaning headstones. Dry leaves crunched under our feet. My sister Jen set up one of the video cameras as we tried to find a comfortable place to conduct the opening dialogue. After filming some general shots of the cemetery, we went back to the car to do a cursory interview.

"We are at Martha Chapel Cemetery," Jen said. "We've set up video recording equipment around the area, including both the cemetery and several points along Bowden Road. Aaron, would you please describe what we're doing here?"

"We're here to document evidence of paranormal activity," I offered.

She turned the camera around to face herself for a moment, a ridiculous close-up.

"He means we're ghost hunters."

I turned the camera back to me, shaking my head but not able to hold back a smile.

"Amateur paranormal researchers. We're not just looking for ghosts, but any evidence of paranormal occurrences, particularly those related to the afterlife."

"You're not an amateur," Jen corrected. "You've done this before. Can you tell us a little bit about one of your excursions, perhaps the Woman Hollering Creek trip?"

"Oh yes," I replied. "*La Llorona*, or 'The Weeping Woman', between San Antonio and Seguin on I-10." I stroked my beard, remembering that weekend to be a rather dull camping trip where I met with dozens of mosquitos, but no apparitions. "There are a lot of variations on the story, but the basic premise is that there is a female ghost who weeps at night because her children were drowned or killed and tossed in the river. It's probably just a cautionary tale to keep kids from playing in the water. There is hardly any evidence of apparitions there besides personal accounts."

"What about Moody Mansion?"

"Eh, most reports are just of disembodied footsteps and ambiguous discolorations that have shown up in photographs. There is no other documented evidence of paranormal activity in Moody Mansion. It's an eerie Romanesque mansion just begging for a good old fashioned ghost story… but unfortunately, it seems that is not the case."

"That's a shame."

"Yeah, you're probably better off checking out Hotel Galvez if you want a good Galveston haunt, although I didn't have any luck there either."

"What other places have you investigated?" My sister was attempting to sound serious. If we did get evidence, she didn't want it discredited because we looked like we didn't know what we were doing. Although I'd done this many times before, it was all new for her.

"I've done hunting expeditions at the Driskill Hotel, the Spaghetti Warehouse in Houston, the Granbury Opera House, Parker Cemetery, the Bonner house west of Lufkin and Inverness Castle in Fort Worth."

"So you've mostly stayed local, exploring haunted locations in Texas?"

"Mostly. I've been to a few places in Louisiana too— Myrtles Plantation, LaLaurie House, the Bentley Hotel—and I've gotten the same unimpressive results. Vague photographs, purely static EVPs and negligible EMF readings."

"That sounds disappointing."

"It is," I said. I felt the disappointment anew as I admitted the failure of those investigations. "I've studied ghost hunting procedures and interviewed quite a few paranormal experts myself. But I've never come close to anything conclusive. It is disappointing."

"So why do it?" she asked, knowing full well why. It was the same reason she was here too. But this was for the camera, for others who might watch this if we did gather substantial evidence. We had to be open and honest about everything, including our motivations. The tone of the conversation became somber.

"I think you have to be patient," I started, and then reconsidered. "My brother was killed in a car crash last year. I barely escaped the accident myself. That night has stayed with me, consuming my thoughts. I want to know about the afterlife and if there is anything beyond death."

"Why Bowden Road? Why did you choose this place specifically?"

"I think my brother Alex could try to contact us here. There has been an influx of reported hauntings since he passed away. Bowden Road is less than ten miles from the crash site. I want to know if this is more than a coincidence."

"What are you hoping to get out of this?" she asked. I paused, wanting to express this just right. I thought of the uncertainty that I lived with every day, wondering where Alex was, or if he was anywhere. I thought of all the failures that had come before, and why I still persisted. I rolled my shoulders back and looked right into the camera.

"Irrefutable proof of the afterlife. Contact with spiritual entities. A real haunting. It's all I want. I want to know there is something beyond death."

"I hope you get it," she said, a wistful smile on her face. She glanced out the window. Our back-up had just pulled up in a Nissan Altima.

"So who's joining us?" Jen continued. She turned the camera on our arriving group member, a red-headed woman in her mid-twenties. She wore black from head-to-toe and had two noticeable eyebrow piercings.

"That's Roxy Halton, a retrocognitive—it means she sees things in the past. We'll also have Sahria McNamara joining us, a clairvoyant. She sees dead people, and she's also into demonology and the occult."

"Wait, I thought there were supposed to be three psychics?"

"The precognitive cancelled on us."

"What does a precognitive do?" Jen asked. I thought she was inquiring for the sake of the documentary, but her eyebrows crooked like she was confused.

"He senses things that haven't happened yet."

"Wait, so you mean the only one that can see the future is staying home? That's comforting." She shook her head as a worried expression crossed her face. "Did he say anything to you about why he's not coming?"

I shrugged. "Just some ominous message about visions of impending doom. You know, the usual."

"Haha, very funny," Jen said, playfully slapping my arm. Her tone sounded annoyed but she smiled.

Roxy waved at us as she approached the vehicle. I got out and shook her hand. We exchanged greetings, and she turned to Jen. When they shook hands, Roxy tensed her jaw and grimaced.

"Something wrong?" Jen asked.

"No, I'm fine," she said, reverting back to the friendly smile she'd had before. "I think I'll walk around, get a feel for the place."

She passed through the cemetery gates, and Jen and I exchanged confused looks.

"That was strange," I said. Jen nodded.

Sahria showed up fifteen minutes later. It was a pleasant meeting compared to the peculiarity of Roxy's exchange with Jen. Sahria was a middle-aged woman with a serene disposition. Her gentle handshake sent waves of calamity through me, and she hugged Jen despite the camera pointed in her face.

"Sorry, you just looked like you needed a hug. I'm a bit of an empath."

Jen smiled. "That's okay. Maybe I did need one. Maybe we'll all need one after this is over."

We chuckled over that. We talked over the financials—Roxy and Sahria weren't there out of the goodness of their hearts after all—and then they set up the séance.

The four of us sat around a Ouija board, illuminated by white candles as the scent of sage wafted through the air. Anticipation beget disillusionment. Strange, low moaning emerged from a distance, but I rationalized that it was probably animals or even teenagers making out in the woods. I did feel a fifth presence at one point. It was only a feeling though. I couldn't document it. I couldn't even really explain it. We sat there for hours spinning the planchette in circles, no rational messages coming through no matter how much we asked Alex to speak to us. At least Roxy and Sahria were honest about the spirits being quiet, and didn't try to fake it so I felt like I got my money's worth.

After the unsuccessful séance, I decided to go around and check the cameras. I played back some of the footage, checked on the camera angles and made sure they were still rolling. A few minutes later, I heard a scream.

I raced back to the place we had gathered earlier, and saw Jen laying on the ground with her hand over her heart. She had a shocked expression on her face and was panting.

"What happened?" I asked. I knelt beside her and brought her into my arms. Her whole body trembled.

"I saw him," she said. "Aaron, I saw our brother."

She rambled incoherently as she tried to describe what happened. I had to ask her twice to slow down. Sahria told her to take deep breaths, and once Jen calmed down, she told us the details.

"I was looking toward the woods, I just felt a presence, you know? Like during the séance, except a lot stronger. So I walked toward it, not really expecting anything. And then I saw Alex. I wanted to call out to him, or to call out to all of you to come with me, but I was afraid if I did he would disappear. So I approached him quietly. I said his name, and he walked up to me. I touched his hand, and then when I thought we were going to hug, his eyes turned red and he scared me, so I screamed. And then he vanished."

"I knew it," Roxy said. "I saw it. When I shook your hand earlier, I had a vision of you. I saw a guy who looked like Aaron with red eyes touching your hand. Wow, this is crazy."

Roxy seemed almost as agitated as Jen. She pulled on the sleeve of her jacket. "I've never predicted the future before. I only see the past, usually the distant past. Time must work differently here."

"That concerns me," Sahria said. "Time manipulation is more common with a demonic presence than an apparition. Tell me Jen, what did it feel like when you touched him?"

"It was...warm. Comforting. It felt gentle and kind."

"Are you sure it was warm?"

Jen nodded.

"That's bad. Ghostly entities are supposed to sap heat from the room, not generate it. Heat spots are typically demonic. It could be a ghost, but it is sounding more and more like a demon."

"But it could be Alex though, right?" I asked. When Jen mentioned seeing our brother, I couldn't believe it. Just as quickly, I didn't want to let the thought go.

"Even if it is him, it may not be the same Alex you remember. People can change personalities as they die due to the trauma of their death. They can also become tainted by demonic forces after death, as I suspect is the case here. You said his eyes looked red. That's a sign of spiritual hostility, usually by demons or ghosts that have been driven insane by anger, vengeance, or guilt."

Sahria paused for a moment and took both of Jen's hands in her own. She gave her a sad smile and spoke in a soft voice.

"It's not Alex. I'm almost sure of it. Demons target people who are desperate to connect with a deceased loved one. You may receive your answers about the afterlife, but it will come with a cost. A cost I am not willing to pay, not even for ten times what you paid me. I'm sorry, but I'm leaving."

"I'm leaving too," Roxy said in a scared voice. She tugged on her ear and glanced around with paranoid eyes. "Things are about to get bad. I can feel it. And the fact that I can feel it is freaking me out."

I nodded. I couldn't make them stay. The place was starting to unnerve me as well, and I had wanted this. I turned to Jen and saw a troubled scowl on her face. Her arms wrapped around her abdomen as if she had a stomach ache. She looked up at me.

"I know you want proof of the afterlife," Jen said. "I know you want something to believe in—but after hearing Sahria, I think I agree with her. I don't think this is Alex. It may look like him, but it's not."

I groaned. My eyes surveyed the landscape as I thought it over. All of the evidence pointed to something paranormal going on. I was as excited and curious as I was fearful. I'd only hoped I might see Alex. Any contact with the other side would have been a victory, and the chance to see my brother again made it worth staying despite the danger. Trying to persuade Jen would be too challenging, though. Roxy and Sahria had freaked her out. Contacting Alex at the risk of frightening Jen was too high of a price. I would come back later on my own. I nodded my head and agreed it was time to leave.

"Thank God," Jen said. "I thought this road would never end."

I saw the Bowden Rd. street sign. We both let out sighs as we turned onto 1791.

"Are you really okay with us leaving early?" Jen asked.

I shrugged. What was done was done. There was no going back now that we'd packed everything up. We drove in silence for a few minutes when I felt Jen touch my arm to get my attention.

"Do you see that?" Jen asked. She pointed to a sign that said Bowden Rd.

"That's weird. Guess somebody fucked up," I said as we drove past it.

"No, that's more than just weird. Stop the car and go back, I want to record this."

"Are you serious? I thought you wanted to leave."

Indecision flickered across her features. She bit her thumb, and then nodded. "Yeah, I do. Forget it. Let's just keep going."

We drove a few minutes more. I thought it strange that we didn't pass any side streets since 1791 was full of them, but I was tired and didn't think much of it, only that perhaps we'd gone in the wrong direction or that there was more distance between the streets than I remembered seeing on Mapquest. I didn't usually come this way, so it was unfamiliar terrain. Jen suddenly grabbed my arm and squeezed.

"Look!" she shouted, pointing to the street sign we were approaching. Bowden Rd. Again.

I slowed down and then pulled over to park. I took my hands off the steering wheel and sat there numb, trying to comprehend it.

"What the hell is going on, Aaron?" she asked. Her voice squeaked when she panicked. She maintained her tight grip on my arm. I wished Sahria was here to tell us what was happening. I imagined the answer would be the same though: demons. It made sense. If demons could play with time, surely they could play with geography too. My heart pounded in my chest, but I didn't want to scare Jen any more than she already was.

"Maybe we got turned around," I said, trying to keep a normal voice. It was a lame excuse, but I couldn't think of anything else.

"We haven't even turned around," Jen replied. "So that's impossible. And where are all the side streets? I didn't see any, and we drove long enough that there should have been a side street. I'm really freaked out."

"Well...let's just keep going. The road has to end sometime."

"Does it?" she asked. I couldn't answer her. We both stared at the sign for a moment. I put my hands on the wheel. Before I could bring us back onto the road, the sign blurred, and then the letters shuffled. The letter B dissolved. The W rotated to become an M, and the rest of the letters rearranged themselves to form a different word.

Demons.

"Aaron," Jen gasped. Her hands covered her mouth. She brought her legs up to her chest and whimpered.

"I see it," I said as we pulled back onto the road. My hands trembled. I pressed hard on the pedal, bringing us from 30 mph to 70. I didn't know or care what the speed limit was. Something as normal as a speeding ticket would be a welcome intrusion into whatever we were experiencing. A minute later we passed another street sign. *Demons Road.*

Jen didn't say anything, but she was curled into a ball and trembling. She buried her face in her hands.

"It's okay," I said. I was tempted to floor it, not that I thought it would do any good. "It's fine."

"It's not fine," she said in a low voice, as though she were in a trance. "It's definitely not fine."

We drove all night and we still didn't escape Demons Road. We passed the same sign over and over again. Our gas dwindled. We both tried to ignore the low gas light signal, but I had to admit the futility before we wasted all our gas and ended up completely stranded. Jen tried calling for help on both of our cell phones, but, of course, there was no reception.

"What do we do?" Jen asked. I hated that she thought I had all the answers. I'd been on ghost hunting expeditions before, but never a successful one. Sahria was the only one with knowledge about demons.

Dawn was breaking, and I was grateful we would be out of the darkness soon. A part of me felt that maybe we could drive away and hit 1791 if we just waited until daytime. Surely strange occurrences like this could not abide daylight. Unexplainable stories usually took place at night, and were rationalized and forgotten the next day.

"I don't know," I said. "I guess we could start watching the footage we recorded. See if we can find anything useful. Then try to leave again in the daytime."

Jen nodded. In that moment, she probably would have agreed to anything I said. I sensed she was just grateful I proposed a plan. She pulled a couple of cameras from the back, and we watched recordings. I didn't see any orbs or strange lights. There was nothing of importance. The odd sensations we all experienced and the psychic visions couldn't be documented.

Although something was happening, there was no proof of any of it. I told Jen that once we got back on the road, I wanted her to record the road signs.

"Maybe if we try to record it, it will stop?" Jen asked. I shrugged.

"Not the worst idea," I said. "Demons are probably camera shy."

There was a nervous edge to her laugh, but the joke did seem to lighten the mood. With the sun rising and no street sign in sight, the anxiety began to taper off. I began to think we might be alright.

Recording the road didn't help. We drove until we ran out of gas. We didn't see a sign again until the car rolled to a full stop. Then the same sign popped up out of nowhere, as though mocking us. I rubbed my temples, feeling a headache coming on.

"So we walk now?" Jen asked.

I shrugged. "We walk or we wait, I guess. And we try calling for help again."

"I don't think you get reception in purgatory," she quipped. She took a swig from her Aquafina bottle.

"I'm glad you can joke about this. And you need to save the water."

We packed up the remaining water and food and left everything else. We trekked for miles. The same sign followed us like an obnoxious relative that can't take a subtle hint, or knows they are annoying and just doesn't care. Realizing this plan wasn't working, I suggested we try going through the woods.

"Are you serious? After what I saw last night?"

"Well, walking into a forest full of demons isn't exactly my idea of a good time, but neither is the highway to hell. Or the backwoods side road to hell.

Either way, we need to change our strategy because this isn't working."

Hiking through the woods proved to be just as futile as travelling down the road. Every half mile or so, we'd end up back on the same road, the Demons Road sign waiting for us like a creepy butler.

"I give up," she said. She leaned against one of the trees beside the road. We were exhausted, and the air was getting warmer despite the approaching dusk. We agreed to rest for the night. I tried checking my phone for reception. I noticed that the day, month and year had changed to August of last year, the day Alex died.

My stomach twisted in a knot. I asked Jen if I could use her phone to try to get a call out. I checked the date and saw that it was normal. I smiled out of nervousness as I returned her phone. Her tired, defeated face still managed to smile back. I couldn't bring myself to tell her about my phone.

"Aaron! Aaron! Wake up!"

I hear Alex crying out, but I'm too out of it to move, either because I'm still drunk off my ass or I'm too dazed from the crash. Perhaps it's both. He's jostling me with one hand, trying to wake me. The smell of smoke registers, and after a second of initial panic, I react. One of the backdoors is hanging open, so I just roll out of the backseat and collapse onto the ground. Alex's screams escalate. I lift my head and try to see what's going on, but everything spins. I see doubles of everything: two smashed cars, fists beating against glass windows, then two sudden explosions. I'm thrown back from the impact of the blast. Hot metal scorches my chest and abdomen, causing second and third-degree burns that will linger for months. But I'm alive because

Alex woke me up, and he's dead because I didn't realize he was trapped until it was too late.

"Aaron. Aaron. Wake up."

Jen shook me awake. We walked miles before we slept, and woke up in exactly the same place we started. Our car was visible not far from the street sign. I sighed.

"I don't know what to do, Jen," I said. I shook my head. "God, I'm so sorry I dragged you out here. This is all my fault."

"I'm glad you did," she said. She put her dainty hand in my large, hairy one. "I wouldn't want you to go through this alone."

Her choice of words combined with the hellish memory my psyche just conjured gave me a new perspective on our situation. I didn't want to propose the idea, but I had to. The road looked infinite in both directions. The woods were a useless detour. We had no provisions, no gas, and no other options.

"I think I do need to go through this alone."

"What?" Her eyes widened. Her voice was so vulnerable then, I almost wished I could take it back.

"What happened to Alex was my fault. If it is Alex, then I need to confront him alone. Maybe then he can forgive me, or get revenge, or do whatever he needs to in order to settle this."

"And if it's not Alex?" she asked.

"If it's a demon, maybe it can only follow one of us. I think it's feeding on my guilt. If I'm not with you, maybe you can get away."

"That's a big if."

"What else can we do, Jen? We're running out of options."

She glanced toward the woods, perhaps wondering if we might try that way again. We exchanged skeptical looks, both believing that it would be another exercise in futility. She bit her lip and then agreed with my plan. Her arms wrapped around me tightly before we said good-bye. I walked away from her. She followed me and hugged me again.

"Be careful, okay?" she said. She buried her face in my chest and trembled. She kissed me on the cheek as tears formed in her eyes. "I really don't think it's Alex."

It felt like days since I parted ways with Jen, but it had only been hours. The heat emanating from the asphalt blistered my feet, so I trailed beside the road in the grass, where it wasn't quite as hot. The road was long and winding. The idea that I could ever reach the end seemed ludicrous. Each step I took seemed to require more steps, but I couldn't stop. I had to face Alex. I had to help him move on. Maybe then Jen and I could go home.

The road taunted me, whispering that I would die alone. The deer and other wildlife that seemed all around us before were gone. The birds went silent. The wind became still. I may have been the only living thing for miles.

Sweat dripped down the curve of my spine as the scorching sun continued to beat down on me. My clothes clung to my flesh like a second skin. I tore the cotton t-shirt off and used it to mop up the wetness. The cloth absorbed the moisture that rolled off my burned, scarred skin. A faint smile spread across my dry lips as I beheld a glorious sight: Martha Chapel Cemetery.

The gates squeaked as I pulled them open. The sky darkened as I entered. A grey twilight encompassed the sky above. I searched for a presence. Whether or not it was Alex, I would face it head on.

"Alex! Are you here? It's me, Aaron," I said.

Hope filled me when I saw a faint shadow behind a tree. I hurried to the other side of it and found him standing yards away.

Stumbling across him in this way felt too easy, but I couldn't help going up to him. I tripped over an old, crumbling headstone and fell onto the ground.

Alex was on me in an instant. He jumped on top of me and plunged something into my side. He repeated the motion again and again. I screamed each time the sharp object penetrated my flesh. Blood tears streamed from his bright red eyes. He wept as he smiled.

"Alex, stop!" I managed to get out. I crawled away from him, and when I glanced up, he had disappeared. I didn't understand why he attacked or why he vanished so quickly. It didn't make sense.

"Who are you?" I screamed. "Who are you? What do you want? *Tell me what you want!*"

There was no answer. I searched for something to stop the bleeding. I found one of the bags with our gear sitting in a patch of tall grass. I didn't remember missing anything when we packed up, but it was possible I left something useful in there. I thought perhaps it was the bag that held the first aid kit, although I wasn't counting on it.

I unzipped it and found a single voice recorder. Pain jolted my entire upper body. I felt lightheaded from blood loss. A sense of dread filled me as I pressed play.

Who are you? What do you want? Tell me what you want!

I swallowed hard as the recording played back my own voice. Alex, or the Alex-like entity, came up from behind one of the trees, smirking. His hand toyed with a long piece of jagged glass. Windshield glass. He ran his fingers along the edge. He strolled toward me as Jen's doubtful voice emerged from the recorder.

I really don't think it's Alex.

He opened his jacket, revealing red, raised skin. The angry burn scars melded together in intersecting lines like spider webs of flesh. I knew these scars well, despite doing everything I could to avoid seeing them on a daily basis. Beneath that disfigurement, blood trickled from small punctures in the gut, confirming what I suspected. It wasn't Alex, or a demon. This thing was me.

What are you hoping to get out of this?

Jen's voice again. The recorder shook in my trembling hand as the voice log continued, answering her question.

Irrefutable proof of the afterlife. Contact with spiritual entities. A real haunting. It's all I want. I want to know there is something beyond death.

An energy surrounded us, permeating my body. Somehow I could feel myself splitting, separating, becoming two entities at once. I was both alive and dead, a person and an apparition. He was me, and I was him. Although he was my future, we both co-existed in that same moment.

Time must work differently here, Roxy's voice ventured, as I plunged the windshield glass into my past self. The glass tore into my gut, ripping open my scarred abdomen. Blood sprayed from the wound. I screamed as I tried to apply pressure, but the red liquid gushed out, completely coating my hands within seconds. He sunk the glass shard into my gut again, and I instinctively tried to kick him. I knew I was going to die, but acceptance of the inevitable didn't mitigate the pain or instinct for self-preservation. It only lessened the fear. Blood dripped from the jagged glass onto the blades of grass. A smirk graced the apparition's face. That would soon be me, grinning down as I watched myself writhe in agony and die.

"You'll never feel whole until you know," it said to me. "Neither will Jen. This is the only way to gain the answers you seek. You'll see."

"I know," I said. It had become so obvious. He knew that I knew, yet I confirmed our thoughts just the same. "This is the only way," I repeated, closing my eyes for the final time.

Two weeks later, Jen is alone in her bedroom at her desk. I watch her as she documents in the expedition log how she woke up alone in the middle of Demons Road with all the evidence lying a few feet away from her.

Maybe I could have been more subtle and left it on the side of the road, but I wasn't about to let her leave without the evidence I gave my life for. She would have the answers we both wanted so badly. She deserves it. She deserves a lot more, too, but this is all I have left to give her. Perhaps she will gain closure as well. I hope so.

She is going through the evidence we collected— EVP recordings, EMF readings and video footage of the repeating signs. She watches the interview we did at the cemetery. She notices a white mist in the background of the video that wasn't there before. She hits pause and zooms in. She presses play, and the figure she must assume is Alex appears. Only now she sees the burn marks along my chest and realizes it is actually me. She covers her mouth in shock.

"What are you hoping to get out of this?" Jen asks, her tone seeming far too joyful and optimistic in retrospect. My eyes possess a heaviness I didn't notice the first time I watched the playback. They're bloodshot. Now all they possess is knowledge, a knowledge something like contentment. But I know why the dead are rarely content.

A real haunting. That's all I want.

Luke's Lost Manuscript
by Jeremy Hepler

In contrast to the rusty, bumper-less, dull gold '64 Plymouth Belvedere that he sat in, and the stew of cheeseburger wrappers, crushed Coke cans, moist cigarette butts, empty Ding Dong packages and worn Luke Steele paperbacks sloshing around his twitchy feet on the floorboard, Seth Holcomb looked dashing and smelled pleasant.

He was clean-shaven, his hair trimmed and styled. He was wearing black slacks and black shoes and a white long-sleeved button up, all new, and had applied what he considered the perfect amount of cologne—two squirts.

He chugged the last of his three customary morning sodas, tossed the can onto the floorboard, and glanced at his wristwatch.

Ten-fifteen. Two minutes until go time.

In the second book of Luke Steele's Beast Series, *The Beasts on the Move*, Seth's favorite, a character referred to as Uncle Leo tells another character named Mark that everyone has two special times each day. Two times when God's light shines a tad brighter on them. Two times when their actions would have an above average influence on their fortune. Two times, that if used correctly, could alter the course of their entire life. These two times, he said, were the hour and minute, both AM and PM, that mirrored the month and day of their birth date.

With this in mind, Seth exited the Belvedere. He grabbed the brown leather satchel from the back seat, rifled through it to reassure himself that the envelope, Newports and loaded 9MM were still there, which they were. Then, leaning into the aggressive Panhandle wind, he headed toward the enormous box-framed farmhouse that he'd been parked in front of for nearly an hour.

His left knee hitched and ached as he lumbered through the tall prairie grass toward the front door. Two weeks earlier, on his way to take a piss in the middle of the night, he'd tripped over his poodle Lucky and taken a nasty fall, partially tearing a couple of ligaments. His doctor said he'd need surgery to repair the damage, but his insurance company was giving him the runaround about covering it due to his weight.

He struggled up the wooden steps leading to the front door and glanced at the crooked mail box. Large white stickers peeling away at the corners confirmed that this was indeed 35 Matador Lane. After making sure his shirt was snugly tucked, he checked the time.

Ten-seventeen. Perfect.

He drew in a deep, inspirational breath and knocked.

Almost instantly the red door creaked open, but only a bit. A scrawny man with a weathered face peeked out of the small opening. "Yes?"

"Mr. Steele? Luke Steele?"

"Yes," the man replied. His brown eyes looked grotesque, bulging from his tiny face.

"Hi, Mr. Steele. My name is Seth Holcomb."

Seth extended his hand. Luke stared at Seth's stubby fingers for a few seconds before easing the door open and extending his own bony hand.

Luke didn't look or sound anything like Seth had imagined he would. He'd expected Luke to be young, wear all black and have aggressive eyes, a dominant posture and a hauntingly deep, intimidating voice—someone capable of conjuring nightmares on command. Someone formidable.

But here was scrawny Luke Steele—*The* Luke Steele, The Lord of Darkness, author of the critically acclaimed Beast Series, multiple winner of International Horror Guild Awards—with an oversized blue flannel shirt tucked into Levis held afloat by a thick brown belt. His voice was weak, his hair stringy and thin. He stood hunched over. He looked tired and depleted and paranoid. Anything but dominant or intimidating.

Despite his disappointment, Seth's stomach knotted up with anxiety as they shook hands.

"Mr. Steele, I'm sorry to show up unexpected like this, but I have something that I need to give you." Seth started rummaging through his satchel, his hand shaking. Beads of sweat were popping out on his temples. "I received it about a week ago by mistake," he said, "and I thought you should have it back. Here it is."

He pulled a large manila envelope from the satchel and held it up.

"It's addressed to *Dead Man's Literature Review*, but the P.O. Box number must be wrong because I found it in my box last Tuesday."

"Oh, my," Luke said as he inched forward and awkwardly plucked the envelope from Seth. "I must've labeled it wrong. Sometimes my glasses give me a headache, and I take them off but still insist on finishing what I've started." He glanced at Seth. "And look what happens."

Seth smiled as Luke stepped back into the doorway. Looking down at the envelope, he felt compelled to explain why it was opened.

"I opened it because there was no return address on the front, but then I found your name and address on the cover letter. There was no phone number, and you're not listed in the phone book or I would've called first, and since I've been a member of your fan club since your first book, I thought I'd bring it by personally. I couldn't resist the opportunity to meet you in person. Not that I'm a crazy stalker or anything. Promise. Just a fan."

"Thank you," Luke said, his bulbous eyes darting around the porch as if searching for some mote-sized treasure.

Seth leaned forward but kept his feet planted. Seconds passed that felt like hours. He wanted to go inside but didn't want to ask. Surely he wouldn't have to force the issue.

"I'm sorry," Luke suddenly blurted out, as if some etiquette ghost had crept up behind him and whispered into his ear, reminding him of common courtesy rituals. "Would you like to come inside? I've got some coffee and I'll sign a few books for you if you'd like."

"That'd be awesome. A real treat, Mr. Steele. Thanks."

Luke led Seth into a dark foyer. There was a sparse living room directly to his left, a bookroom with a fireplace to his right. Splintered, wooden archways shaped like spades adorned the entrance to each room. Seth couldn't stop grinning, his smile so wide that it exposed both rows of teeth. He was inside Luke Steele's house. *The* Luke Steele. Charlie Bucket and those other misfits from his favorite childhood book had nothing on him.

He followed Luke down a long corridor on the left side of a wide staircase. Two closed doors and two open doors lay on each side of the corridor. Seth paused to glance in the open ones.

The house was everything he'd dreamed it would be. Dark, colorless and unaccessorized. The wooden floors creaky. The furniture elderly. Cobwebs grew from ceilings to walls and from walls to floors in random patches. The air was chilly and heavy and tasted stale.

Luke pushed through a swinging door at the end of the corridor and led Seth into a dimly lit kitchen that looked like it hadn't been used or cleaned in decades. The curtains were stained a thick grease-yellow, the linoleum missing in places. And mold-encrusted pots and pans and plates and silverware were piled up on every inch of available counter and table space and scattered across the floor.

Seth chuckled at the sight. "Wow," he whispered.

Without responding, Luke opened a wooden screen door at the back of the kitchen and led Seth out onto an enclosed patio that overlooked Lake Meredith.

"Have a seat," he said, gesturing toward one of the two chairs separated by a small wicker table. "I'll go get the coffee, books and a pen. Be right back."

As Luke walked away, Seth asked him if he could smoke.

"Yes," Luke answered.

Seth pulled a pack of Newport Menthols from his satchel and dropped the bag next to one of the chairs. He lit the cigarette and looked out at the lake. A simper creased his lower face. Newport Menthols were what Luke smoked. He was sure Luke would notice and approve. He knew Luke smoked Newport Menthols because of an interview Luke had given to *Fangs Magazine* two years earlier—the one and only interview he'd ever agreed to, and only after years of nagging from his agent who he'd never met face-to-face.

Mary Waters, the reporter who interviewed Luke, met him at a neutral location and agreed not to ask questions about his family or describe his physical appearance in her article. He'd always refused to participate in book signings or readings, and his books came without a photo or bio. But Mary did say that he chain-smoked Newport Menthols throughout the interview and smelled of Stetson Cologne.

After reading the article Seth switched to Newport Menthols and started using Stetson. He'd bought a new bottle the weekend before making the two day drive from Charlottesville, Virginia to the Texas Panhandle to deliver Luke's manuscript.

Luke walked out onto the enclosed patio a few minutes later balancing two mugs of coffee atop a stack of all the books in his Beast Series—*The Beast in the Attic*, *The Beasts on the Move*, *The Beasts in Ireland*, *The Beast in the Cellar*, *The Beasts on the Boat* and *The Beast in the Toilet*.

Cigarette dangling from his lips, Seth grabbed the two mugs and set them on the small wicker table next to an ashtray.

Luke plopped down in one of the chairs, Seth, the other. The worn chair moaned under the strain of Seth's weight as the armchair cushions, like the hungry jaws of an exotic flesh-eating plant, closed around his huge thighs.

Seth struggled with the chair for a moment, then held up the pack of Newport Menthols, fully extending his arm and jiggling the pack. "Want a smoke?"

Luke didn't look up. He pulled a pen from his chest pocket. "No, thanks."

Seth held the pack in place for a few extra seconds, hoping Luke would look and approve, but he didn't. After dropping the pack into his satchel and pounding out the last half of his cigarette in the ashtray, Seth glanced around leisurely, trying to appear normal. "Nice house," he said. "Lived here long?"

Luke was already on the third book. "My whole life."

"Raised here, huh?"

"Yep."

"I bet your parents are proud. Because of your fame and all."

Luke sighed. "My parents died when I was three."

"My God. I'm sorry. I didn't know. How'd they —"

"A car accident. Don't be sorry. It was a long time ago. I don't really remember them at all."

Seth bit down on his lower lip to fight smiling. Not because Luke's parents were dead, of course, but because nothing about Luke's personal life had ever been revealed to the public.

"Well, I bet their dying probably helped make you a better horror writer, huh?"

Luke's hand froze in mid-scribble. "Yeah...sure."

Sensing disapproval in Luke's tone, Seth fidgeted in his chair, as much as he could anyway, disappointed at himself for choosing the wrong words. You'll always be stupid, so get used to it. It was one of his father's favorite choruses. The words echoed so close and so real it was as if his father had been standing right next to his chair.

Seth gave his eyes a solid rub, then asked, "So...who raised you after the accident?"

"My Uncle Leo."

"Not...you mean...like Uncle Leo who raised Mark in the series?"

"Yep."

Seth threw his head back and chuckled. "Cool," he whispered. After a brief pause, his eyes tightened into giddy slits, as though struck by a moment of genius, and he leaned toward Luke. "Tell me something, do you ever scare yourself with the ideas you get for your books?"

Luke didn't answer.

Seth glanced at the book Luke was signing. "Like that one there, The Beast in the Toilet. Did that idea freak you out when you first came up with it? It sure as hell made me scared to sit on the toilet after I read it."

"Not really," Luke mumbled without looking up.

"How'd you come up with an idea like that anyway?"

Luke didn't answer.

"Well?" Seth urged.

"I don't know."

"What do you mean? It's your idea. You have to know where it came from."

Luke didn't answer. He signed the second to last book. His hand was slightly shaking.

"I'm only asking because I'm a writer, and I think that I write really good. Kind of like you, actually. I've just had problems when it comes to finding my—what did Stephen King call it? *My Idea Well*. Yes. I figured maybe you could give me some pointers since you're the master of good ideas. You know. Writer to writer and all."

Seth had only written four short stories in his entire life—the first when he was seven for his mom, a few months before the cancer took her (she always told him he was very creative and would make a great writer someday), the second when he was eighteen as an assignment for an English class and the third and fourth, both unrevised, over three years ago. But when people asked him what he did for a living at the bars and jazz lounges he frequented on weekends and dollar-drink-Wednesdays, he always gave the same answer: "Odd jobs. But only to pay the bills. I'm a writer. Born and bred." Then, when they asked if he'd ever had anything published, he'd wax contemplatively: "No, but I just got my first manuscript in the can. It's a contemplation of horror in the vein of Luke Steele's Beast Series. I think it's going to make quite the splash." Sometimes, Seth added an "If you'll pardon the pun" after "splash." At that point, if theretofore skeptical inquirers had had any doubts, he knew the heightened vernacular and shop talk disarmed them. Real writers referred to their works as manuscripts. And real writers didn't finish manuscripts for publishers. They got them in the can, like film-makers.

Luke looked up, but out at the lake, not at Seth.

"Just a little help would do me a world of wonders, really," Seth added, feeling a little frustrated, rejected.

The corners of Luke's mouth rose just a tad, hinting at amusement, as he opened the last book and started signing it. "Well, *Mr. Hokum*—

"Seth," Seth interrupted. "Please call me Seth. And it's Holcomb."

"Sorry, Mr. Holcomb," Luke corrected. "Seth...but my well is my secret."

"That's exactly what you told Mary in the *Fangs* interview. You know that's a cop-out, man. Give me something here. *Mono y mono.*"

The misused mispronunciation almost made Luke smile, but he simply pushed a greasy lock of hair behind his ear and laid the last signed book on the table.

"Come on, Luke," Seth said. "Tell me about your first book, *The Beast in the Attic*. Where'd you get that idea?"

Luke slowly shook his head. "I don't know."

Seth slapped the chair armrest. "Don't be like that. I know you know. I'm not stupid."

Luke stood up. His eyes met Seth's for the first time since they'd entered the house. "I think you should go," he said as firmly as his genetics allowed. He picked up the stack of books and handed them to Seth. "Thank you for returning the manuscript. I'm sorry for the mistake."

Seth threw his hand up in front of Luke to stop him. "If you're upset that I opened your manuscript, or that I showed up in person, I'm sorry," he said with urgency, like a kid trying to talk his way out of a beating he knew he deserved. "And I'm sorry for bugging you about your ideas. I just figured if I met you in person and you got to know me, you'd give me some pointers and help get me started on a book. I didn't mean to upset you. Sit down, please. Let's talk some more."

"I'm not mad. I just think you should go. I have things to do."

"But—"

"I'll walk you out."

Seth took the stack of books off his lap, slammed them back on the table, and then struggled to pry himself from the chair's grasp. Once up, he grabbed his satchel, nonchalantly pulled out the 9MM, and thrust it in Luke's face. All he wanted was some advice. Some help. A little one-on-one, certainly no big deal between writers, especially if one had been a member of the other's fan club for over a decade. And Mr. Big Shot Luke Steele—just like Seth's Father—didn't think he was worth it.

"So, that's it, huh?" Seth said, waving the gun. "Just like that? You're giving me the high hat? You're too good for me?" Seth leveled his aim and turned the 9MM sideways, like he was a character in one of the books he had yet to write. "I came here at my special time," he continued. "You know, just for you. I brought your favorite cigarettes, wore your favorite cologne, complimented your work, and you couldn't give a shit."

Without being asked, Luke raised his hands half-heartedly up by his ears. "I don't...I..."

"Not so good with words now are you? All I wanted was a few tips and you—"

A knock at the front door startled them both.

"You expecting anybody?"

"No."

Another knock. Louder. Faster.

Seth pressed the tip of the barrel firm against Luke's nose. "Who is it then?"

"It's probably Mr. Aames, the mailman," Luke said, keeping his eyes on the barrel of the gun. "Sometimes when my agent sends my fan mail, there's too much to fit in my box at the post office and it piles up. Mr. Aames brings it by sometimes to keep the clutter down since I don't go into town often."

"*Weh-heh-hell*. Too much, huh?"

Another knock. Even louder.

"He won't go away," Luke said.

"Then you'll go talk to him. But you say one word about me, and I won't hesitate to finish you both off. Nobody knows I'm here. Nobody even knows I received your manuscript."

Luke spun around and Seth guided him through the kitchen, down the corridor, and up to the front door, digging the muzzle of the 9MM into his back.

"Don't open it all the way," Seth insisted. "And make it quick."

Luke opened the door just enough.

"Morning, Luke."

"Good morning, James."

"I got another batch of letters for you. It never ends. You get more mail than the Pope."

"Thanks," Luke said, nudging the door open far enough to grab the bundle of letters. They were tied together with twine. James had done that for Luke for almost five years now.

"You feel all right today?" James asked, peering over the top of his bifocals. "You look tireder and weirder than normal."

They both chuckled—James's genuine, Luke's not. Seth had twisted the gun into his back hard after that last question.

"Fine," Luke said. "Just staying up late trying to finish a new book."

"Bet your fans can't wait to read it. I'm a Hemingway man myself."

He said that every time.

"I know."

"See you next time, Luke. Get some sleep."

"Bye, James."

Luke closed the door and when he turned round, Seth clocked him in the side of the head with the handle of the gun. Luke fell against the window next to the front door. The bundle of letters slapped onto the floor. Seth picked up the stack, ripped one out, tore it open and read it aloud. With sarcasm.

Dear Luke,

Do you remember my other letters? I'm one of your greatest fans. I've read all your books at least a hundred times now. They're magical, which I know I've written before. I wrote this time to ask you for another autographed copy of The Beast in the Attic for my friend Alicia. I can't convince her to join the fan club and get the free one, so I thought if I showed her how generous you are that she'd join. Please help. You're the best.

Forever Dedicated,

Leanne Fowler

"How cute. *Forever Dedicated*. But you won't help her will you? You won't help anyone."

Seth punched Luke in the stomach with the gun, doubling him over.

"I didn't want it to be this way, you know. All you had to do was just give me a little advice."

Struggling to stand up, Luke said in a pained whisper, "I really don't have a good imagination. I couldn't help you if —"

"Bullshit!"

Seth hit Luke in the head again, dropping him back down onto a knee, a rivulet of fresh blood trickling down his forehead.

"You told the mailman that you're finishing another book. Is that true?"

Luke nodded, rubbed his head, and noted the blood on his fingers.

"Take me to it. Give me that idea. You can have the next one. If I can just have one, that's all, just one, I'll make it. It'll kickstart everything. I know it."

Luke nodded again and gave Seth a weird look that he couldn't read. It wasn't quite defiance, but it wasn't submission either. Seth bent forward, pulled Luke upright, and pushed the barrel of the gun to his head.

"It is loaded, you know. I've gone to the range once a week for fifteen years so don't try anything stupid. Now, where's this book?"

Luke mumbled, "The closed door in the corridor. On the left."

"Then let's go, old man."

Seth walked Luke to the door, stifling his laughter as they went, his stomach swarming with butterflies. He was about to see a Luke Steele book that the world would read and love and think was written by Seth Holcomb, an up-and-coming star of horror fiction. What a gem, he thought. His first bestseller. Finally. What would Father think of him now? Of course, he'd have to re-title the story. And change the characters' names and ages and occupations. And the setting. And some of the plot details. But those things were trivial. Uncle Leo had been right after all.

"So what's this one called?" Seth asked as he placed his hand on the cold brass door knob.

Luke didn't answer.

Once the door was ajar, Seth looked down at the wooden staircase. "You write down there?"

Luke nodded.

"You may not look like a Luke Steele, or sound like one," Seth continued. "But you sure as hell are strange like one." He nudged Luke forward with the gun. "You first."

Luke shuffled forward but stopped firmly at the edge of the stairs. Then without warning, and as unpredictably slick as a cornered feline, he sidled left and side-kicked Seth's left leg with all his might.

Pain exploded in Seth's knee, sending hot barbs rippling up and down his leg. He dropped the gun, and it ricocheted off his leg and rolled down the staircase, clanking on the concrete floor below. He fell to one knee on the edge of the stairs, howling, tottering.

Panic-stricken, he craned his neck to look back at Luke, and Luke immediately jammed his thumbs into each of Seth's eyes, all the way up to the knuckles, and gave them a good twist. The pain was immediate and intense, like someone had fired a flare gun directly into Seth's brain. He fell sideways against the doorjamb, cupping his hands over his eyes, screaming in terrified agony. He didn't hear Luke hop back to get a running start. He only felt Luke's knobby shoulders drive into his back, hard. He crumpled forward and tumbled halfway down the flight of stairs before slamming to a stop up against a pocked cement wall.

While trying to twist around and sit upright, Seth heard a soft click at the top of the staircase, and then the steps beneath him suddenly straightened out, morphing into a wooden ramp that sent him rolling down the remainder of the stairs. Writhing in pain on the cold cellar floor, he heard Luke say something about a well.

As Luke eased the cellar door closed, a shrill, unsettling scratching sound rose from the darkness. After all these years he didn't have to watch to know what would happen. He knew that the beast in the cellar, the spiny black one with four arms and sparkling green eyes that lived in the dried up well in the corner, had smelled Seth and was scratching its way up to feast.

Luke walked into the kitchen, washed his hands, wet a paper towel, and dabbed at the blood on his forehead. He cocked his head and smirked when he heard Seth's horrific screams a few seconds later.

Seth Holcomb had turned out to be just as predictable as most of them who'd come, though he was only the second to bring a gun. Luckily, Luke had watched him hobble up to the front door and knew he had a bad knee.

Almost all of Them showed up at their special time and made it a point to tell Luke that, hoping to impress him. And most of Them, like Seth, were writers and wanted to know how Luke came up with his ideas and if he'd help them with theirs and read or critique their writing. Most of Them also quizzed Luke, digging for an insider's peek into his personal life, something they could share with their friends, which he always made it a point to give Them—information on his parent's death, his uncle Leo, his new book, or whatever—before they died. It made Them feel special and calm and comfortable, which made it easier for him to reel Them in. Usually.

Luke retrieved the manuscript Seth had brought back and walked upstairs to his bedroom. He'd ditch Seth's car in the deep end of Lake Meredith after sunset. He sat down at his computer and wiggled the mouse. The dark screen hissed and brightened, revealing the open Word document he'd been working on that morning, his latest book, *The Beast Within*.

Another work of nonfiction.

He hadn't lied to Seth. He had an average imagination at best. He wrote what he knew, which was about the four beasts that Uncle Leo had introduced him to when he was eight years old, and the stories he was told about them. Beasts of different size, shape, color and form—including the wispy one that needed a human host, the one Uncle Leo had passed into Luke with his dying breath—that all had different preferences for food and living conditions. Beasts that didn't age, or as far as Luke knew, die. Beasts that had been protected and cared for by Uncle Leo before Luke, Leo's father before that, his grandfather before that, his great-grandfather before that and his great-great-grandfather in Ireland before that, before the boat ride to America.

Luke glanced away from the screen when a series of soft crunching sounds, bone crunching sounds, drifted from the vent on the wall.

Considering Seth's size, the beast in the cellar would be sated for at least three years, but Luke only had a week or two until the beast in the toilet would need its annual meal.

He closed Word, logged onto the internet, went to his author website and, after using the administrator password, found the list of the fifty-thousand people in his fan club, and clicked on a name. As the profile picture and personal information loaded, he pulled the manuscript from the manila envelope Seth had brought back, the only manuscript he'd ever written using his imagination, the one he'd never sell, and slid it into a new envelope.

Copying the information down from on the screen, Luke labeled the envelope.

Fiction Editor
Dead Man's Literature Review
5305 5th street
Wichita, Kansas 78501

The address was Leanne Fowler's. She was thirty-five, single, and, according to her online bio, had no kids.

When Seth had read her letter aloud earlier, Luke had remembered her previous letters, letters which all screamed "obsessed fan." He hoped that she would be another sure bet.

One of Them.

He jotted her birth date, 12-16, on the palm of his hand with a permanent marker so he'd remember what time to watch for her, hopefully sometime next week.

The Consequence of Thought
By Aaron Milstead

One might wonder what a French philosopher and the leader of a southern white Neo Nazi skinhead movement have in common. Here it is: each morning Clifford Brennan puts on a tight t-shirt that does nothing to compliment his loose bulk, slips on a loose pair of army trousers—which are supported by a black leather belt with a swastika-shaped buckle—and tightens the laces of a pair of combat boots that have stomped on the heads of countless niggers and kikes; and then he stares at a poster that shows him standing next to Adolph Hitler. The only (but overly obvious) clue that the image has been photo-shopped is that the image of Clifford's superimposed person is in color and the Fuhrer stands in stark black and white. Clifford shouts "Sieg Heil!" and offers a Nazi salute, then lets his attention drift to a framed quote below the poster that he needle-pointed while he was still in the joint. It reads:

History is the only laboratory we have in which to test the consequences of thought.

Etienne Gilson

Clifford's lips move in mute accordance as he considers the sentiment.

Clifford Brennan's functional IQ is less than 70 which officially classifies him as mentally retarded. He spends a lot of time with a Thesaurus, however, and he considers himself a visionary and an emissary and possibly even a luminary. He lives in Silsbee on a vast plot of land that appears to hold a dozen identical chicken houses, but they are a front. The horrible stench that constantly hovers around the area is a product of far more sinister activities than countless chickens defecating on each other while they murder and feast upon their weak and infirmed.

Clifford climbs into a golf cart that has a black swastika spray-painted on the hood and cruises down a gravel path that leads to one of the elongated chicken houses. He parks, steps up to a steel door and punches his secret code into a sophisticated lock: 1-2-3-4-5-6. The massive door opens and Clifford steps into an air-conditioned room containing several young men with closely shaven heads and tattooed bodies who quickly jump to their feet and chorus: "Sieg Heil!"

"As you were," Clifford says, and they return to their former positions behind ultra-centrifuges, micro-centrifuges, a molecular dynamics phosphor-imager, a Betascope blot analyzer, electroporators, UV crosslinkers, thermocylers, spectrophotometers, mini-fluorometers, speed-vacs and several hybridization chambers. Each young skinhead has an area of expertise that is so specialized that dissertations could be written based upon their unique perspectives; however, most of them cannot write and they lack the appropriate diction to express their proficiencies, referring to the mini-fluorometer as a calculator and the spectrophotometer as a Nintendo.

Clifford walks down the long aisle and glances dumbly at the machinery, but he grunts and nods knowingly when the young skinheads look up at him. Toward the back of the large chicken house, an obese man in blue overalls is standing in an impressive makeshift lab staring at a large glass cylinder that's filled with a thick pinkish liquid. The man's name is Robert Herrington and he's been tasked with monitoring the small fleshy object suspended in the pink substance.

Clifford places a hand on the fat man's shoulder. "How's the lima bean?"

Herrington looks up and smiles weakly. "Six is coming along perfectly. Will this be the last one?"

"Heck if I know," Clifford replies. "Do I look like God?"

Herrington turns back to the glass cylinder. "You promised me we'd only do the one and then just two and—

Clifford quickly places his free hand on Herrington's opposite shoulder and leans in, sinking his fingers into the soft meat and squeezing hard. "Who saved your bacon back in Huntsville?"

"You did," Robert Herrington mumbles, turning away from Clifford's breath. "You know I appreciate it."

"Sometimes I wonder," Clifford says, as he releases his grip and slaps Robert Herrington on the back. "This is for certainly sure the very last lima bean. Okay?"

"Sure," Herrington says. "I believe you."

Robert Herrington's IQ is almost three times higher than Clifford's, but he was sent to the joint in the late 70's because he was in the wrong place at the wrong time; more specifically in his dorm room screwing the corpse of a sorority girl that he had strangled and snuck up the elevator under the auspices of severe drunkenness at the precise moment that the campus police decided to raid his room for a miniscule amount of homegrown cannabis. Herrington considers life truly unfair, and karma an archaic concept best discarded. Men who make love to corpses are unfairly lumped into the same category as pedophiles and Robert's life expectancy in Huntsville penitentiary was only slightly higher than that of his sphincter, the pitiful band of muscle fibers that only exists to maintain a necessary orifice. One day Herrington and his uninitiated orifice were surrounded by five African Americans in the showers who seemed intent upon doing them both irreparable harm, when a heavily muscled man with a swastika tattooed across his chest stepped onto the scene. In Herrington's reluctantly reverent memories of the scene, rising hot shower steam served as a dramatic backdrop.

"You black niggers need to get on out of here," Clifford had calmly remarked.

Herrington had started to relax and take his next breath, but before he could offer a proper 'Thank you' his knight in shining prison tattoos added "That's *my* bitch."

The African Americans vacated the showers and gave the man a wide berth. Herrington's savior was Clifford and he controlled all the whites on the inside, as well as most of the Mexicans and a fair number of the guards. Besides that, the odds were only five to one and that favored Clifford by a wide margin.

The two men became close friends over the next few months, though Herrington has managed to block most of it out of his memory. Occasionally, a discomforting snippet of recollection hovers along the periphery of his mind, threatening to reduce him to a fetal ball, but he reflexively begins humming Benny Mardones' "Into the Night" and pleasanter visions take center stage in his daydreams, like the time he strangled a dainty sorority girl when she called him creepy.

Mostly the Huntsville memories were good and pure because, realizing he had a real-life genius under his wing, Clifford had the guards bring in all kinds of books that Herrington devoured and assimilated. Clifford was due to get out in ten years and he wanted a business that was more lucrative than extorting, pimping, slave trading and contract killing. It was nickel and dime stuff. Clifford wanted his own piece of the independent pharmaceutical industry. Limitless opportunity and high profit margins. Herrington read dozens of chemistry books and one day he popped Clifford the question.

"How about a potent nervous system stimulant which affects your neuro-chemical mechanisms?"

"Does it get you high?"

That was how meth took its foothold in the south. It had actually been around since 1893 when Japanese chemist Nagayoshi Nagai synthesized it from ephedrine. Clifford was pleased to learn that Hitler himself was given intravenous injections of methamphetamines by his personal physician, Theodor Morell, from 1942 until his death in 1945. That meant it clearly passed the WWHD test. Besides that, it was ridiculously easy to manufacture; you could make it at home yourself if you purchased concentrated hydrochloric acid from the hardware store and some drain cleaner, starter fluids and Vicks nasal inhalers from Wal-Mart. You just needed some glass bottles, a porcelain bowl, coffee filters, a small jar with a top, a Pyrex baking dish and a single glass test tube. Gather it all up and you were in business—but if Clifford caught you selling it in his territory (anywhere south of the Mason-Dixon Line) he'd have you gang-raped and hanged by your own intestines.

Clifford barely even thought about meth anymore. Sure, he let the cash from it keep on rolling in, but he funneled it into what became his true passion: the fleshy little lima beans.

The first one was created over ten years ago.

"When's the show?" Herrington ventured.

"Pretty soon," Clifford replied. "Pretty soon."

"Good luck," Herrington said.

"Back to work," Clifford ordered.

Clifford strode back down the aisle, nodding at the young skinheads while they worked. Herrington watched him apprehensively until he was out of sight.

Seven hours and thirty minutes after Hitler's death, he and Eva Braun and two dogs were discovered in a shell crater by Ivan Churakov of the 79th Rifle Corps of the Red Army. After an autopsy that recorded gunshot damage to Hitler's skull and glass shards in his jaw, his remains were buried in an unmarked grave beneath a paved section of the front courtyard. The location was kept secret.

In 1970 this plot of land, which was still controlled by the KGB, was scheduled to be handed over to the East German government. KGB director Yuri Andropov feared the Hitler burial site might become a Neo-Nazi shrine; therefore, he ordered a covert KGB team to secretly exhume the body and thoroughly burn it before dumping the ashes in the Elbe River. The body was, in fact, secretly exhumed; but it was also secretly not destroyed. Instead the bones and hair and bits of putrefied flesh were sold underground to buyers ranging from those who lost relatives to the concentration camps to those who idolized their Fuhrer. Mementos. Treasures. Echoes and memories. A reminder that everything and everyone was transient.

Or not.

In '83 Clifford Brennan was introduced to a Japanese entrepreneur named Masaharu Matsushida, who became a billionaire after creating an Eco-Taxi service. After shrewd negotiations he obtained a metacarpal and a proximal phalanx from Hitler's left hand and three strands of hair set in an amber pendant. Those trophies cost Clifford a shit ton of meth, three original snuff films and two dozen Mexican girls who hadn't even had their first periods. The trophies were handed over to Herrington and the first lima bean was produced almost a decade later.

Clifford strolls up to a second chicken house and inputs his secret code, 1-2-3-4-5-6, and steps into an air-conditioned room. Lima beans four and five are in the middle of story time sitting Indian style in front of Wanda Willington. She smiles at Clifford and continues to read, "…and the Big Bad Jew ate Red Riding Hood's grandmother and climbed into her bed and hid under the covers and waited."

No. 4 just turned two years old and though No. 5 is almost three months younger, they look like identical twins. They sit so close that their knees touch and their gestures seem synchronized. They glance back at

Clifford and smile and then their attention returns to Ms. Wanda. She is the closest thing to a mother they have ever known. No. 4 is named Alois, which was Hitler's father's given name, and No. 5 is named Wolf, which is the translation of Adolf into English. After story time they will have German lessons for forty-five minutes, then history, then a nap and then art lessons.

Clifford is trying a gentler approach with Four and Five after what he considers to be a failed beginning with No. 2 and No. 3, and, of course, the outright disaster that is No. 1. The precious dark-haired boys stare up at Ms. Wanda with confident smiles on their round faces and Clifford allows himself some measure of hope.

Clifford waves goodbye and strolls over to another chicken house. The air within is stale. It is dark except for the faint glow from a flat screen television mounted on the wall. No. 3 is sitting behind a school desk and staring with rapt attention at the screen: a black man is being electrocuted to death and blood is pouring from his ears and eyes. No. 3 is four years old. Dr. Kurt Tungsten is standing behind the boy and, spotting Clifford, hurries over and shakes his hand.

"How is Adolph doing?" Clifford asks.

Dr. Tungsten shrugs. "Better I guess. He no longer cries when I show him the *Faces of Death* movies. But I think he's convinced himself that the scenes aren't real."

Clifford stomps over to the boy and points. "That's real," he deadpans. "This is the world we live in."

On the high definition screen, a hostage is having his head sawed off by a terrorist whose face is covered by a burlap sack with eye slits.

The boy looks up at Clifford. "Okay," he says.

"Those are camel niggers cutting off that white man's head," Clifford continues. "You understand? You got to hate them. You hate them, right?"

The boy shrugs. Clifford takes Dr. Tungsten aside.

"What's the problem? Ain't nothing in this world easier or more natural than to hate."

"He's so young, Mr. Brennan. He needs time."

"We ain't got time," Clifford hisses. "The War is coming. We need a leader. That boy don't look like he could wipe his own ass."

"He just turned four a few weeks ago. What do you expect?"

Clifford takes a deep breath and stares at the subject. "We can't dick around. Give him his first cat. Once he's done twenty of them, give him a puppy. Then—"

"Mr. Brennan," Dr. Tungsten interrupts. "It's too soon. You're repeating the same mistakes that were made with No. 1 and No. 2. You brought me in as an expert in human behavior...and the modification thereof. How can I help if you ignore my recommendations?"

Clifford frowns. "Are you really such an expert?"

"As you are well aware, Mr. Brennan, I was a Psychology professor at the University of Ottawa specializing in—"

"Yeah, yeah," Clifford interjects. "And you were fired for fucking coeds in exchange for passing grades. Does that make you an expert in human behavior?"

Dr. Tungsten smirks. "Absolutely."

Clifford chuckles. "You got a month to teach No. 3 how to hate and if you can't then it's time to start bringing in the cats."

"Fair enough," Dr. Tungsten says and then returns to his post behind the boy. On the screen a black woman is being gang raped.

Clifford heads over to the next chicken house feeling frustrated. As he enters the secret code his anger builds. He knows No. 2 is hiding in his room, a meticulously planned staging area where countless cats and puppies were stabbed, drowned, burned and tortured in every conceivable way. A dungeon where the death rattles of so many creatures have shaken their last that a residue clings to the walls and dying murmurs seem to encroach on the silence.

Clifford surveys the gloom and begins removing his belt. "You got a beating coming to you, boy," he says. Clifford scans the room and spots the boy hiding behind a book shelf. "Come and take it like a man, son."

As a young boy, Hitler was often beaten by his father. Years later, he bragged about it. "I resolved never again to cry when my father whipped me. A few days later I had the opportunity to put my will to the test. My mother, frightened, took refuge in front of the door. As for me, I counted silently the blows of the stick which lashed my rear end."

Clifford beats No. 2 unmercifully, and the boy cries out with every blow. It's a disgusting display of viciousness and, as Clifford wipes the blood from his belt and watches the child cower in the corner he wonders if it all hasn't just been a waste of time.

A package of Sharpie permanent markers on a school desk across the room catches Clifford's eye and he walks over. He runs his index finger across the colors and stops on black. He takes the black Sharpie out of the package and marches over to No. 2, lifting him off the floor by his dark, unkempt hair.

Clifford glares at his creation. Nothing of the greatness he came from is reflected in the boy. Clifford flips the lid off the black Sharpie with his free hand and then raises it to No. 2's face, growling "Be still."

No. 2 complies and Clifford draws a crude square between his nose and upper lip. Then, he sets the boy down.

Clifford retrieves the Sharpie lid and replaces it on the marker. His gaze low, the boy remains motionless.

"I'm sorry," Clifford says.

No. 2 raises his eyes in something akin to hope, but Clifford continues.

"I'm so sorry you were ever born."

No. 2's gaze sinks back into the gloom and Clifford exits without looking back.

Clifford has one final stop left, the greatest disappointment of them all. Lima bean No. 1.

Clifford had held No. 1 in his arms, fed him formula, changed his diapers and rocked him to sleep practically every night. He spoke of the greatness to come and named No. 1 Hitler, insisting that everyone else refer to him as the Fuhrer. Clifford's heart was full, so full, that tears streamed down his cheeks on several occasions as he looked down into No. 1's eyes.

"You will lead us all to a new world order," Clifford had said, wiping the tears with Adolph's blankie. "A world where there is one true pure race to rule over all others (sniffling)...and we have exterminated every last fucking mongrel."

Those early days were filled with such promise.

Clifford had held an almost constant vigil while No. 1 slept, conjuring images of his greatness, inferring motives behind every furrow of his brow and every toothless grin, goo-goo and crying fit. It was as if he'd created a time machine and he was watching history unfold. No—better put, he was unfolding history, one shitty diaper at a time.

After a few weeks No. 1 became colicky and then it was four months of constant crying and screaming.

Clifford turned over rearing duties to a skinhead youth. By the time No. 1 was sixteen months old, night terrors were a constant and by the age of two, asthma was kicking in. No amount of beatings ever corrected these deficiencies and as No. 1 matured he grew more and more feeble.

Clifford expressed his disappointment in predictable ways.

After another short stroll and his secret code, the door to the final chicken house opened. It is a day of reckoning for No. 1. Graduation day. Flunk or fail.

No. 1. is ten years old today and his room is filled with high ranking local members of the Neo-Nazi, Aryan and white supremacist movements. They are gathered around an elevated, wooden stage with maroon curtains in the back. The stage is adorned with vintage Nazi propaganda posters, Nazi flags and black and red balloons, and a dusky man with nervous brown eyes is chained to a steel, folding chair in the center. The chains are wrapped around his ankles and chest, and his wrists are handcuffed and left to languish in his lap. The audience has been throwing eggs and tomatoes at him and his bruised face is covered with filth.

The onlookers salute Clifford as he enters, and he flashes mock bodybuilder poses as he shuffles to a spot in front of the stage. His back to the crowd, Clifford contemptuously regards their captive. "That there is a real-life nigger Jew," he shouts, stoking the audience. "I shit you not."

Clifford strolls onto the stage and the audience rises as one and claps. Clifford takes advantage of the moment. He fake-punches the captive and snorts as the helpless man flinches and trembles. The onlookers roar.

"Are you ready to build our own true Fourth Reich here," Clifford continues. "In America, our second Fatherland?"

Clifford allows the crowd to hoot and clap louder for a moment and then brushes the volume down with his hands. Then he nods and continues to nod, almost as if in cadence. The audience follows Clifford's every gesture, and then he stops.

"Is there anyone here ready to see their once and future Fuhrer?" Clifford asks finally.

The mob begins stomping in stationary goose step, pounding their chests and expressing tribute in repeated Nazi salutes. The gathered white patriots are beside themselves, gleeful and practically gushing, and Clifford returns their affection with a long, reciprocal Nazi salute, holding it for effect.

Then, a gangly, fragile boy begrudgingly steps out from behind the maroon curtains and the onlookers go silent.

Dressed in a Nazi youth uniform, No. 1 seems impossibly thin and deathly pale. His hair is dark and, due to his slumped posture, his long bangs cover his eyes. Clifford turns and leads him to the man who is chained to the chair.

No. 1 stares at his feet while the chained man in front of him trembles.

A young skinhead steps onto the stage and hands a firearm to Clifford. It is a 1911 9MM filled with .45 caliber hollow point shells. Fired at close range it will splatter the contents of the chained man's skull and drench the maroon curtains behind.

Clifford has serious doubts that No. 1 will even pull the trigger. The boy refused to kill cats, let alone puppies, and he closed his eyes during the propaganda film screenings, ignoring the graphic scenes regarding the enemy's treatment of patriots and the patriots' methods of retaliation. No. 1 passed out every time he was physically punished in any way and even a harsh word could render him faint. He was weak in every conceivable way and an absolute failure. The only thing he ever showed any interest in or cared about was his brother and only playmate, No. 2.

And that was Clifford's down card.

Clifford knows this display will likely be an embarrassment, and certainly a failure, but the financial investment in No. 1 was shared by many and now it was the time to roll the new model out into the showroom.

Clifford hands the 1911 to No. 2 and leans in. "You shoot that kike or I'm going to kill you and No. 2. I'll feed you to this crowd and then skin him alive. You got me?"

No. 1 nods and then quickly reaches into the front pocket of his Nazi Youth shirt, pulls out an inhaler and takes a long drag. Then, he replaces the inhaler and brushes his bangs out of his eyes.

No. 1 raises the 1911 and points it at the ceiling and the room grows silent. The man chained to the chair begins to twist and writhe, horrified. No. 1 leans down and whispers something into the wild-eyed captive's ear, and the captive's eyes grow wilder and he becomes increasingly panicked. Clifford's eyebrows crook and he momentarily allows himself to entertain the notion that the christening will turn out okay.

No. 1 cocks the gun and flicks off the safety with his thumb. Then he slowly lowers it and aims it at the captive's temple. The chained man begins to scream.

Clifford's eyes suddenly and unexpectedly well up.

It's the overture to the Wagnerian symphony he was waiting for and trying so hard to conduct. But just as the young Valkyrie is about to take wing, he spins and shoots Clifford pointblank, between the eyes, and his headless body lingers for a few beats, arms raised—as if about to conduct an orchestra—and then collapses at the front of the stage.

Young Adolph's second shot pops a black balloon and strikes a high-ranking member of the Aryan Nation in the chest. His third shot kills a fat man with a handlebar moustache.

As the staging room of the chicken house begins to empty, Adolph shoots a previously fanatic member of a local white supremacist contingent in the back, and the man begins to sob and cry. His wails are drowned out by the screaming captive still seated behind Adolph who, oblivious to the pandemonium, smiles for the first time.

Then, Adolph stands center stage, facing the empty peanut gallery. As he raises the muzzle of the 1911 to a point between his throat and cleft-less chin, he experiences an intoxicating sense of deja vu.

Then, he forcefully and authoritatively exclaims "Heil me!" and pulls the trigger, splattering his brains all over the remaining black and red balloons.

His body falls next to Clifford's.

The Deal
by Samantha Andrasko

Gravel crunching, the rumble of the ancient engine, and her father's wailing were the only things Amberlee could hear as she drove down the pitch-black Farm to Market road. She'd had the radio on when she started her trip, but the signal cut out an hour into the drive. But it was okay. She found the road noise of this particular trip more soothing than the bass-heavy classic rock songs of her father's presets.

She flinched when she hit a deep pothole in the road, checking her rear view to see if any of her cargo had been thrown out of the back of the truck. Nothing. There were only pained moans coming from the back, which she now realized were probably the result of Floyd's head bouncing off the bottom of the flat bed. Amberlee smirked and swerved to hit the next one she saw.

The crossroads was exactly where Floyd said it would be. The first truth her father had ever told her. Not that his honesty really counted when it was given with a shotgun aimed at his knee. But she supposed she shouldn't split hairs when she was where she wanted to be. Amberlee slammed on the brakes at the stop sign and cut the engine, climbing out of the cab as the clock on the dashboard read eleven fifty-nine.

She dragged her father from the bed of the truck forcefully, but careful not to disturb the rest of the contents, and pushed him into the center of the crossroads. She pulled his hunting knife from the pocket of her dress as his body hit the ground. Amberlee felt the hairs on her skin rise when his pupils dilated with fear. She cut the gag off his mouth and wasn't able to hold down the corners of her lips as his screams permeated the black night. She didn't have to tell him there was no one around to hear him scream. She knew she hadn't gotten her intelligence from her mother; besides, she had been waiting so long for the fear. She could hold onto the few seconds she had alone with it. Savor it. Burn the pitch and terror into her ear drums for the days when she needed a reminder of why she did what she did.

Still, her phone alarm broke through the screams at midnight and Amberlee had a meeting to make. She approached her father, knife in hand, holding it up to his cheek. Her other hand was on his neck to hold him still as she pierced the thickest flesh on his face and pulled the knife down. She found the blade duller than she had expected as she opened his face and spilled his blood in the center of the crossroads.

Amberlee didn't back away from the gore that spattered her legs, the red and white fat shining under the moonlight. She stood above her father as he screamed in pain, his fear temporarily gone as the worst had come for him, and waited. The blood poured from the veins inside his cheeks, Floyd screamed, and Amberlee watched as it faded from red to black and smoke rose from it, burning the ground as a man in a crisp suit stepped through.

"Hello," she said, calm and patient as she waited for him to get his bearings. "You look different than I imagined you would."

The demon tilted his head at her, barely registering her sacrificial offering. "I don't usually deal with pairs."

"You won't be tonight either," Amberlee informed him, threading her fingers into her father's thinning hair and pulling his head back to expose his neck. Floyd's Adam's apple bobbed in his throat as he stared down the demon dealing with his daughter. "He won't be here much longer."

The demon's lips quirked up at her, but he still didn't spare her father a glance. "Most people don't bring the soul they wish to bargain with to these meetings."

"I'm not here to do anything half-way." Amberlee slammed the butt of the knife into the side of her father's skull as he begged the demon for his life.

"Most don't understand the sacrifice of their own soul they make when they offer someone else's," he continued.

"Trust me, I understand what's on the line here," Amberlee reassured this devil. Her father's knife cut a soft red line into the flesh of his neck.

The devil gave Amberlee a slow grin. "His soul for what, then? True love? Fame and fortune? Just fortune?"

"I'm not here to make a deal. I'm here to undo a deal that's already been done."

The devil raised curious eyebrows. "We've met before?" He stared hard at her face with a frown before finally shaking his head. "Impossible. I don't recognize you."

"You're very old." The girl didn't mean any offense and the devil was very hard to offend. "Do you normally recognize everyone whose soul you take?"

The devil nodded. "When they've sold them to me, I do."

"Well, there's your answer. I didn't sell my soul to you."

He understood instantly. "Ah. What's your name, First Born?"

"Amberlee Mitchell."

The devil listened to her name and considered it for a moment before it fell into place. Recognition lit up his face. "Floyd Mann," he nodded at her father finally. "Nice to see you again. I see you finally reunited with your daughter. It's nice to have that loose end tied up before you leave this plane, isn't it?" The devil and Amberlee wore matching grins.

"We made a deal!" her father screeched, his last words echoing out in the empty night surrounding them.

"We did," the devil agreed. "We both upheld that deal. You with your endless supply of money and women. Oil that never stops flowing, tapped from the void where your daughter's soul so clearly isn't."

Both man and demon looked up at Amberlee's blank face together. Floyd crumbled into sobs when he saw the demon's truth in his daughter's eyes, the utter nothingness reflected back at him.

Amberlee rolled those eyes before she plunged the knife into the side of her father's neck and pulled it around to the front of his throat with a strong, practiced motion. Her face went hard as she watched his eyes go wide in shock and in pain, choking on blood no longer contained by his neck and mouth, unable to scream around it as she ripped through his vocal chords. She focused on her task, pulling the knife around his neck, opening it in a perfect bloody circle before pulling on his head to carve through his spine and cut through the rest of the tendons with several loud snaps echoing across the empty West Texas fields. He died before she was finished, but not by much. Amberlee threw her father's head at the feet of the demon and looked up at him expectantly as Floyd's body dropped to the dirt at the center of the crossroads.

The devil was unimpressed. "You expected it to be that easy? An even trade, a soul for a soul?"

Amberlee shook her head and wiped her father's viscera on her clean white dress. She backed up to his truck, opened the tailgate, and nodded to the severed heads lined in neat, even rows along the bed of the pickup in varying states of decay. The heads of only men with features that mirrored her father's almost perfectly. Row after row of pained, tortured expressions topped with tufts of brown hair splattered with shocks of white and red. The demon noticed her newest kills were toward the front. Her older ones in the back, though partially masked with the rot that had set in over time, and the maggots getting fat on that rot, exposed her previous inexperience. "I do expect this is an even trade though," she answered.

The devil's smile was slow and wide, cutting across his face like Floyd's knife had cut across his own at Amberlee's hand. "You made him ride the whole way here in the back of that truck with all those heads?"

Amberlee shrugged. "We didn't really have all that much to say to each other."

The demon nodded. "Much as I appreciate the gesture, and believe me I do. No one's ever tried to trade me, what? Thirty? Forty heads?"

"Forty-four. Well," she nodded to her father's head, "forty-five."

The devil smiled, though not warmly. "Very impressive, Miss Mitchell. But I'm afraid it's still not enough."

Amberlee's self-satisfied smile fell from her face as she rose up to her full height, hands on her hips. "I don't understand."

"Yes, I can see that." The devil kicked Floyd's head back toward her, creating a bloody trail in the dirt. "Why didn't you use your own blood to call me forth to make this deal?"

"I did, my father's blood is my blood."

"Very clever." The devil nodded patiently. "But you know what I'm asking, so don't play the child."

Amberlee looked away with a frown, her arms moving higher to cross over her chest. "Why scar myself when I could further his pain?"

"If you're going to make a deal, I'm afraid you have to use your own blood."

Amberlee sighed and walked toward the devil, stopping in front of him and holding out her hand. She plunged the tip of the soiled blade into her palm and dragged it along her heart line, frowning when there was no blood and no pain. "What is this?"

"That appears to be your hand," the devil answered.

Amberlee scowled. "I come to make a fair trade and you play tricks?"

The devil shook his head. "No tricks, Amberlee. A soul cannot exist without a body, nor a body without a soul."

Forty-four decayed heads hit the dry Texas earth at once and Amberlee jumped, turning around to find the truck gone. Yet her skulls still lined in the neat, even rows she put them in. "What is this?" She sighed exasperatedly, staring at the ground where her father's truck should have been parked.

"Your desire for vengeance sustained your delusion of life as long as it was out of your reach, but now I'm afraid it must come to an end. You have work to do."

Amberlee frowned and turned back to the devil. "Work?"

The devil nodded and waved a hand. The skulls and her father's rotting body sunk slowly into the crossroad she had offered them to, the blood soaking into the dirt until she couldn't see them at all. "Someone's on their way here to make a deal tonight, and you, Amberlee Mitchell, have proved yourself more than talented at this job."

Headlights broke the horizon, driving in from the opposite direction Amberlee swore she came in from. "I don't understand," she tried to argue.

"You do, you just wish you didn't."

Amberlee stared into the headlights headed toward them. "When?"

"You died on your twentieth birthday, fulfilling the contract I made with your father."

Amberlee closed her eyes, suppressing the scream she felt in her throat by balling her hands into fists at her sides, acutely aware of the pain she couldn't feel from the bite of her nails into her palms. "Three years?"

The demon nodded as the car came to a stop in front of them, cutting its lights. "You were very prolific in that time. You should be proud."

"It was never going to be enough, was it?"

"It never will be," the devil clarified, staring at her though she refused to meet his eye. "Your soul belongs to me as a part of that contract with your father. That's not a debt but an ownership, and it cannot be repaid."

"This whole time, I thought I was a body without a soul," Amberlee said as she watched a girl, not much older than her, climb from the driver's seat of the car. The devil waited for her to continue. "But I should have known. I was so angry. It cut through me and never stopped running. That's not a lack of a soul, is it?"

The devil shook his head in agreement. "You did more with your soul than I could have done with it in twice that time. And we have more souls to steal yet, Amberlee."

The young woman with tear stained cheeks opened her wrist and spilled her blood at the center of the crossroads where Amberlee stood, alone with her now.

"I wanna make a deal," the girl choked out as she sank to her knees before Amberlee.

Amberlee tilted her head. Her now red dress covered her like a sheet of blood as the moon was overtaken by storm clouds above them. The devil smiled slowly down at the girl. "It'll cost you."

A Dark White Postscript
by E. R. Bills

The figure was as black as sackcloth and it moved awkwardly in the dark. Tieg Bertram sensed it before he saw it.

It had an odor, like it was badly burnt. The wreak was almost overpowering; but it was also familiar. Something Bertram remembered from his past.

The figure moved closer.

Bertram lifted himself up on his elbows and looked around. An elderly man, his eyesight was bad in daylight, even with glasses. But at night, without them, he might as well have been blind. He didn't notice that only the form's lidless eyes and the front teeth of its lipless mouth caught light. The rest of its body was dark and indiscernible. Bertram could hear it, though. Its rough hide cracked as it moved.

"Hello," Bertram said. "Hello? Who's there?"

As Bertram sat up and fumbled for his glasses, the creature stopped.

Bertram retrieved his spectacles from the nightstand and placed them over the bridge of his nose, securing the temple arms over his ears. Then, he flipped on the bedside lamp.

When Bertram's bleary eyes finally adjusted to the light, they abruptly widened and his jaw dropped. Before him stood a dark, twisted figure, solid black. His mind had problems processing it.

The creature stood motionless.

Bertram pushed the sheets and comforter away, swung his legs off the bed and faced the dark form. Except for its eyes and teeth, the scorched figure was as black as the grave. And with no lips, its countenance was frozen in a hellish grin.

"Hello," Bertram repeated weakly. The creature remained mute.

In Bertram's mind's eye, he knew this shadow, this grim form in the shape of a man. Its blackened contour, which looked as if it had been hewn from coal, now glistened in places where secretions of pus, pink with blood, gathered at the cracks in its hide.

It was grotesque, but Bertram was not afraid. There was something recognizable about this being. Something he knew.

Bertram's memory was dim, but his mind began reaching back, sifting through the sedimentary layers of a long life. The creature was a man; or it had been a man. Bertram was sure of that.

The shadow remained motionless, its hands at its sides. The pungent smell it arrived with lingered like gloom. Bertram continued to stare.

A speck of memory flickered in one of the far corners of his consciousness, an inkling at first, evolving slowly, quietly. He turned his head and saw his face in the mirror above a chest-of-drawers.

The reflection of Bertram in the mirror was young and lean. His eyes were bright and his face was handsome and angular. His glasses were gone. It occurred to him that he couldn't have looked like that when he was any older than a teenager—and then it came to him.

He stared away for a moment and then turned back to the silent apparition. He looked it up and down slowly and his bottom lip quivered.

"That's not possible," Bertram said, as he looked back at the mirror, the face there now his face, the face of an old man. "*That's...*"

Bertram's protestation trailed off. The apparition stood idle, an unstirring totem.

Bertram turned back to the figure and peered into its lidless eyes. They stared straight ahead, above him, beyond him, the orbs seemingly immobile. Bertram lowered his gaze to one of its legs, a thick vine of charred sinew. A tear ran down Bertram's left cheek. Then, he looked, again, at the creature's eyes.

"Petty," Bertram said. "*Pettigrew Smith.*"

The apparition's eyeballs shifted then, directly observing Bertram for the first time. Its bloodshot orbs seemed the only thing alive against its blackened head and torso. The rest of its burned carcass remained motionless.

"Is it really you, Petty?"

Bertram knew the answer.

He removed his glasses and wiped his eyes. Then, before turning back to the creature, he sniffed and folded his glasses and placed them on the nightstand.

"Oh god, Petty. It wasn't..."

Bertram placed his hands on his knees and then clasped them and let them rest in his lap.

"I'm sorry, Petty."

The dark creature moved then, unsteadily stepping towards Bertram, but Bertram didn't flinch or cringe. He held out his hand. The creature came close and slowly lifted its rigid right arm.

"Sorry, Petty," Bertram repeated.

The apparition touched Bertram's white, wrinkly fingertips with the nubs of its shriveled, charcoal knuckles, and Bertram burst into blue flame. The blaze roared orange and then yellow as it encompassed Bertram's body immediately and en masse. Bertram grunted, but nothing more.

The dark apparition stood over Bertram as the flames raged. When the fire began to die down, it turned and shuffled away.

Sheriff Dunphee got the call on the radio about seven o' clock the next morning, just as he was leaving his home in Harkin.

Edna Jenkins in Troup had phoned the Sheriff's Department and said something had happened to her granddad, Bertram. But she couldn't explain what. When the dispatch officer pressed her for details, she grew agitated.

A little strange, Dunphee thought. But he knew Edna was harmless and getting up there in years. Their families were both from Harkin and Dunphee had even met Bertram once or twice, in Daingerfield or Ore City, he couldn't decide. Bertram had known Dunphee's grandmother, but had left Harkin when he was a young man. Dunphee had wound up back in Harkin after college and Edna had moved to Troup ages ago when she married.

Troup was just southeast of Tyler and not far out of Dunphee's way. When he traveled through there he always drove by the Troup Boxing Gym. It had originally been named after at a 16-year-old African American boxing phenom named Byron Payton, but the novelty and memory had worn off. Sheriff Dunphee had boxed against Payton in the late 1970s and lost in a decision; but only, he suspected, because Payton had gone easy on him.

Most of Dunphee's family and friends had been at the fight and assured him he was cheated, but he knew better. There was a way things were where they lived, and Payton's success simply ruffled feathers.

Payton had been the total package, a knockout punch (with either hand), a devastating jab and uncanny fist and foot speed. In retrospect, Dunphee knew that he was lucky he had even made it out of the ring alive and fairly sure he couldn't have beaten Payton even if there'd been an extra Billy Dunphee in the ring with him. Payton's talent and determination had been spectacular. Dunphee had just been a tough country boy who was pretty good at taking a punch.

Payton had won the Texas Golden Gloves State Championship twice and was on his way to making the U.S. Olympic team in 1980—the year Reagan boycotted the summer Olympics. But Payton never got the chance to experience that disappointment. He and twenty-one U. S. boxers, trainers and coaches had perished in a plane crash en route to Poland a few months prior.

As Sheriff Dunphee drove through Troup, he wondered at it all again.

Payton's invincibility in the ring had meant nothing in the end. All that was left was a statue dedicated to him and the others in Colorado Springs and an on-again, off-again annual boxing tourney held in his name at the

Troup Boxing Gym. Dunphee sat ringside every year it was held.

When Dunphee had heard the news of Payton's death on the AM radio in his old pick-up truck in 1980, he hadn't believed it. It didn't seem possible. Now an officer of the law for over twenty years, he knew anything was possible and sometimes the worst things. Dunphee realized that maybe the best thing he'd ever done, perhaps the closest he'd ever come to a brush with greatness, was the match he'd had with Payton. And the fact that the young man was gone still pained him.

The boxing gym was one of the only things left of note in Troup, but Troup was practically cosmopolitan compared to Harkin. Harkin had showed some life early in the 20th century, but it sputtered out in the mid-thirties. Harkin barely had a post office. Tyler was beginning to expand out past them both, and Dunphee was thinking about moving away when he retired.

The Jenkins place was on a couple dozen acres just off State Highway 135 heading to Arp. When Sheriff Dunphee turned off on the gravel drive and crossed the cattleguard, he drove slowly, so as not to disturb the handful of cattle and two nags that had run of the pasture. He parked under one of the big oak trees that sat out in front of the house, and Edna immediately appeared on the porch. She was nervous and fearful. Dunphee stepped out of the patrol car and took off his hat.

"Are you okay, Edna?" he asked.

"I don't know, Billy—Sheriff Dunphee."

"You can call me Billy, Edna. You know that."

"Billy—I don't know what happened. I'm not sure what I'm seeing. I went in the spare bedroom I keep for my granddaughter when she visits, and he was..."

Edna cupped a hand over her mouth and started to cry. Dunphee placed his hand on her shoulder and gave her a moment.

"Show me," he said.

Dunphee followed Edna into the house and recoiled when the stench hit his nostrils.

"It's bad, I know," Edna said. "But I didn't want to touch anything."

Dunphee put his hat back on and they took a left down a hall. Edna stopped at the last door on the right and held the doorknob. There was a towel at the base of the door, tucked there in an attempt to contain the odor.

"He's in here," Edna said. "I think. I didn't touch anything. I think it's him."

Edna opened the door and led Dunphee in. The smell got worse.

Noting the odor when he stood in Edna's entry, Dunphee had prepared himself for a charbroiled cadaver, but there wasn't one. There was just a large pile of black and gray ash on the near side of the sheets on the queen bed, and a smaller collection on the floor in front of the bed, settled in and on a pair of fairly new, leather moccasins. The pile on the bed was still smoking.

"I think that's Bertram," Edna said, breaking into tears.

While Dunphee was staring at the ashes on the bed, he pulled a handkerchief out of his pocket and covered his nose. If that was Bertram, he thought, he'd lost a lot of weight or the fire that consumed him had gotten incredibly hot—so hot that it probably would've burned down the whole house. Dunphee glanced at the house shoes and then the shape of the ash piles. It looked like Bertram probably burned to death, but Dunphee continued to scan the room for clues. When he turned back to Edna, she was still crying.

"Did Bertram smoke?" he ventured.

"No."

"If I didn't know any better," Dunphee continued, "I'd say someone poured gasoline on him and lit him on fire. That or jet fuel. But I don't see or smell any gasoline and jet fuel is tricky to handle. And if gasoline was poured on Bertram, what are the chances that someone could do that without spilling any... or cause him to burn up without burning anything else up?"

"So you think it's him? I mean, there's hardly anything left."

Dunphee spotted something on the bed and took a ballpoint pen out of his shirt pocket. He stood next the bed and picked at the ash pile that appeared to have been the head. He isolated a clump of cinder that contained a small, twisted bead of silver.

"Did Bertram have fillings?" Dunphee asked.

"I think so."

"This looks like part of a filling. And I assume those are Bertram's house shoes?"

"Yes."

"I guess this is Bertram. Is there anybody else it could be?"

"No."

Dunphee took her at her word, but there was still the job.

"Edna."

"Yes."

"I don't mean to be indelicate, but I have to ask. You didn't do this, did you?"

"No, Billy."

"I had to ask.

"I know."

Dunphee tried to lighten the moment. "Edna—this ain't some old cowpoke you hooked up with, and things went south?"

"Oh, goodness, no," she said, with a weak smile. "Since I lost Arthur, you know I never. I don't need another man to take care of."

"I hear you. I've felt the same way since Linda passed."

"Oh, I still can't believe it," Edna said. "She was so young."

"Yes, she was."

Dunphee nodded and Edna managed another weak smile.

"What happened to Bertram, Sheriff?"

"I'm not real sure."

They stood there silently considering what Dunphee assumed to be the remains of Bertram. He dialed the office and requested a couple of deputies and a Crime Scene Investigation unit. He led Edna out of the room, closed the door and replaced the towel. Then, they went out into the yard to wait in fresher air.

When the deputies and the CSI unit arrived, Dunphee headed to Tyler. Old man Bertram's odd remains had ruined his appetite, but he knew he should eat something. He got to Nat's Dine-In just after 10:00 a.m. and had the place to himself. He took a chair in a wall booth that featured a crooked, 8X10 snapshot of Nat (a tall African American man and the long-time, sole owner and proprietor of Nat's) standing next to Earl Campbell, Tyler's most revered native son. Nat's hair was black and full in the picture, but of late it had faded white and was receding. Nat appeared and poured Dunphee a cup of coffee.

"What'll it be, Sheriff?"

"One egg over medium," Dunphee said, adding "one piece of bacon—make that two—and side of grits."

Toast?"

"One piece of wheat toast."

"Coming right up, Sheriff."

Nat was close to Bertram's age, and also from Harkin, but he grew up in Kilgore. Dunphee had known him almost all his adult life.

Nat had served in the military and relocated to Tyler in the 1980s. He started the diner and made it into a local landmark, popular because it was folksy and Nat was the genuine article. When the uninitiated made or inquired about to-go orders, Nat was known to point at the sign out front and remind them he ran a dine-in establishment. If they wanted fast food, he'd add, they could take their business to the Whataburger down the street.

Nat was black and—excepting Earl Campbell—black was underappreciated in Tyler. But Nat's Dine-In reminded folks middle-aged and older, black and white, of what things used to be like in East Texas before everyone bent their knees to hurry up and plunked down in front of cable TV.

Dunphee sipped on his coffee. He had to see his grandmother later and he didn't relish mentioning Bertram's passing. His grandmother and Bertram had known each other when they were young. She also knew Nat.

Nat appeared with Dunphee's breakfast momentarily. The bacon smelled good, perhaps especially after the olfactory trauma he experienced at Edna's.

"How things goin?" Nat asked.

"Okay," Dunphee answered. "But it's early yet."

Dunphee finished his bacon.

"When you going to retire, Nat?"

"The day after never. How's yer grandmama doin?"

"She's alright. I'm going to see her at the home tonight."

"Please send my regards."

"I will. But I think she'd rather me bring her a piece of your pecan pie."

"Bring her by later. I'll have it made fresh."

Dunphee picked at his egg.

"How long have you known my grandmother, Nat?"

"Since I was around six. She was older, I think eleven or twelve when we left."

"Did you know Tieg Bertram?"

Nat looked directly at Dunphee and then glanced out the front window. "Hmm. You could say that. *I knew of him.*"

"I think my grandmother knew him."

"Probably so. It wasn't a big town back then."

"Still isn't."

"No. It isn't." Nat rolled up his sleeves. "Tieg Bertram left Harkin 'round same time my folks did, been gone since forever. Why you askin' about him?"

"I think he's dead. I just saw what I took to be his remains over at Edna Jenkins's place."

"Here?" Nat asked abruptly. *"In Smith County?"*

"Yep. I just found him in a pile of ashes."

Nat's face changed. He stared at the egg left on Dunphee's plate.

"You okay, Nat?" Dunphee asked.

Nat continued to stare.

"That's sad to hear," Nat said, dazed.

"Nat?"

"Yes, sir?"

"What's wrong?"

"Nothing, Sheriff. Nothing. There's just some water under that bridge. Bertram and some others caused some trouble for us back in the day."

"I never heard that."

"We don't talk about it. Nobody talks about it."

"Can you tell me about it?"

"Rather not, Sheriff."

Dunphee leaned back and stared at Nat, surprised. Nat stared back.

"It was a long time, ago, Billy Dunphee," Nat said pointedly. "I think we'd all be better off if we left it there."

Dunphee was surprised, but he didn't show it. Nat had always been oak solid, and here he was, rattled. Harkin wasn't big enough for secrets. Hell, neither was Tyler.

Nat noticed the crooked 8X10 of him standing next to Earl Campbell and straightened it.

"I gotta' get back to the kitchen," he said nonchalantly. "Anything else I can get you, Sheriff?"

"No, thanks."

"Thanks for coming by!"

"Thank you."

Dunphee set a ten dollar bill under his coffee cup and left.

He got into his patrol car, turned on the ignition and sat for a moment, stunned. Then he called the Department and told his secretary to hold his calls, except for those regarding the investigation into Tieg Bertram's death.

Dunphee sat for several moments, thinking, and then turned off the car's ignition and went back inside. Nat was still in the kitchen.

Dunphee sat down at the same table and waited. After a few moments, Nat returned to bus Dunphee's dishes. He was carrying a rag and a plastic bus bin.

"We need to talk," Dunphee said.

"That right, Billy?" Nat replied coolly. "You askin' as a friend? Or you telling me in an official capacity?"

"You know me better than that."

"Do I? I know—as a friend—I just asked you to leave this alone."

"I'm aware. But I'm trying to find out what happened to Bertram."

"Doesn't matter."

"What does that mean?"

"Maybe he got what was comin' to him."

Nat regretted the statement as soon as he said it.

Dunphee's eyes narrowed and he considered what Nat said carefully. He doubted Nat was involved in Bertram's death, but the way he initially responded to the news was peculiar.

"I see them wagon wheels turnin' in your head," Nat continued. "Don't let this thing get stuck in yer craw. Won't do you no good. Won't do any of us any good." Nat started gathering Dunphee's dishes. "I know you got a job to do," Nat added. "But this one—it's ancient history. Let the dead bury the dead."

"You have any idea how crazy you're sounding?"

"Yes, Billy. I do." Nat turned to head toward the kitchen with the dishes and then stopped, but didn't turn around. "I'm an old man, Billy. You oughta' let me alone. I slipped up. That's all.

"This just gets worse and worse," Dunphee groaned.

Nat turned around, laid the bus bin aside and sat back down with Dunphee.

"Remember the 'slaughter rule?'" Nat said. "In little league baseball...when you were a kid?

"Yes."

"This is like that, my friend. For a long time, white folks around here ran up the score, but there was no rule against it. There were hardly any rules against killing black people. Or raping black women. And the game went on and on. White folks just kept on goin'—black folks just kept on dyin. And suffering. It was before your time, most of it. But I'm gonna say this, and you need to hear me, Billy. We're friends and you need to really hear me."

Dunphee nodded.

"What happened to Bertram ain't got nothin' to do with anything goin' on today. It's a game that started a long time ago...and was bound to finish. You're grandmamma obviously didn't tell you about it...she had her reasons. I can't tell you about it now. It ain't my place.

"No one told you and no one told anyone because they were scared or ashamed. And it's been like that here since Johnny Reb came home after the war. My family left Harkin 'cause of it. And our home town is still a nothing little smudge on the map 'cause of it."

"What are you saying?" Dunphee asked.

"I'm sayin' what happened to Bertram may have been a long time coming, probably because he stayed away."

"Stayed away. Stayed away from what?"

"What he did, Billy. *What he did*."

Dunphee sat in the booth dumbfounded. He suddenly felt like he had no idea where he was from or who the people he grew up with were. "Nat," he said. "I can't let this stand. I feel...I feel undermined."

"Sorry," Nat replied. "But that's a fine word for it. That's exactly how I might've put it."

"You know I gotta' know," Dunphee added.

Nat looked Dunphee directly in the eyes. They stared at each other for a long moment and then Nat nodded.

Nat told Dunphee he had to get ready for the lunch crowd, but that he would meet with him later. At the library, at 3:00 p.m. Dunphee hadn't been to a library in years and he regretted it. He decided to move up his date with his grandmother.

Dunphee's grandmother's nursing home was not too shabby and had been her idea. He had protested, but Emma Jean, as his grandmother preferred to be called, usually got her way. When he entered her room, she was sitting on the side of her bed, staring out the window.

"Emma Jean," he said.

She turned her head slowly.

"Hello."

"Hello. How are you?"

"I'm alright. What about you?"

"Doing okay."

"How are my great-grandbabies?"

"Still off at school, one at A & M and one at UT."

"That'll make for an..." Emma Jean trailed off.

"An interesting Thanksgiving," Dunphee said, finishing her sentence. "Yes."

"Thanksgiving? Already?"

"No, Me-Maw. Not yet."

"Seemed awful soon."

"Yep. We've got awhile."

Dunphee looked around the room at all of Emma Jean's old pictures. The TV was on but the sound was turned down.

"I saw Nat," Dunphee added.

"How's he doing?"

"He's doing well. He sends his regards."

"Oh, I miss him. He's a sweet man."

"He's a good guy. Always was."

"Yes."

Dunphee walked over and sat in a chair next to Emma Jean's small couch. Then, he stared at her. She kept her white hair neat and her nails filed, but she was visibly frail. She tried to carry herself well, but advancing age was really starting to show. Emma Jean noticed that he was staring.

"Can I talk to you about something?" Dunphee asked.

"I suppose...so."

"Okay. You may have to put on your memory cap."

"Okay. I can do that."

"Do you remember Tieg Bertram?"

Emma Jean looked away and was slow to answer. "Bertram. Yes. He moved away."

"Yes," Dunphee said. "What do you remember about him?"

"Oh. He was a bully."

"He was?"

"Yes."

Dunphee waited for her to elaborate, but she didn't.

"Yes," she repeated. "Why do you ask?"

"Well, he came back over the weekend."

"Back..." Emma Jean said. "Here?" She turned to face Dunphee. "Bertram is here?!"

"Yes."

"Is he okay?"

"No."

Emma Jean clasped her hands and brought them to her face, her knuckles just under her nose. She appeared to be praying, but Dunphee knew she wasn't. It wasn't her way. Or his.

Emma Jean's hands were clasped tightly and they started to shake. She unclasped them and placed them at her sides. She held them there for a moment and started to sob. Dunphee came over and placed his arm around her shoulders.

"Are you okay, Emma Jean?"

"No, Billy," she said, between sniffs. "I'm very tired." Emma Jean wiped her eyes. "Sorry," she continued. "I'm just so tired."

"You need a nap?" Dunphee asked, perplexed.

"I don't know. Just let me lie down. I'll be better in a minute."

Dunphee hugged his grandmother and then helped her lay back in the bed. She closed her eyes and he stood over her, wondering what the hell was going on. When she fell asleep, he left.

Dunphee walked out to his patrol car and put the Department on the horn. The CSI unit had wrapped up and Bertram's remains had been transferred to the Coroner's Office. There was no official word yet.

Dunphee was frustrated and it was still early.

Emma Jean had finished raising Dunphee after his parents were killed in a car wreck. He was eleven at the time, about to turn twelve. He spent the rest of his adolescence on his grandparents' farm, milking cows, driving tractors and hauling hay. He hunted and fished and canoed the Nueces and Sabine Rivers. And he played sports.

Dunphee's grandfather passed not long after he graduated high school. His name was Roscoe and he was from Valdosta, Georgia. He was a tall, quiet man, patient and witty. Dunphee had loved him and his grandmother dearly, and now Emma Jean was all he had left. His aunts and uncles still all lived close, but he didn't see much of them. Especially after he came back from Sam Houston State University and joined the Sheriff's Department.

They had all been there on the night he fought Payton, like he was Harkin's own Great White Hope. His grandparents had remained composed after he lost, Emma Jean giving him a tight, loving hug, and his grandfather winking at him and nodding, realizing how hard he had worked to even put things in the hands of the judges. There had been no doubt in Dunphee's mind who won, but at least he went the distance. His aunts and uncles raised redneck hell.

That Nigger cheated.

Goddam spear-chucker!

Dunphee knew Payton had heard them, because Payton had looked at him the way black people you know and like look at you when a racist antagonist interrupts the common consideration or friendship you've shared, and the black person knows the circumstances will force you to agree with the antagonist or hold your tongue, a betrayal either way. But the way things were and sometimes still are.

Dunphee had lowered his head then, soundly defeated. And ashamed.

Twenty years removed, Dunphee sat in his patrol car hoping Payton had understood that. That he had been ashamed.

The dead don't bury the dead, he thought. The living do. To make things easier. To make it easier to betray them.

To Dunphee's way of thinking, the best way to bury the dead was to live right by them, and he figured that's why Byron Payton had remained a friendly presence in his mind all these years, like his parents, his granddad and, more recently, his wife. They weren't meant to be disposed of. They were supposed to stay with you, in memory and spirit, guides as much as reminders. And they still made Dunphee as much of who he was as anything else.

Nat's advice had done no good at all. What happened to Bertram and whatever it was he may or may not have done to deserve it, stuck in Dunphee's craw and vexed him something fierce. The cryptic talk, the warnings; he knew Nat was being straight. But the missing pieces, which seemed to indict Bertram and the entire town of Harkin, disturbed and frustrated him.

Emma Jean slept fitfully.

She kept mumbling a name under her breath, inaudible at first, but finally plain.

"Petty," she moaned.

She was back at her parent's place, early in the Depression. Up in her bedroom.

Her parents were out front, watching a group of Harkin citizens leave on horseback. They were followed by a one-horse wagon. A black boy was lying unconscious on the worn planks on the bottom of the wagon. It was Petty. His lips were smashed and he was bleeding from his side and his head above one eye. His hands were tied behind his back.

Emma Jean moaned again, barely audible.

She had been forced to do something that day.

Not by the black boy lying in the wagon, but by her parents and their neighbors and their friends. By the community.

When they had brought Emma Jean out and she had seen Petty in the wagon, she thought he was dead. There was so much blood.

When her parents had asked her to do what she did, she thought it wouldn't matter because Petty looked like he was already gone. And her parents had told her to do it. Told her that if she didn't do it, they could lose the farm. Told her that if she didn't do it, their neighbors might turn against them and run them off.

Did she realize they could lose everything? Did she realize they might have to move away to make a living?

Emma Jean had done what her parents asked. Emma Jean had done what she was told and they had kept the farm and their friends and stayed in Harkin.

From that day forward, however, there were unintended consequences. Emma Jean suddenly enjoyed small town celebrity, importance, pity—as a victim and maybe even a survivor.

It was all a lie. And Emma Jean resented the lie.

Petty had been her friend. Petty had taught her how to catch crawdads and trap fireflies in jars. And she was trying to teach Petty his letters.

Emma Jean remembered hearing her parents argue that night after they carried Petty away in the wagon.

It's our fault, what they done to that boy.

How could we have known?

She shoulda' known better.

We shoulda' known better.

Petty wuz just a boy, a good boy.

Don't matter a lick. You know what the talk woulda' been.

Emma Jean hadn't seen what happened. She was told later, by a neighbor's bragging son. It had turned her blood cold, and she didn't think it would ever thaw.

And it didn't for a long time.

What happened to Petty was never forgotten; it was just never spoken of. Emma Jean was not inclined to forget, but it was an ugly thing to bear. She busied herself with her chores and schoolwork. It had everything to do with why she was late to marry.

Emma Jean had plenty of callers, but they were all from the Harkin area. One by one, she politely turned them away. Her mother began to worry she would be an old maid. Her father wondered if she was simply doing it out of spite. Emma Jean didn't believe the cold in her would ever subside, but it did. Life went on.

She met Billy's grandfather and she grew to love him. Their courtship was prolonged, because she had grown comfortable in the cold. She may have felt she owed it to Petty. But Roscoe was persistent and when he proposed, she told him about it, tested him with the truth, the shame of it, her long sadness and her soul laid bare. And a curious thing happened.

Roscoe didn't comfort her or try to help her rationalize it. Roscoe understood.

There had been a similar incident, maybe even worse, outside Roscoe's hometown. He had some experience with the same kind of revulsion. He was afflicted with some of the same guilt and doubt and sadness. They were both disfigured on the inside and she realized they could shelter one another. And they did. And when Roscoe passed, Emma Jean had Billy. Her surviving sons and daughters had become little more than East Texas detritus, subject to the same ebbs and flows of the communal neuroses that had seized the citizenry of Harkin when she was young. But Billy was different. Billy was like her and Roscoe, capable of empathy. Conscience. And he, too, was alienated by his own decency in the midst of dimwitted hayseeds and slack-souled buffoons. They were everywhere and all at once, the products of dangerous mob mentality that seemed to thrive in environs of red dirt and pineywood forests.

Idiots like Tieg Bertram and his kind had fed off frenzy and reveled in it. Men like Billy usually stood back, and away, and tried to keep some perspective.

In Emma Jean's dream, Petty was awake and being drug by a rope tied around his chest and arms. He hadn't been dead in the back of the wagon and this disturbed her.

Petty was being led to a large tree stump by a dozen white men. He was crying and calling out to the ones he recognized, to the ones he had worked for or grew up around—but they all ignored him. Disassociation was necessary. It made what they were about to do easier.

"Petty," Emma Jean repeated weakly.

Her eyebrows furrowed and she began to turn.

Though distracted, Nat worked the lunchtime crowd with his usual, imperturbable contrarianism. And customers still managed to spill coffee, forget to tip the waitpersons and asininely inquire about catering or "to go" orders.

When the lunch customers began to fritter out, Nat thought on Dunphee's line of inquiry while he bussed tables.

It had never occurred to him that the lynching of Petty Smith would ever come up again—especially in a conversation with a white man. White folks were great at forgetting history that presented them less than favorably and even better at portraying folks who viewed them unfavorably, well, unfavorably. It was a crippling one-two punch and Nat had heard it all.

Jim Crow was a long time ago.

Reverse discrimination is the real problem.

If you people will just quit belly-aching about race.

He marveled at the simplicity of white avoidance and almost admired the sheer and utter gall of it. It was as if white folk really believed that black folk were incapable of keeping track of what had been done to them. It had been less than a year since James Byrd, Jr., was beaten severely and then dragged to death behind a pick-up truck carrying three, young white men, and the first reporting on the crime had focused on Byrd's past issues with alcoholism. And once white folks at large got their head around the actual facts concerning the murder, they acted like it was the first time anything like that had ever happened in Texas.

Nat shook his head and checked the time. It was 1:45 p.m.

Nat was also dumbfounded that Bertram had come back. Nat was a young man in the early 1950s when the last incident occurred, and it had happened the exact same way. Lester Grissem had returned home for a funeral and one funeral became two. Lester was cremated before cremation was even a thing. And they had all known damn well or at least suspected the truth of it then. But everyone had just gone on back about their business. Black folks and white.

Could Bertram have forgotten?

Nat found that hard to believe, but Bertram was getting old. Maybe he had gotten old enough he didn't care. Maybe he thought something had changed.

Nat thought on what it had meant to his own family. They had had some hard years after, forced to start again in a new town. Grissem's death had absolved them all. But too little, too late.

Nat finished cleaning a section of tables and carried his bus bin to the kitchen. Then, he abruptly told the girl behind the register he was taking off for the rest of the day.

Nat decided to go to the library early. He had started participating in a local African American genealogical research group on the weekends. He quickly learned his way around the library and was well-familiar with the microfiche machine. He figured he'd go on down and locate some of the articles he wanted to show Dunphee.

Dunphee was in trouble.

Bertram's death was inexplicable, his mother's reaction to it was puzzling and Nat's insinuated secrets about them both were unsettling. And when Dunphee remembered the phrase that seemed to describe what happened to Bertram, he immediately wished he hadn't.

Spontaneous human combustion.

It was straight out of *Night Gallery* when he was a kid. Or maybe it was *Kolchak: The Nightstalker*.

Oh well, he thought. He was up for retirement soon. Maybe he could buy the old Troup Boxing Gym.

When Dunphee arrived at the library, Nat was waiting for him. There was a short row of three microfiche machines in the back corner and Nat had them all to himself. He had microfiche spools installed in all three.

Nat smiled, stood up and shook Dunphee's hand. "You ready for this?" he asked.

"I don't know," Dunphee answered. "It doesn't matter. I need to know."

"Okay," Nat said. "First, let me give you some background. Last week you were on the news for that memorial the city put in on the west side of the courthouse square. The one for the fallen law officers."

"'Fallen Heroes.' Yes. Fire department and law enforcement personnel who died in the line of duty."

"And the ceremony was moving and the water pool was pretty and you had a good turnout."

"Yes."

"Have you ever noticed how you don't see a lot of black folks down there? Except to report to the courthouse across the street?"

"Not a lot, but some."

"Probably only a few. Nice memorial dedication, right? The courthouse, the monuments. You like it down there?"

"It's alright, I guess."

"Only 'cause you don't know any better."

"Well, tell me then."

"And the same thing is true of Harkin. But I ain't ready to talk about Harkin. Or Bertram. Tyler first. We'll take a look at Tyler, first."

"Okay."

"You sure?"

"Sure."

Nat sat down at the middle microfiche machine and had Dunphee sit at the one on his left. He gave him brief instructions on how to scroll the microfiche forward and back and how to focus in and enlarge. Then, he enlarged a story on a page that he had already pulled up for Dunphee. It was from the October 30, 1895 edition of the *Dallas Morning News*. The title read "Roasted to Death."

Nat had Billy glance at it and then lean over and examine the article on the newspaper page he had pulled up. It was from the October 31, 1895 edition of *Wills Point Chronicle*. The title read "Burned at the Stake."

"Is this the same guy?" Dunphee said.

"Yep."

"He was burned at the stake?"

"Yep."

"Where?"

Nat nodded at the microfiche machines. "Take your time," he said.

Dunphee began reading.

He learned that in late October, 1895, a black man named Robert Henson Hillard had been the only suspect in the alleged sexual assault and murder of a young white woman. Except the victim, the only eyewitness, was dead. But Hillard hadn't faced a judge or jury. Dunphee learned that one of his predecessors, Wig Smith, had discovered Hillard asleep in a cotton pen near Kilgore. On Smith's way back to Tyler, a large white mob surrounded him and relieved him of his suspect. Then, the mob finished Hillard's transport, planted a steel rail from the railyard in the ground in the present-day memorial section of the public square and burned him alive in front of a crowd of thousands. Dunphee also learned that Hillard's lynching party had taken its time, starting, extinguishing and restarting the fire over and over, letting it rise a little higher and burn a little longer each time, so Hillard would cook as slowly and painfully as possible.

"Oh...my..." Dunphee sighed.

Dunphee also learned that halfway through the ghastly proceedings, Hillard had begun smashing his head back against the rail he was bound to, attempting to bash his own brains in to escape his long, horrendous suffering. And his agony elicited hoots and snickers from his tormentors.

"Is this for real, Nat?" Dunphee asked.

"Real as you and me sitting here."

Dunphee finished.

"The same part of the square where we erected the Fallen Heroes Memorial?"

"Yep."

"Damn."

"Damn is right. Now look at the story on the last machine."

Dunphee moved to the last microfiche machine in the short row. It displayed an article from the May 26, 1912 edition of the *Dallas Morning News*. The title read "Negro Meets Death at Stake in Tyler." The African

American victim was Dan Davis. Like Hillard, Davis was accused of attacking a white woman, denied a trial and due process and burned at the stake on the west side of the courthouse square in front of a mob of thousands. When the flames had begun to consume him, he begged his executioners to slit his throat; but they ignored his pleas.

Dunphee finished reading again. His gaze met Nat's momentarily, and then he averted his eyes. "You think you know a place," he said. "There are bad things, but you assume the good outweighs the bad. But this...How could folks not know about this?"

"Some do," Nat replied. "Not many. But they're all black and old-timers like me. No one talks about this. No one wants to hear it."

Nat and Dunphee remained silent for a minute or two and then Nat sat down at the first machine and began rewinding the microfilm.

"Those are just the ones they burned in town," he continued. "They burned more at Camp Ford, northeast of town on State Highway 271. It was the largest, Confederate prisoner of war camp west of the Mississippi. They burned several black men there, black men enlisted in the Union army or black Union sympathizers."

Dunphee turned back to the machine he was sitting at and mimicked Nat. They rewound the rolls of microfilm and reinserted them in the small boxes they came in.

"Someone should answer for this," Dunphee observed. "Davis and Hillard ought to have a memorial themselves."

"That's all well and good, sure. But, if you ever suggest it you'll lose your job or they'll bury you under the damn thing if it's ever erected. This is just what went on. It started during the war out at Camp Ford and continued after Reconstruction. There was no slaughter rule. There were no rules at all where blacks were concerned. Remember those three boys that dragged 'ol James Byrd to death in Jasper, last year? That one that received the death penalty? He'll be the first white man that ever received a death sentence for killing a black man in Texas. Think about that."

Dunphee shrugged. It was a lot to take in.

"What can we do?" he asked.

"Nothin," Nat replied. "But we know. You know—I know. We can know. And maybe later we can tell more people. Right now, no good'll come of it. People don't wanna' know and wouldn't believe you if you told 'em. Let's talk about Harkin."

Nat told Dunphee what he knew. The Tyler atrocities were a primer; but as bad as they were, they were tame compared to what happened in Harkin.

Pettigrew Smith, a thirteen-year-old black boy, had simply been accused of being sweet on Dunphee's grandmother, nothing more. Petty's mother had worked in the fields with and for Emma Jean's folks, and it was natural that Emma Jean and Petty started playing together, running the pastures and exploring the creeks. But the townsfolk took note and were not unfamiliar with how their neighbors in Tyler handled their "negro" problems.

The town of Harkin was the proud hometown of two Confederate war heroes, both deceased, and the youngest son of one was still insanely bitter about the "War of Northern Aggression" and Lincoln's attempt to turn Dixie into "Nigger York." This yokel, whose name escaped Nat, had been the instigator; seven Harkin boys, including Lester Grissem and Tieg Bertram had done the deed.

With the son of the dead Confederate hero coaching, Petty was accused of making eyes at Emma Jean and beaten. Then, "making eyes" became "making advances." More young men beat on Petty and by the time he was brought unconscious before the town elders, his guilt was a foregone conclusion. All that was missing was a semblance of proof.

Petty was taken out to Emma Jean's home and she was coerced to give it. Then Grissem, Bertram, Tom Huff, Jack Walls, the son of the Confederate hero and three others took Petty to a clearing heading out of town (towards New Summerfield), and bound him to a broad, tall tree stump with rope. Then they cut his tongue out, castrated him and bullwhipped him until he was unconscious.

The soaking, antiseptic sting of kerosene revived Petty, just in time for Tom Huff to apply the torch. Huff ridiculed him first, asking him if he had any last words. Blood poured from Petty's mouth and tears streamed down his cheeks. As the others laughed, Huff set Petty aflame.

"Even without his tongue, they say he wailed for several terrible minutes," Nat said. "Eventually the flames burned through the ropes holding Petty up. He fell over. And even after the fire had burned him chimney chute black, something inside held on. Right as Huff walked over to poke Petty's charred body with a stick, Petty suddenly writhed and contorted, twisting away from the coals."

"Oh, god," Dunphee said.

"It scared the hell out of the lynching party. Bertram supposedly yelped out loud and Huff threw up. The son of the Confederate hero fell down to his knees. But Jack Walls and one of the others started stomping on what was left of Petty and kicked him back into the fire. Huff gathered some more brush and struck Petty's head with a chunk of it a few times, revealing his white skull plain through his charred scalp. And then they just piled the rest of the wood on top. When Petty had burned down to cinder, they left. And that's when things got really scary."

"When did my grandmother find out?" Dunphee asked.

"I'm not sure. Once her folks got wind of what happened, I think they kept her locked up for days."

Dunphee's phone rang and he answered it. He nodded a few times and said "yes" and "thanks" and hung up. Then he turned back to Nat.

"That was the lab," he said. "Those are Bertram's ashes."

Nat and Sheriff Dunphee left the library and went to the courthouse square. Dunphee gave Nat a ride and they parked on the west side. Then, Dunphee went over and stood in front of the Fallen Heroes Memorial. Nat joined him.

"It's a nice monument," Nat said.

"It is," Dunphee replied. "I certainly prefer it to the one dedicated to the Confederacy back towards the courthouse—but you didn't hear me say that out loud."

"I understand," Nat said. "I do."

Dunphee sat down on a park bench and Nat joined him. "It doesn't seem like a bad place, does it?" Dunphee asked.

"No," Nat replied. "It's not too bad. It's a lot better than it was."

Dunphee laughed out loud. "Sorry," he said.

"No," Nat said. "I understand. It's crazy. Sometimes I still feel like we're still living without slaughter rules...Here at home and overseas. Other times, I think we've come a little ways."

"So what you told me so far wasn't scary?"

"It was scary, but not real scary. Not hide-under-your-bed, tooth-chattering afraid-scary. White people had burned plenty of black boys in Texas before this."

"Shit."

"Yep." Nat looked around to make sure no one was within earshot. "The thing is, the next morning Petty's remains were gone."

"Yeah?"

"Yep. The tree stump was burned all to hell, but Petty's ashes were gone."

"Holy crap."

"It frightened the lynch party at first, but then they decided it was some kinda' prank or black folk just tending to their dead. Just went on. They told some folks, and later, after some time had passed and they were no longer afraid, they did some bragging. Word got around. Nothing was ever done about it. Petty's mom moved away. Dallas, I think."

Dunphee took off his hat and placed it on his knee.

"About a year later," Nat continued, "Tommy Huff disappeared. Got up early one morning to milk cows, and all they found was three or four piles of ashes under a cow. Sound familiar?"

"Human remains?" Dunphee asked.

"They didn't have high technology in those days, Billy. Whadda' you think? They suspected, but they didn't know for sure. Didn't even singe the bone-dry hay around the ashes. But Huff was gone and no one ever heard from him again. Then, Jack Walls and two of the others disappeared the following week. All the same way—out in the dark, missing, a pile of ashes in one of the places they were supposed to have been. And that's when we had to leave."

"They couldn't explain what was happening," Dunphee deduced. "But they started to think they knew."

"Yep. A black boy had been burned at the stake and now white folks were disappearing."

"They thought someone in the black community might be responsible."

"Exactly. They thought we were retaliating somehow."

"Wow."

"Yep. But we weren't. We weren't stupid. In that day and age, angry white folks could run black folks out of entire cities, even counties. My family fled and so did the rest. Gave up our land and homes, whatever we couldn't carry. We started over.

"The son of the Confederate hero hung himself a few months later and the 'disappearances' seemed to stop. But what really happened—"

"Bertram and Lester moved away," Dunphee blurted.

"Bingo," Nat said. "And you know most of the rest. Grissem came back for a visit in 1951 and got burned to a crisp. They called it a freak accident. I think any of the old-timers who'd convinced themselves that it'd been us behind the burning disappearances, finally considered otherwise. And, of course, Bertram stayed away almost for good."

"Was there anybody else involved? I mean—not that I'm buying a charbroiled Pettigrew Smith still walking around like some kind of vengeful ghost—but was there anybody else Petty could be targeting?"

"No one else still alive was directly or even indirectly involved, Billy. Except maybe your grandmother."

"Oh, shit."

Dunphee dropped Nat off at the restaurant and headed back over to the nursing home. Emma Jean was waiting.

When he saw her, he hugged her as if he hadn't seen her in years.

"Take it easy, kiddo," she said, smiling.

"Just glad to see you, Me-Maw."

"Glad to see you, too, Billy. But it's only been a few hours."

Billy smiled. She was feeling better.

Emma Jean turned off the silent TV and they sat in the chairs in front of it.

"It's a little before your time, Billy," Emma Jean said. "But do you remember those old cathedral-looking radios?"

"Maybe. I think so. I know I've seen pictures."

"We used to have one when I was younger. A Philco 90. It was a tired, old thing, that would lose the signals. You could set it on and leave it on your favorite channel, and then, when you turned it on again, the signal would be gone or it wouldn't be there all the way. We'd turn it off and when we turned it back on a few hours later, the channel would be working fine. Never could tell when the signal would be all there."

"You want one of those old radios, Emma Jean?" Dunphee asked.

"Oh, honey," Emma Jean replied, laughing. "I am one of those old radios."

"Emma Jean."

"No, William Taggert Dunphee, I'm serious."

"Okay."

"I'm not always around—and I know that—I wasn't completely around earlier when you came by. But I'm here now."

Emma Jean took one of Dunphee's hands and squeezed it. He squeezed hers back.

"I'm glad," Dunphee said.

"Me, too. But I need you to take me somewhere."

"Let's go do something. You want to go out to eat? You want to see a movie?"

"No, no. Nothing like that. Thanks, though. For offering. You're such a good boy, and a strong man." Tears filled Emma Jean's eyes. "I'm so proud of you."

Dunphee's eyes welled up. "Thanks, Mee-Maw. You know how much I love you."

"You know how much I love you, too, boy." Emma Jean got up and hugged him. He hugged her tightly again, and she laughed. "I wish I would remember to say things like that more often."

Dunphee released her from his embrace. She walked over to her closet and took a light jacket off a hanger. "I need you to take me back to Harkin, Billy."

"What?" Dunphee said, standing up. "No, Emma Jean. Why?"

"You don't know why?"

"No, ma'am."

"I called Nat's Dine-In inquiring after you a little while ago. I guess you were on your way."

"Oh, Emma Jean."

"It's okay. I know you know. But I'm glad you know. I sure miss Nat. You forget my piece of pecan pie?"

"We can go there, right now. I'll buy you the whole pie so you can bring it back here. And we'll get some vanilla ice cream to go with it."

"Maybe later, Billy. Maybe later. Please take me back home to Harkin."

"Why, Mee-Maw? Why?"

"They did keep me locked up for a spell," Emma Jean said. "But eventually things went back closer to normal—except Petty was gone. My best friend. I didn't know everything that had happened until later. I hadn't even been aware of some of the boys disappearing, or what they said was disappearances. But there were rumors."

Emma Jean walked to the center of the room and continued.

"They said on the days those young men disappeared, there was a black boy playing, just off a clearing on the road to New Summerfield."

"There's no clearing there now, Emma Jean. It's thick woods. Through and through."

"I don't doubt you, but I have to try."

"Try? Try and do what?"

"I'd like to see him again, Billy. You don't know what it's like. All these years. What happened. I'd just like to see him one more time."

"I doubt he's out there if he ever was. And if he is out there, he may not be the same."

"Maybe not. But I can try. Tieg came back and he's gone. Petty is here. I know it."

"What if he's looking for you?"

"Then there's no sense in hiding. Please, Billy. I'm ready. I been ready. I'm old. I'm not even myself some days."

"But I don't want you to go. I don't want to lose you."

"You'll never lose me, Billy. You never lost your granddad. You never lost your parents. I see all of them in you...when the dial on the radio is working.

"I never lost your granddad. I never lost your mama or your daddy. And I never lost Petty. And now he's back. What would you give to see Linda again? Or Papa Roscoe? Or your mama and daddy?

"Please help me, Billy. Please."

Dunphee took a deep breath as he approached Harkin. His place was located down a turn-off opposite of the old county road to New Summerfield, and he thought about just driving his grandmother there. But she wasn't having it.

Emma Jean was light and anxious. She talked about Dunphee's granddad and his parents. She talked about his baseball games. Dunphee wished she could stay like this, suddenly full of vigor and familiarity. But he knew she was right about that part. The channel would come and go. And eventually it would fade away.

They took the county road towards New Summerfield just as it was starting to get dark. Dunphee was having second thoughts about the whole crazy narrative and still wasn't sure they'd see anything—but that's when they did.

Dunphee started to speed up, pretend like he didn't notice; but his grandmother grabbed his arm.

"There he is," she said.

The dark figure was off to Dunphee's left, right at the edge of the thick woods. It was a curious sight and Dunphee felt his stomach drop.

He slowed down, pulling over about twenty-five yards in front of it, on its side of the road. When Dunphee opened his car door, the smell stung his nostrils and he drew his gun. His grandmother was already out on her side of the car and spryly walking around it towards the creature.

It didn't seem to notice either of them, until Emma Jean said its name. Then it stopped.

"Petty," Emma Jean repeated. "Petty, it's me."

The apparition turned to Emma Jean and then stepped in her direction.

Dunphee screamed "Stop!" and ran toward the dark figure.

The figure turned back to Dunphee and limped stiffly forward. Dunphee yelled stop, again, but it kept coming.

"Billy," Emma Jean said. "Please. *Please*."

The dark figure approached Billy, its roasted hide cracking, its eyes bright red and its ghastly smile offering a profound image of menace. Dunphee stopped and watched it disbelievingly and then took aim.

As Emma Jean approached, the creature stopped and stood stock still, approximately fifteen yards from Dunphee.

Dunphee stared at it, a blackened human ligament. Twisted, repulsive. He could hardly believe what he was seeing—but he couldn't look away. He held his aim steady.

"Stay back, Emma Jean," Dunphee said.

She stopped, but Petty turned toward her and took an awkward step. Dunphee began firing and emptied his clip

The dark figure was rocked backwards and sideways, tripping and then stumbling, every bullet producing a flash of yellow-orange flame as it penetrated or passed through the creature's blackened form. But it never collapsed.

As Dunphee reached for his spare clip, it slowly steadied itself and began coming at him. Emma Jean began screaming.

"No, Petty, no! STOP, PETTY. *STOP!*

The apparition froze in its tracks, its lidless eyes still aimed forward in the direction of Dunphee. Emma Jean stepped closer.

"No, Emma Jean," Dunphee cried. However it was too late.

The creature turned its head slowly, almost mechanically. Its grotesque face and teeth were expressionless. Emma Jean beamed.

Dunphee raised his gun again, but he couldn't fire. He screamed "Mee-Maw," but Emma Jean didn't hear. He aimed his gun, but his grandmother took another step toward the creature and extended her left arm. The creature turned its body slowly and stood awkwardly, raising its right.

Dunphee watched helplessly.

Emma Jean's fingertips touched the creature's charred knuckles and there was a bright flash of blue flame.

In the glowing light, Dunphee saw Petty, a young black boy, at the edge of the woods. He was dressed in well-worn britches with suspenders slung over his over-sized, white, hand-me-down long-johns. And facing him stood a young Emma Jean in a light, cotton dress, with more life in her than he thought he had ever seen before. Both of them were bright and happy, both before it all. And they were smiling.

Smiling.

Dunphee started to cry.

Then, Emma Jean and Petty were laughing and Dunphee was no longer there.

As Emma Jean and Petty turned to run, the blue glow flashed yellow and orange and became flame. And then they were no longer there.

Finally taking a breath, Dunphee wiped his eyes with the sleeve of his gun hand, and then re-holstered his weapon.

He walked over to where they had stood last and saw two separate sets of ashes.

He began crying again, but this time he didn't stop. He dropped to his knees and let everything out.

Dunphee sat next to the two sets of ashes for half an hour, crying like a child, for everything that had gone on and for everything that had gone wrong. Then, he drove home.

At the house, he parked the patrol car and went inside and changed. He came back out with two empty, 5-gallon plastic buckets and a shovel. He drove back out to spot where he'd left Emma Jean and Petty. He shoveled them into separate buckets, put them in his truck and then transported them to his house.

The next day he drove out to the old, overgrown Harkin cemetery and buried them in two separate sections of his grandmother's reserved plot, next to his grandfather's.

Tieg Bertram's cause of death was ruled a possible "Spontaneous Human Combustion."

Local and state media outlets had a field day with it, but Dunphee refused to comment. He even turned down a call from the *National Enquirer*.

Emma Jean's remaining children filed a Missing Persons report after she had been gone for a week. They wouldn't have known, but the nursing home called.

Dunphee's aunt and uncles pushed for the county to issue a death certificate after six months, and he stayed out of it. When the certificate was filed, his aunt and uncles fought over what was left of Emma Jean's bank accounts, which wasn't much. And they never concerned themselves with purchasing a headstone for their mother's presumably empty grave.

Dunphee eventually bought one that matched his grandfather's and placed it at his grandmother's plot himself. He had the initials "P. S." etched into the center of the back of Emma Jean's marker in four-inch letters and didn't think anyone would notice.

And for a long time, no one did.

Lying Eyes
By Shawna Borman

O liver pushed the scalpel into her eye socket, careful not to damage the globe. He sawed through the four extraocular muscles and deftly pried the eyeball from its home. As he pulled the eye away from her face, slicing through the optic nerve, he noticed the green contact lens that now clung to her cheek. He frowned at the brown iris that was staring from his palm.

"This is what happens when you try to hide your true self."

He had met the girl two hours ago. She was hitchhiking when he picked her up. As she approached the passenger's side door he watched her in the rearview mirror, catching sight of her green eyes. As soon as she opened the car door and he looked at her directly he knew she was wearing contacts but it was too late; the urge was irresistible once it started. Something would click in his brain and though he wasn't sure why, he knew what he had to do. She asked if he knew a place she could stay for the night and she accepted when he offered the spare room at his cabin. He thought it was almost too easy, but it was starting to rain and she seemed desperate to get away from something or someone.

"Well, it's not entirely your fault. Sometimes I just get overzealous and can't stop myself." He shrugged and set the eyeball aside. "But you're right, now's not the time for lectures."

Brushing away the colored lens on her remaining eye, he set to work removing it as well. He hummed quietly as he worked, almost as if attempting to soothe a patient. When he had the globe in his hand, he picked the other up and looked at them.

"What to do with you..." He stared at the eyes then looked down at the girl beneath him. "I think I'll leave them with you."

Oliver placed the globes back in the sockets and took off his gloves. He removed the wire from the girl's neck, frowning at the red ring it had created. He always hated seeing the blemishes left behind after the struggle. In his own form of recompense, he would make sure that she rested peacefully in a clearing in the woods behind the cabin, along with the five that had preceded her. Each grave had its own subtle marker, reminding him where each girl was from; each had come from a different area along his trip between the cabin and home. He also despised the crushing sleep that followed such acts because it made the dreams that much more vivid. Unfortunately, both sleep and the dreams were unavoidable. No matter how hard he squeezed his eyes closed after he woke up, the memories that were called forth by the dreams enveloped him.

Ollie? Oliver? Ollie, Ollie, oxen free!

The voice was soft, almost a whisper, as it called to him.

When his eyes opened, he was surrounded by toys, clothes, shoes, all of the important things that had a way of getting lost in the bottom of a closet. He was six again. He slid the door open a crack and peeked through. Her dazzling green eyes were the first thing that greeted him.

"Found you." She pulled the closet door open and beckoned for him to come out.

He held himself, rocking back and forth, and shook his head. His eyes followed her as she moved to sit at the foot of his bed. Her strawberry blonde hair glowed in the late afternoon light that flooded through the window. He could barely hear it but he knew she was humming his favorite song, "Return to Pooh Corner," knew that she would keep humming until he went to her. He stared at her profile for what felt like hours, never making eye contact but constantly aware of the shining jewels that kept flickering in his direction.

When he finally left his haven, she pulled him into a hug. "You okay?"

He nodded but the fresh bruises that peeked out from under his sleeves were more honest.

"I'm so sorry that I was late, Ollie."

"Where'd you go, sissy?"

"I had to go to the library after school. I thought I'd be home sooner. Mom seemed better today. I thought it'd be okay. I... I'm so sorry." Tears glistened in the corners of her green eyes.

He smiled and hugged her. "I'm okay, sissy."

She was crying silently and a quiet buzzing penetrated the air surrounding the two. It grew steadily louder as the room dimmed. He blinked and when his eyes opened, he was staring at his current self in the bathroom mirror, his alarm clock ringing in the next room. He rubbed the images from his sight and went to turn the alarm off.

"Time to head back. Pity, really. I could use a vacation."

After a small breakfast, he made the three-hour drive back to Dallas. As he entered the outskirts of the city, he stopped at a small place that he frequented, where the sign simply said "Diner," for a cup of coffee. It was the type of place where the waitresses all called you "hun" and the chocolate pie was always homemade. As soon as he entered, he was greeted with a smile and told to sit anywhere. He chose his favorite table closest to the door. A new waitress set a menu in front of him.

"What can I get'cha to drink?" Her voice was soft, almost musical.

He looked up at her; jeans, a grey t-shirt, pale face framed by auburn hair, and a set of jade eyes. The word "perfect" ran through his mind, but all that escaped his lips was, "Coffee, please."

She smiled. "Can do. Anything else?"

He shook his head.

She walked away, humming. He stared out of the glass door as he waited for her to return. He noted that there were three cars in the parking lot besides his. They must belong to the woman, Delores, behind the counter who doubled as owner and cook, the waitress and an elderly gentleman seated in the corner. It was a sunny Sunday afternoon and a breeze was rustling the trees that lined the other side of the road. He was almost lost in the rhythmic swaying when a clatter brought him back to the coffee set before him.

"Sure you don't want anything else?" She stared at him.

He looked around at the counter and gestured toward the displayed pies. "What kind of pies do you have?"

"We have apple, peach, lemon meringue, chocolate, and…" She counted off the pies with her fingers, frowned and glanced toward the display case. "Oh! And coconut crème."

"Uh, and which do you recommend…" His eyes dropped to the nametag pinned to her shirt. "Jocelyn?"

She shifted and glanced away. "It's just Lyn, Mister… Um…"

"Oliver. They just call me Oliver here."

"So they call you Oliver here? Does that mean you're a regular?"

He nodded. "I guess you could say that."

"Well, I may be a newbie here but personally, I prefer the apple or lemon."

"Then I guess I'll try the lemon meringue, please." He smiled.

She nodded. "Okie doke."

He watched her walk away. She pulled a whole pie from the display case and Delores handed Lyn a knife. He stared, mesmerized as the blade sunk into the white topping then came out, almost clean, only to dive back in from another angle. Lyn lifted the small wedge from the circle and transferred it to the awaiting plate with ease. He was impressed with her quickness. He glanced at her as she turned around and set the plate in front of him.

"Thank you."

"No problem. Need any more coffee?" She looked at his cup. It was still full.

He shook his head and reached for the pie. He didn't notice that the fork was teetering on the edge of the plate. When he pulled the plate toward him, it sent the fork tumbling to the floor. She bent forward and he leaned sideways, both reaching instinctively for the fork but he touched it first. He hastily sat up and held the utensil out to her.

She smiled, her eyes sparkling in the sun that was shining through the door. "I'll go grab another fork."

While she was gone, he straightened his shirt which had ridden up on the side and poured some sugar and a cream into the tepid coffee. Amazing, he thought. He never expected to find the perfect pair so soon. His thoughts turned to ways of luring her to the cabin. He didn't have long to plan before she laid a clean fork next to his pie and another napkin in front of him.

"So, you live 'round here, Oliver?" She was smiling again.

He paused before responding with, "I have an apartment in town, yes, for during the week."

"The week?"

"Yes. I usually spend the weekends at my cabin out near Little Lake."

"Where's that?"

"Uh… it's near a little town called Lincoln. It's about three hours away, give or take." He shifted in his chair.

She pushed the hair away from her face. "Wow, that must be nice. Wish I could afford a cabin."

In his best attempt at a joking tone he said, "Well, maybe I could show it to you, if you want."

She laughed.

"You have beautiful eyes."

She looked him up and down. "Thanks. And you have great… skin?" She shrugged and laughed again, as if embarrassed.

"Uh…" He smiled sheepishly and looked down at the pie.

"Speaking of skin…"

He quickly looked up.

"Sorry, I couldn't help but notice." She looked toward his side.

"Huh?"

She spoke quickly. "When you bent over to get the fork, your shirt rode up a bit and I saw the scars. I know this is rude, but I'm curious, what happened?"

He smiled. "Would you buy the line 'if I told you, I'd have to kill you' by any chance?"

"Not really, but I understand." She chuckled.

"Maybe I can tell you about it another day."

"We'll see." She tapped the napkin. "Eat up."

His eyes dropped to the napkin which had a phone number written on it. When he looked up, she was already attending to the other customer in the corner. He ate half the pie and took two sips of the coffee before paying at the counter. He grabbed the napkin and waved at Lyn on his way out. The memory of those eyes followed him the rest of the day, clawing its way deeper into his consciousness until it consumed his every thought. The next morning, he lay in bed with his eyes closed.

The scent of smoke surrounded him, making his chest feel as if it were on fire. Someone was screaming. It was a distant but strangely frightening sound that was growing with every second. It was his own blood-curdling cry. He knew what would happen once he opened his eyes, and he fought to keep them closed, to pass this by, but it was no use. When his eyes flew open, he was confronted with a dull green gaze partially obscured by a fringe of mousy brown that almost matched his own hair.

"It's your fault! You were supposed to keep us together! Why do you have to look just like him?!"

The woman's screams grew incoherent. Her breath reeked of whiskey and she pressed the lit cigarette into Oliver's side again and again until it was extinguished.

"Mom, what the hell are you doing?"

His sister shoved his mother away, pulling him up off the wooden floor. It was late summer and they were vacationing at the cabin. His mother had tried to quit drinking numerous times, each time begging the children's forgiveness and swearing never to hurt her Ollie again; each time she relapsed and the violence was worse than before.

His mother's tired eyes fixated on his sister's vibrant green stare. "It's his fault." She was slurring and swaying as she tried to stand.

"He's eleven," Oliver's sister said. "What could he have possibly done to deserve this?" She gestured to the fiery red welts covering his side, as he cowered next to her. "It was dad's choice to walk out," she continued. "Go find him if you want to hurt someone! Leave Ollie out of it!"

His sister led him to the bathroom as a soft thud from the living room signaled that their mother had passed out. He refused to go to the hospital, so she cleaned and bandaged his wounds with the promise that if they didn't look any better when she changed the bandages that he'd let her take him to the hospital. She helped him get into bed and sat next to him.

"Hey, Ollie, you know, Mike, my boyfriend?"

"What about him?"

"Do you like him?" She ran her fingers through his hair.

He shrugged and winced. "If you like him then he's okay, why?"

"Well, he and I graduate this year, right? And we'll both be eighteen, so we were thinking of getting married."

"Oh."

She smiled. "Of course, we'd want you to live with us. Would you want to do that?"

"What about mom?"

"She'd be fine."

Oliver nodded and closed his eyes. When he opened them, he was staring at the ceiling of his apartment. He was late for work. His boss told him that he was an ophthalmologist's assistant. He knew that with him, it was just a fancy name for a secretary since the other assistant did most of the work, he just answered the phone and told people to sign in, but the title sounded more official. Mondays were never very busy at the office, but he despised being late for anything, especially work.

He pushed through the door of the office, causing the welcome bells to go crazy. "I'm so sorry, Dr. Moore."

"Don't worry about it, Ollie." A graying gentleman waved from behind his newspaper on the sofa in the reception area. "No appointments until eleven, anyway."

"Still, sorry."

"It's fine, really."

He looked around for the real assistant but her crystal blue eyes were nowhere to be found. "Where's Shelly?"

"She called to ask if she could come in around ten thirty. Had to take her husband to work, their other car died." Dr. Moore shook his newspaper.

"I see."

He looked over the list of appointments for the day. There were three check-ups scheduled between eleven and one, then the doctor had an enucleation procedure to perform at the hospital at half past three. He went over the appointments in his head, blue, grey, honey, then the removal of a green eye. He shivered and shook his head. No, Dr. Moore was nice enough to give me this job, I will not mess it up. Never a patient, never someone who can be linked back here. He had to remind himself of this pledge daily. He felt like he was indebted to Dr. Moore since he allowed Oliver to observe the surgeries occasionally. Without Dr. Moore, Oliver would be without a mentor to ask the proper procedures of, though the doctor would never know he was more than a curious assistant.

Between appointments and the occasional walk-in, Oliver spent all day reminiscing about the girl from the café. His mind kept flashing her smile past his eyes. It was an odd experience; he never really noticed anything but eyes. He decided to call her that evening. It rang three times.

"Hello?"

Her voice caused him to freeze.

"Anyone there?"

"Uh… Lyn?" He shifted in his seat.

"Yeah, who's this?"

"It's Oliver."

"Oh yeah! I almost thought you weren't gonna call."

He chuckled nervously. "Would you want to have a drink with me, maybe Friday?"

"Absolutely, just name the time and place." She sounded thrilled.

"Um… do you know July Alley?"

"On Elm? Yeah. You wanna meet there? Maybe around eight?"

"Okay, I'll see you there on Friday at eight."

"It's a date!"

After she hung up, the minutes began to feel like hours. A date? He understood the concept but never quite got the hang of the actual experience. All of his dates had always been strange and uncomfortable events. He wasn't exactly happy with the idea of another one. Every night until Friday was filled with the same dream as Sunday night. Every day was filled with flashes of emerald in his mind. When Friday finally arrived, he went to the pub an hour early. He chose a table in a quiet corner where he could watch the door. She was wearing jeans when she walked in, and a turquoise blouse that accented her auburn hair. He waved her over.

"Hey! I'm not late, am I?" She looked at her watch. It was 7:55.

He shook his head. "I just got here myself. Have a seat." He pulled her chair out for her.

She smiled as she sat. "Thanks."

They ordered drinks, a white Russian for her and a Sam Adams for him. He stared at her as she sipped her drink. Her eyes weren't her only nice feature. He quite liked her high cheek bones and her bright smile. He wasn't opposed to moving slowly with this one.

She tilted her head. "So, Oliver... what do you do for a living?"

"I'm an assistant to an ophthalmologist."

"Oh, so that's why you liked my eyes." She grinned.

He chuckled and looked down at his beer. "And what do you do? I mean, uh, do you do anything other than waiting tables?"

"I'm just doing that to put myself through school. I'm gonna be an aesthetician."

He smiled. "So that's why you said I have great skin."

"Do I get to find out about those tonight?" She pointed to his side.

"Uh…"

She smiled and shook her head. "Sorry, that's so rude of me. I just think scars are kind of… sadly beautiful… ya know? Is that creepy?"

"Kind of." He laughed. "But I think I kind of understand."

They laughed and spent two more hours getting to know each other. She tried to veer the conversation toward his scars once more but he was quick to change the subject. He asked if he could see her again. Over the course of the next few days, they had another "date" that was more like just friends hanging out, dinner and a movie, and numerous random encounters that were never random. His dreams had become less frequent and the memories less intense. He had asked her to go to the cabin but failed to get her to accompany him because she had to work and study, but he hadn't been putting his best effort in. She reminded him of his sister; she was kind and comforting, and she hummed when she knew that he was feeling a little stressed out.

She invited him to her house for the one-week anniversary of their first date. He wasn't especially good at handling events such as anniversaries, but he agreed. He arrived promptly at seven with a bottle of wine in hand. When she answered the door, she was wearing the same outfit that she wore to July Alley.

"Hello." He held out the wine and leaned in to kiss her cheek. They had kissed before, but it was still an awkward detail for him.

"Welcome! It's a bit messy but come on in."

The house was small, but everything seemed to be in its proper place, far from what he would call messy.

"Your house is lovely."

He looked at the pictures that lined the entrance hall, most were of dogs playing in a yard. There was one picture of a young man and woman holding a baby; the man's hand was covered in burn scars. The living room had beige walls, one of which was dedicated to framed posters of bands ranging from the Beatles to Disturbed. The sofa and coffee table appeared to be secondhand but were clean and had no holes in the cushions or chunks missing. There was a vase of yellow roses sitting on the coffee table. There was no television but a stereo occupied a cabinet across from the sofa. The CD cases that lined the shelves around the stereo were in alphabetical order by band and when there were multiple CDs by the same artist they were arranged, from what he could tell, in chronological order by release date.

She smiled. "Sit anywhere. Dinner will be a few minutes."

"Can I use your bathroom?"

"Of course! Down the hall, it's on the right."

He nodded and went into the hall, placing his hand on the door to his left.

She noticed. "Your other right, hun! That's my private room."

He quickly switched doors. When he came out of the bathroom, dinner was being set on the kitchen table.

As there was no dining room, the table marked where the kitchen ended and living room began. She had made roasted chicken with garlic mashed potatoes and green bean casserole. He opened the wine and poured a glass for her before pouring his own. She motioned for him to sit.

"I hope you like it." She smiled as she set a plate in front of him.

"It looks delicious. You didn't have to go through all this trouble."

"It was no trouble at all."

He pushed his fork into the mound of potatoes and watched as the thin brown gravy flowed over the edges of the hollow that contained it. He took a bite as she sliced the crisp skin from her chicken breast and set it aside, he assumed for later. As they ate, he noticed that she was staring at him.

"Hmmm?" He blinked, the fork held between his lips.

She took a sip of wine. "Can we talk?"

He set the fork on his plate. "About?"

She pointed at his side.

"Ah. That's not really a meal-time story." He smiled and took a bite of chicken.

"I'd like to know."

He swallowed hard and coughed a little as a piece of chicken that was slightly too big forced its way down his throat. He took two more bites, one of potatoes and the other casserole, then a sip of wine. Finally, he proceeded in telling her about his past. He was happy that she remained quiet for the most part, only nodding and interjecting the occasional "uh huh," "I see," or gasp. He finished his story about the same time that he finished his first plate and looked at her before reaching for seconds.

"That must've been horrible, Oliver. To be treated that way… I don't know what I'd have done if my parents were like that."

She reached and patted his hand as he was getting a spoonful of green bean casserole.

He smiled, grasping at the available change of subject. "Tell me about your parents."

"Oh, not much to tell. They were good people. They loved each other and they loved me." She gasped. "I'm sorry. You don't wanna hear all that."

"Actually, I do." He was surprised at how true the statement was as it exited his mouth.

"Are you sure?" She was chewing her bottom lip.

He nodded and waited for her to proceed.

"Well, like I said, they were good people." She spread her hands and shrugged, as if considering where to start. "Mom used to volunteer at Parkland, the hospital. That's actually how they met."

"Really?" He took a sip of wine, his eyes never leaving her.

"Yeah," she said. "Dad had tried to light a pile of rubbish when the flames blew back on him. It burned his arm and hand pretty bad, so he was in the hospital for a bit and Mom visited him every day. A year later, I was born!"

Oliver held back a chuckle at her enthusiasm for the last statement and hid a smile behind his napkin as he wiped his mouth. She didn't seem to notice.

"I remember staring at dad's arm for hours after mom told me that story. It was just so beautiful that something so sad could bring two people together."

He nodded.

By the time she completed her story he was finished with his second plate and she excused herself. When she returned, she was carrying two large slices of lemon meringue pie. He laughed as she set his piece in front of him.

"Lyn, this is amazing."

She smiled.

"Do you have any plans for next weekend?"

She shrugged. "Not that I know of, why?"

"I was wondering if you'd like to go out to my cabin." He took a bite of pie. It was good.

"That sounds like an awesome idea, Oliver. I could use a vacation."

He nodded and took a few more bites. Within minutes, the room was beginning to spin. He looked up at her and swayed.

"You okay, Oliver? Not drunk already, are you?"

"Just a little dizzy." He was seeing black spots.

She got up and touched his shoulder. "You wanna go lay down?"

"I'm sorry. If you don't mind."

He leaned on her as she guided him down the hall. He wasn't sure where he was going but it wasn't long before he was laid down. Silence invaded the darkness that had encompassed him. When he opened his eyes, he was in the backseat of his sister's boyfriend's Camry. Sun was shining through the windshield. They were on their way back to the city after picking him up from the cabin. Fields lined the road on either side and he was watching the cows and horses pass by. His sister's boyfriend was driving a little too fast and it had Oliver a bit nervous. His sister was looking back at him through the rearview mirror.

"Well, are you excited?"

He shrugged; he still wasn't comfortable with the idea of leaving his mother to suffer alone. "Yeah."

"Ollie," she was almost whispering, "Mom'll be fine. She's a big girl. She can take care of herself, you know that, right?"

He nodded, nervousness and guilt weighing on his shoulders.

She smiled.

His mother had cried as they were leaving. She begged and promised all the things she had promised repetitively over the years. His twelve-year-old mind couldn't comprehend leaving someone in such a state, but his sister had assured him that it would all be all right.

It wasn't long before they lost all contact with his mother.

The world seemed to move in fast forward. He was fifteen now. He had spent three chaotic years with his sister, Beth, and her husband. His sister's husband, Mike, and he never saw eye to eye. Mike was a former linebacker for his high school football team and he carried himself with the same cockiness and goofy swagger that most former high school football players do. He called Oliver a 'mooch' behind Beth's back, and he and Oliver were constantly bickering over something, usually Beth's attention.

About two years after they started living together, Oliver discovered that his mother died of cirrhosis of the liver. They had a small funeral for her. He left in the middle of the service and when Beth found him, he was sitting under a tree in the cemetery pulling up grass piece by piece.

"Ollie? You ok?" She touched his shoulder.

He shrugged her hand off.

"Ollie?"

He was staring at the small bare spot he had created in the grass. "You said she'd be okay."

"Ollie… this would've happened whether we stayed or not. It was better this way." She reached for him.

He pulled away. "No! I should've stayed with her."

"Why? So she could hurt you more?"

He glared at his sister but didn't argue… couldn't argue.

They spent another year together. He stayed away from the house as much as possible and fell in with the wrong friends which only caused more arguments. He was skipping school, smoking, and had begun cursing, but he never drank or did any drugs besides nicotine. At least once a week, he would find someone to take him to the DART rail, so he could wander around by himself instead of hanging out with his friends. Mike and he still vied for Beth's attention most of the time and he usually won until they found out that she was pregnant; after that, things started going Mike's way. One day while skipping classes, Oliver saw Mike coming out of a hotel and decided to ask Beth about it.

"Hey, sis, where was Mike yesterday?"

She blinked. "He was at work all day, why?"

"He doesn't work near the Sheraton, right?" He took a sip of Pepsi.

"No. Why are you asking about that?"

He shrugged. "Thought I saw him there."

"And just what were you doing over there?"

"Doesn't matter."

She turned toward him, a hand on her stomach. "It most certainly does matter!"

"Just hanging out after school." He had gotten home late which they already argued about and he hoped this would pass as a possible truth.

"I see. Well, it wasn't him." She smiled. "Don't be paranoid."

Later that night, he heard his sister and Mike arguing. From what he heard, his sister had confronted Mike and he had gotten angry because she didn't trust him. Oliver scoffed at the idea of his sister trusting someone besides him. They called him into the living room a few minutes later.

"Ollie, when you saw Mike yesterday, he was coming out of a meeting." She nodded as if this was the only truth.

"Yeah right, the chick with him certainly looked like a professional."

"Ollie!"

Mike stood up. "I don't have to put up with these kinds of accusations, you sister-complex freak."

"Don't call me a sister-complex freak and don't cheat on my sister, asshat."

"Ollie, stop it!"

"I wasn't cheating! It was a business meeting. You believe me, right, Beth?"

Oliver laughed. "Why would she believe such a weak story?"

A loud 'crack' rang in his ears as his cheek began to sting. His sister had smacked him. He resisted the urge to hit her back and took it out on the wall instead, placing a hole in the sheetrock and cracking a knuckle in the process.

"That's enough, Oliver. It was just a business meeting. I trust Mike."

Oliver's behavior became increasingly hard to handle. He was no longer going to school. His sister suggested military school, but he refused and she didn't push the matter. He was also fighting on a daily basis and had hospitalized one of his ex-classmates when he tried to choke him with a shoelace. The incident was written off as self-defense since the other boy had a knife on him, but it was the last straw. It wasn't long before his sister placed him in the state's care.

"I'm sorry, Beth! I'll be good!" He was sobbing as if she had beaten him. "I'm sorry!"

"It's not your fault, Ollie."

"Please, don't send me away." He clung to her protruding waist as she stroked his hair.

"We can't afford to get you the help you need. Maybe you can get it this way."

"I just need you, sissy," he said. It was a word that he hadn't used since he was a little kid and it tasted rusty on his tongue.

She sighed. "I'm just thinking of what's best for you and for the baby. I need to protect my family. All of it."

He looked up at her and her eyes were shining as she looked toward her husband. Those eyes that had protected him and comforted him all those years had looked away from him. He had thought that those eyes trusted him implicitly but it was a lie. He wasn't trusted. He spent most nights in the foster homes dwelling on the lies that those eyes had hidden; the lack of trust, the death of his mother after a promise that she would be fine. A loud whirring filled his thoughts. He closed his eyes against the sound and when he opened them again, he was momentarily blinded by a bright white light.

"Ugh. Where am I?" He tried to rub his eyes, only to find his hands tied above his head.

A dark blur appeared over him, slowly sharpening into Lyn. "You're not supposed to be awake. You're in my private room."

The room came into focus; large pieces of something like fabric were hanging from the wall, almost like tanned animal hides. "Why am I tied up?"

"So you can't run away, silly." She was sharpening a scalpel.

"Wha-what are you doing?"

She frowned. "You really don't know?"

He shook his head.

She touched the scars on his side. "They're beautiful."

"And?" He looked at the scalpel.

"I just can't help myself. Scars are so amazing. They're works of art." She gestured toward the hides on the walls. "I have to collect them. You know how it is, right?"

He could only nod. He understood more than she knew.

She frowned slightly. "So, I guess we're not gonna go to the lake next weekend."

She got on the table, straddling him, and wrapped a rope around his neck, pulling it tight. Her eyes met his and he held that jewel-like gaze as long as he could. He was happy as his lungs began to burn in an oxygen-less fire. As he faded back into darkness, the words "how beautiful" flashed through his mind.

Goat Man
by Bret McCormick

July 25, 1969

"Have you ever seen the Lake Worth Monster?" It was Jimmy who asked the question as he licked red dribbles from his Popsicle off the tips of his fingers. He tucked the wooden stick into the corner of his mouth where it would protrude from his chubby cheek for the remainder of the afternoon, like a harpoon lodged in Moby Dick's hump.

Our nature guide, who was leading us on a tour of Greer Island, turned and grinned. "I can't say I've seen him, but at sunrise I've heard some strange cries emanating from the forest."

"What did it sound like?" This from Todd, the skinniest kid I ever saw, whose huge brown eyes seemed to take up most of his face.

Rick Pratt, the guide, gave this a bit of thought. "Something like a cross between a cougar and a coyote. Not exactly, but that's an approximation. It doesn't sound like anything you've ever heard."

"My dad says it's a bunch of malarkey," said Blake. He was the one who always wore his neatly starched and ironed Scout uniform, hat placed perfectly on his head. He smelled of Dove soap and never, ever used cuss words.

Rick chuckled. "Well, your dad might feel differently if he was standing right here just before sunrise and he heard that strange howl echoing across the lake."

Todd seized the opportunity to poke fun at Blake. "Yeah, your dad would be screaming like a little girl, wetting his pants!" He acted out his proposed scenario, providing a high-pitched shriek, flailing his arms as he stumbled in circles. His enormous eyes looked wilder than ever.

Everyone laughed. Everyone except Blake and Rick. I imagine the guide refrained because he was the only adult present and wanted to set a good example by not joining in the ridicule of one of his charges. Blake, on the other hand...I just don't know. The kid was inscrutable. As far as I could determine the boy was completely devoid of humor. I don't think I ever saw him laugh. He took his Scout merit badges very seriously and could point out edible wild plants like Euell Gibbons, but he was like an old man trapped in a boy's body. It sort of seemed like he didn't have time to waste on childhood. I could easily imagine him as a war hero or the President or something equally grave and grown-up. Blake didn't even like the *Three Stooges*! He said they were stupid. What planet was this kid from?

The Lake Worth Monster had been the subject of a few news stories in the newspaper in recent weeks. Most of the adults in my family attributed the phenomenon to "those long-haired kids on drugs." I hoped it was something more than psychedelic hallucinations. The beast had been seen by more than twenty people and they all described it as a really tall man, hairy on most of its body and a goat's head crowned with gnarly ram horns. To me it sounded like something from Greek mythology or the goat-thing nestled in a pentagram I'd seen in an illustration in one of my grandfather's books.

As we continued the nature walk we encountered multiple squirrels, an armadillo, a really long green snake and maybe a dozen species of birds, the names of which I forgot as soon as Rick had spoken them in his well-intentioned effort to educate us. When we arrived at the amphitheater we found a table arrayed with various insect, leaf and stuffed animal specimens. Rick passed out a two-page quiz with twenty questions we were supposed to answer, so he could determine how much we'd actually learned about nature in our first week of camp.

"A test?" Jimmy whined, almost losing the Popsicle stick from his mouth. "This is summertime. I thought we were done with tests until next September."

"You don't have to take the test," Rick said with simple neutrality. "It's not mandatory, but I'd appreciate if you would."

"Awww…" Grudgingly, Jimmy took the two pages Rick held in front of him.

"Don't take it," Blake suggested. "Then everyone will know you're the stupidest kid here."

Jimmy's pudgy face transformed into a war mask. "Take it back!" he sneered, shoving his sizable belly into Blake.

"Easy fellows," Rick said, authority, but no anger, in his voice. He placed a hand on each of the boys' shoulders and gently directed them away from one another. "Take a pencil from the table and answer these twenty questions to the best of your ability."

All of the boys did as he instructed, their uncertain young eyes darting from the papers in their hands to the specimens on the table. I was the first to finish my test, but I'd just skipped over the questions I couldn't answer, rather than guessing. I handed Rick my paper.

"Done already?" He grinned. "Let's go sit over there," he said, indicating a picnic table at the perimeter of the amphitheater, "and give the others a chance to finish." When we'd seated ourselves, he asked, "Are you enjoying nature camp?"

I shrugged. "It's okay."

Rick frowned. "Just okay? How could we make it better?"

I knew what would make it better, but I also knew my desire was a child's wish and would not be taken seriously by adults. I laughed self-consciously.

"Really," he said, "I'd like to know. Any ideas?"

"Well…" I began, tentatively.

"There are no wrong answers to this question." Rick clearly was trying to put me at ease and it worked.

"I'd like to see the monster. The goat man. I know it's probably just a story somebody made up, but I'd like for it to be real."

"What makes you think it's not real?" Rick asked.

"My folks say its nonsense."

"Sometimes people call something nonsense if it frightens them. They don't want it to be real, so they make themselves feel more secure by saying it's not real." Rick sounded like no other adult I knew.

"You think it could be true?"

"I know it's true." His face was serious, not even the slightest inkling that he was putting me on.

"But, you said you've never seen it."

"Not yet, but under the right circumstances, I know I will."

"What circumstances?"

"Well, to begin with, the more people who believe in the goat man, the easier he will be to see."

This made me frown. "You mean like an imaginary friend? I want it to be really real."

"What do you think makes something real?" he asked.

I shrugged.

"Science has proven there is no objective reality independent of an observer." Rick held eye-contact and spoke these words very carefully, which is why I remember what he said, even though at the time I did not have a clue what he was talking about.

"I'm finished."

It was Blake. He approached us with his folded pages aimed at Rick. Blake may have been second to finish, but I was pretty certain he'd answered every question. And I would've bet my allowance he'd answered every question correctly.

"We'll talk more about this later," Rick said softly to me before reaching for Blake's quiz sheets.

I didn't go back to nature camp that year. Over the weekend I contracted chicken pox and was forced to stay home the following week. The next summer, when my parents gave me the choice of going to nature camp again or spending a couple of weeks on my grandparents' farm, I chose the farm. There I could swim every day in the creek and eat all the blackberries and peaches my belly could hold.

Nature camp and Rick Pratt were soon forgotten, but the goat man showed up in my dreams sometimes and would turn up in conversation once in a while. Every few years there would be a resurgence in sightings of the monster, but I attributed that to copycats trying to breathe new life into the fading urban legend.

July 5, 1991

When I suggested my nine-year-old son, Max, attend nature camp for two weeks, he was less than enthusiastic.

"It's summer!" he proclaimed. "School is out and I thought I was going to get to do what I want for a while!"

"If you give it a chance, you'll probably find that nature camp is something you want to do."

"Yeah, and if not, oh well, I'm stuck there for two weeks. Right?"

My wife gave me a sly look across the table. It conveyed her stance on the matter. You brought this up. You handle it. Don't expect me to intervene.

I already knew that she was not thrilled with the idea of Max going to nature camp. Sylvia preferred tile and carpet (provided both were clean) under her feet to dirt, grass and rocks. She hated all manner of insects with a passion that bordered on psychotic. She was fine with nature only so long as we were experiencing it via a *National Geographic* documentary and even then, only if the other viewing options were sports.

"If you don't go to nature camp, how will you spend your days?" I asked.

Max looked down at his plate, considering my question. "Just whatever I feel like doing."

"Which means about eight hours a day playing *Mortal Kombat*."

Max shrugged. "What's wrong with that?"

"They say video games do help develop hand/eye coordination," Sylvia interjected.

"There are plenty of ways to do that," I snapped. "One of them is by being out in the real world experiencing new things!"

Her eyes widened with indignation, but she said nothing.

"Okay," I said to Max, "go to nature camp for three days. If you don't want to continue after that, I won't force you."

Max pursed his lips, wondering if he should negotiate further. He glanced at his mother. Sylvia nodded quickly, indicating that he should accept my terms. Their collusion did not dampen my enthusiasm over what I felt was a solid victory. My son was going to nature camp.

Max loved it.

On the final day, when I went to the Nature Preserve to pick him up, I arrived a little early, so I sat in the air conditioned car listening to music and reviewing some notes on a project that was due the following week. For some reason my mind wandered back to my own childhood experience at the Nature Center and I found myself thinking of Jimmy. When I glanced up from my notebook I saw a kid not twenty feet in front of my car that was the spitting image of Jimmy. For an instant I was startled. It seemed as if my memory had coalesced into a flesh and blood kid. I watched the boy as he walked to the Ford truck that was parked beside me. As he opened the door I caught a glimpse of the driver. The heavyset guy at the wheel had to be the real Jimmy. I just knew it.

Before the kid closed his door, I rolled down my window and called to the man, "Hey, are you Jimmy?"

"Yeah…" he answered hesitantly, like maybe I was going to serve him papers or something. I explained, telling him who I was and concluding with the fact that his son looked just like him.

He forced a laugh. "Yeah, small world, eh? So, how you been?"

"Fine." I gave him the Reader's Digest version of what I'd been up to for the last twenty plus years. "This place hasn't changed much."

"Yeah," he said, "nice to know some things stay the same."

"Remember our counselor, Rick?"

"Rick?" Jimmy's brow furrowed. "Was that his name?"

Jimmy's son chimed in, "Just like our counselor this year."

"Isn't that something?" Jimmy mused. "What are the odds of that, eh?"

"You remember Rick telling us about the Lake Worth Monster?" I asked, getting caught up in the nostalgia.

"Yeah…" he was saying, 'yeah,' but his expression was saying 'not so much.'

"You remember Rick, don't you?"

Jimmy shrugged. "Don't get me lying, dude. That's been a long time ago." He turned the key in his ignition. "Listen, guy, great to see you. Hope your boy had as much fun as mine did."

"Glad we got to talk." I smiled and nodded as Jimmy and his boy each unwrapped a lollipop and tucked them into their cheeks before the truck pulled out slowly. "Time marches on," I mused.

I was roused from my reverie when Max bounced into the car. As he buckled his seat belt, he said, "Dad, do you remember a guy named Rick Pratt?"

Distracted, I didn't really take in his question. Mentally fumbling I said, "Who?"

"Rick. The nature guide. He said he remembers you from when you were a kid."

"Oh, yeah…" This was too much! A smile formed on my face. "So he's still here after all these years?"

"Yep. He said to tell you he never got a chance to finish talking to you about the goat man."

My smile vanished. How could the guy remember me after all this time? Why would he recall an unfinished conversation with a boy that had occurred more than twenty years earlier? A chill disturbed the hairs on my neck and the muscles around my stomach tightened.

"What's wrong, Dad?"

I looked down to see Max staring at me confused and concerned.

I forced a smile. "Nothing. I just remembered something I need to do," I lied.

"Oh." The lie satisfied my boy. "So anyway, Rick would like to talk with you when you have the time."

"Talk? About what?" I asked, unable to filter the apprehension from my voice.

Max laughed. "About the goat man, of course. I'd really like to get a look at him, wouldn't you, Dad?"

"Where is this Rick?" I asked, my tone all business, not at all in the spirit of speculative monster talk.

Max straightened up in his seat and peered through the windshield. "There he is." He pointed at a young man standing near the Visitor Center building. A young man in his early twenties who looked exactly like the nature guide I'd known in the summer of 1969. Just then, Rick looked directly at me, smiled and waved.

My son grinned at me. He waved at the impossibly young nature guide. "Aren't you going to wave back at Rick?" he asked.

I put the car in reverse and drove quickly away from the Nature Preserve.

July 17, 2015

I was working on an article for a fan magazine when my phone rang. It was Max.

"Hey, Dad," he said. "I have a favor to ask."

"Sure," I said, glad to hear from him. "What can I do?"

"I'm tied up at work and I haven't been able to reach Naomi. I'm supposed to pick up Stephen. Since I can't get through to her, would you mind picking him up?"

I didn't have to think about it. Spending time with my grandson was pretty much at the top of my to-do list ever since Sylvia had passed away. "Of course," I said, grabbing a pen and notepad. "Where is he?"

"He's at nature camp."

The words hit me like a gut punch. My energy drained away. "Stephen's at nature camp?"

"Yeah. Isn't it great? Remember how you had to coerce me into going?" He laughed.

I said nothing, but Max must not have noticed, or if he did, he attached no meaning to my silence. He continued. "I loved it so much, I figured he would, too. And guess what...he loved it! Today's his last day. I'm sure he'll have plenty to tell you."

"All right, Max," I managed to say. "I'll get the boy."

"Great. Thanks, Dad."

"My pleasure." The uncanny feeling was lessening, so I made an effort to cast it off entirely. "All right if I take him for ice cream?"

"Sure. As long as you're willing to take the heat when Naomi hears about it."

"I'll accept full responsibility," I said, forcing a laugh.

"Thanks, again. Hope to see you tonight. Maybe you can stay for dinner?"

"I'd love to."

"I'll set it up with the boss when I'm able to reach her."

"Sounds good."

"Bye now."

Max hung up and I sat for a moment, confused, feeling a bit like I'd been pushed over a cliff and was now enjoying the peaceful feeling of weightlessness as I fell toward the inevitable collision with Earth.

I was impressed by how little that part of the county had changed. Everything looked exactly as I remembered it, even though I'd had no reason to visit the area since Max was a boy. When I pulled into the parking lot, I was surprised to see Naomi's car. She and Stephen were in the front seat. I pulled into the space beside her and rolled down my window.

"What's up?" I asked.

"Sorry for all the confusion," Naomi said. "My phone was dead earlier and when I got it charged I tried to call you, but got no answer."

My hand slapped automatically at my pocket where my phone was not. "Must've left my phone at home."

"I would've been glad to let you pick up Stephen and spend some time with him, but he has a birthday party to go to tonight. We still have to shop for a gift." The disappointment must have shown on my face. She frowned with empathy. "Can you come for dinner tomorrow? That way you can see Stephen and we can all catch up."

"Sure. No problem." I offered what I hoped seemed a not-bothered-at-all smile. I could roll with the punches. I was firmly committed to not becoming one of those crotchety old guys who couldn't gracefully handle life's little upsets.

"Great!" Naomi exclaimed. "I'll make lasagna. Hopefully that will compensate you for the wasted trip."

"I'll be looking forward to it." That was no lie. Naomi's lasagna was the best.

Stephen, who'd been staring at me patiently, waiting for the adult business to be squared away, gave a little wave and said, "See you tomorrow, Grandpa."

"See you then, Stephen." I smiled and nodded.

"Grandpa, do you remember Rick Pratt?" the boy asked eagerly.

Before I could muster a reply, Naomi said urgently, "Stephen, we've got to go. Now. You can tell Grandpa about that tomorrow when he comes for dinner."

Stephen slumped in his seat, no happier than I was with our curtailed visit. Naomi offered me a wistful smile before putting her car in gear and pulling away.

"You do remember me, don't you?"

I jumped. My heart felt like it would beat its way out of my ribcage.

There, leaning into my car through the passenger window was Rick Pratt, looking exactly as he had that summer when the goat man made his first big splash in the papers.

"Ever heard of Roswell?" Rick asked. We were sitting now in the garage apartment where Rick said he'd lived since 1969. He had requested a ride home and I, after decades of trying to ignore this mystery, realized it was finally time to face it. Time to confront the impossible turn my life had been trying to take for over forty years. He placed a cup of tea on the coffee table in front of me. I sipped it. Orange spice. It was a pleasant flavor and I found it calmed me just a bit.

"You're not going to tell me you're an extra-terrestrial are you?" I asked. "Weren't they supposed to have died in the crash, anyway? Little guys with big heads? Not like you."

"No, not like me." Rick agreed, sipping his tea. "Ever heard of Baphomet?"

I sighed and placed my cup on the table. "The goat man."

"Yes. The goat man. Know anything about him?"

"His picture is on Tarot cards. His image turns up in medieval grimoires. I've heard it said the Freemasons have some connection with Baphomet, but I'm not a Mason, so I have no firsthand knowledge. Do you?"

"Yes." His eyes lit up. He threw his head back and laughed at the ceiling. "I have firsthand knowledge. I am the Baphomet."

"So you shaved and had your horns removed?" I must have sounded disdainful.

"How old were you when we first met?" he asked, his eyes narrowing.

"I was almost ten."

"How old are you now?"

"Fifty seven."

"And I look exactly as I did forty seven years ago?"

I nodded.

"That alone should buy me a modicum of suspended disbelief, don't you think?"

I could not disagree. "Yes." Again, I nodded.

"Your reality has been challenged. Humans don't like that. It makes them feel insecure."

"So clue me in. Throw me a bone." Though I could not imagine how, I was clinging to the hope that this nonsense would resolve in a rational manner. "What's this got to do with me? And what about Roswell?"

"The atomic bomb brought them back."

"Brought who back? From where?"

"The races who pilot the disks. Not the big-headed little fellows, but their masters. They…we…left Earth after the fall of Babylon." He paused.

"I've got so many questions I don't even know where to start," I said half-sarcastically. "How about I just let you talk for a while? I'm in no hurry. Not now that you've finally caught up with me."

"Right," he said, rubbing his forehead, leaning back on the sofa. "Earth was not always as dense as it is today. It used to be something like a lucid dream, malleable and flowing. No hard and fast rules. Even gravity was sort of arbitrary back then. All worlds start out this way, but they solidify into much more rigid constructs as time goes by. Depending on the prevailing thoughts and desires of the indigenous consciousness, a world can become one thing or something entirely different. You humans chose a rockier path than most."

I nodded vaguely, lips pursed, taking in his words and striving for the suspension of disbelief he'd requested.

"My race thrives in a state of being humans can only describe as chaos. Our chaos is actually just a larger reality than the minds and sensory organs of humans are capable of perceiving. There is a sort of order to this higher reality, but it is so complex that most of your kind are incapable of contemplating it. Those who do are usually called psychotic. Or theoretical physicists.

"All your myths and strange legends from prehistory are attempts to describe the actions of my race in that early dawn of the world before the local reality formalized."

"Okay," I interrupted. "Let's assume for a moment that I accept what you are saying is true—or at least some version of truth—why are you lingering here? Why do you want to talk to me of all people? Why haven't you just scooted off to another lucid dream planet somewhere?"

"Good!" He laughed. "Your questions indicate that you're at least taking my premise seriously enough to allow me a foothold in your mind."

I nodded grimly. It was not my desire that Rick, or Baphomet, would have a foothold there.

"The short version of the story is…"

"Yes! Please. Let's stick to the short version." Somehow I felt the less information I had, the more power I'd have to resist unwanted intrusions into my consciousness.

"Agreed. Consciousness is a living thing. Every material manifestation in the observable universe is just another costume consciousness is trying on for size. I am of an earlier order. What amuses my race may seem terrifying to you humans because you perceive yourselves as finite. Once you understand nothing ever really dies, you are better equipped to enjoy the show. But, you're afraid to come out of your box and play. You are terrified of demons and angels alike because both lie outside your limited purview.

"Those of my race move from one fledgling planet to another, sowing the seeds of possibility. But, we are not allowed to force indigenous consciousness into one path or another. In this way diversity is allowed to flourish among the worlds.

"There is a hierarchy of agendas throughout creation. My race created the people who pilot the disks. In a manner of speaking, they still serve us. They in turn created the small servants who are referred to in your popular culture as the 'Greys.' The humans of Earth, though not created by the Greys, have through a series of free-will choices over the course of millennia, placed themselves in a subordinate position to them.

"When I departed Babylon, it was the Greys who transported me to other worlds. Because my experiences have no direct temporal link to Earth-time, I experienced a virtual infinity of adventures in other realms before I was returned to your planet. The atomic bombs of World War II sent a warning through the field of consciousness and the craft, in which I was a passenger, was dispatched here to be shot down in Roswell."

"I'm glad you're telling me the short version!" I exclaimed disparagingly, feeling I had not moved much closer to understanding what this was all about.

"One of the many curses of the path you humans have chosen is that you have little patience. You prefer the quick explanation to the accurate one. And consequently, you are very slow to learn from your mistakes." He stared at me. There was that nervous discomfort again as the hair on my neck stood up and a tingling sensation swept over my entire scalp.

"Sorry," I said. "Please go on."

With a grim smile he continued. "Ever since 1947, your planet has been under quarantine. As soon as the alien craft were delivered into human hands, travel to and from this world was halted."

"So we actually shot down an extraterrestrial craft?"

"Yes and no. Yes, you shot it down. No, you would not have been able to had they not desired it. It was a sort of Trojan Horse maneuver."

The implications of this were not lost on me. "So we've been infected, so to speak, by alien technology? Disease? Some form of mind control?"

"All of the above. You will be under quarantine until you prove yourselves capable of mastering a higher reality. Or until you destroy yourselves. In the meantime, I am stuck here with you."

"Why are you here if you were on a craft that crashed in Roswell?"

"The remains of the craft were initially sent here to Carswell Airforce Base. One of the local commanding officers examined the contents, not wanting to be left out of such an important loop. He pilfered a few items from the collection before forwarding the rest to Ohio. The storage device containing my sleeping consciousness was among the artifacts he kept here in Texas. It wasn't until 1969 that some local aerospace engineers figured out how to open the device and unwittingly released me into the local environment."

"The Lake Worth Monster."

"One of the many names I have been called on this world. This brings us to the present...and why I needed you."

"Yes. Why did you need me?"

"You are a beacon."

"Beacon?"

"Yes. In your chosen paradigm, there is about one beacon for every ten thousand individuals born into your race."

"What does that mean?"

"It means you have influence. Even now, the reality you inhabit is always evolving. Tell me, haven't you ever noticed that others are unusually receptive to your ideas, your likes and dislikes? Haven't you realized that otherwise complacent people become enthusiastic when exposed to your enthusiasms?"

"They do?" As I mulled it over I could recall many episodes in my life when things had gone my way despite odds to the contrary.

"Yes. They do. When you were a child your desire to see the Lake Worth Monster was exactly what I needed to help sustain me. You see, if you boost my life force by allowing for the possibility that there is a goat man, then I am better able to survive in this rarefied, and to me toxic, environment you humans have engineered."

"Toxic environment? Here you are, still alive and well for almost fifty years. You don't seem to have aged a day. That hardly seems toxic."

"I can't expect you to fully understand it, but my being here, under these circumstances, is something like asking a human to live for years in a closet. A very small closet. For the last twenty years I flicker out of this reality a good deal of the time."

"Flicker out?"

"Yes. If you were to visit me in the dead of winter, you'd find me fading in and out of your visible spectrum, like a ghost in some old movie. I live for the summer when I get to talk to the kids at nature camp about the Lake Worth Monster. There are always a few who become very excited at the prospect of seeing the monster. But, as time passes, fewer and fewer of the children have even heard of the Lake Worth Monster. And only rarely have I encountered a beacon like you. I store up as much psychic energy from the children's enthusiasm as I can coax out of them and that carries me through to the next year."

"That sucks."

"You have no idea. Life on this planet was so much easier before you married your minds to science."

We sat in silence for several moments.

"So, what do you want from me?" I asked.

"I need you to want to see the goat man. I mean really want it with the most fervent desire." He stared at me hopefully.

I considered his request. Did I still want to see the monster? Yes. I think, deep down, I'd never stopped wanting to see the goat man. Could I generate the enthusiasm he needed to charge his psychic battery? I didn't know. All I could do was try.

I closed my eyes and thought my way back to that summer, when the articles about the Lake Worth Monster first appeared in the *Fort Worth Star-Telegram*. I replayed memories of myself talking about the mysterious beast with my friends. There it was. Yes, I definitely had a handle on that original emotional response. I felt the excitement swelling within me and then I felt a burst of energy like the wind from an atomic blast.

I opened my eyes.

My heart still races when I recall what I saw in that small garage apartment on the west side of Fort Worth. There, perched on the opposite end of the sofa, was the goat man. Not the way I'd imagined him, but much, much larger. Even seated, he was bent over in order to fit under the low ceiling. His legs sprawled across the floor. The Baphomet roared. And I literally wet my pants. It stretched its arms and one enormous fist knocked a large hole in the sheetrock overhead. The sight was too much. I closed my eyes and felt an imposing shift in the energy within the room. There was a ringing in my ears. When I finally dared to look, I saw Rick peacefully sipping his tea. He winked at me. The hole was still there in the ceiling and the floor was littered with chalky debris.

"I'll have to patch that before Mrs. Murphy sees it," he said, then added, "Thanks. That feels so much better."

"No problem," I answered, my voice shaking. I was painfully aware of the wet stain on my pants and eager to get home and into some dry clothes. "Need anything else from me?"

"Yeah," he said. "I want you to write a story about all this. And I want you to make sure it gets published."

I swallowed hard. "Okay," I answered in a whisper.

"That's a good beacon," Rick cooed.

A Night at the Spring
by Dennis Pitts

It had been a hard, dry, hot two days for Doggett. He was, himself, hard and dry, a compact man with leathery skin stretched over prominent bones. But Doggett was about at his limit, as was his horse. Both canteens strapped to his saddle were empty. He'd done everything he could imagine to avoid thinking about his thirst, but he had to admit that he was about done for if he didn't find the spring.

He'd been riding since before sunrise after two long days and dark, dry camps at night.

This was always dry country, rocky and uneven with a scattering of prickly pear cactus, mesquite trees and low, sparse brush. The cactus and brush were all a dry gray-green, the only color in a sea of light tan dirt and rocks, all baked by an unusually dry spring and a very hot summer. Even the few mesquite trees looked more gray than green. One water hole where he had counted on finding water yesterday morning had been dry. But there was a spring in this general area that Doggett had visited a few times. It always had water, even in the worst of times. However, he prayed—an unusual action for Doggett—that he would come close enough to see the few trees that always grew around the spring.

He had sweated through his clothes, again. It had been days since he'd had a bath. He wasn't sure which smelled worse, himself or the horse.

His horse tumbled somewhat, bringing Doggett out of a near-stupor. Being a Ranger was hard on a man. But it was harder on the man's horses. Doggett wasn't sure how many horses he'd ridden to death or broken down. It was so many that he'd quit naming them. This hard-boned, rough-riding nag that he rode now was horse number...well, he wasn't even sure how many horses came before this one.

Doggett was on his way to Ft. McKavitt looking for a Mexican reportedly hanging around the post. A Mexican wanted for murdering a deputy sheriff in Ft. Worth. But the Ranger knew he wouldn't make it to the post if he didn't find the spring.

Scanning the area around him, he began to question his own judgment. He thought that he should be in the general area of the spring. But if he was very far away from the spot he'd never see it.

Reining in the plodding horse, he stood in the stirrups and pulled down the brim of his greasy, salt-stained hat to shield his eyes from the glare of the afternoon sun. There! Off to his left he thought that he saw a small spot of green along the horizon.

Taking a firm grip on the reins, anticipating the thirsty horse would rush toward the spring when it smelled water, Doggett turned the horse to the left. After a few minutes the horse snorted and picked up its head. The tops of a few cottonwood trees soon showed above the rocks and dry brush that screened the spring. Doggett smiled inwardly, proud of himself for his dead reckoning in such a god-awfully desolate place.

From the top of the rocky depression that contained a small pool of water Doggett could see an area of mud around the water and a little tall grass growing in the mud. On the opposite side of the muddy patch were the few small cottonwoods that he had seen earlier.

The horse fought Doggett's control in an attempt to rush down the slope.

Doggett had the animal under control until the horse stepped on some large loose rocks and stumbled sideways.

The Ranger was nearly thrown from the saddle as the horse fought to keep its own balance. Doggett swung his left leg over the horn of the saddle and jumped awkwardly off the horse in case it fell. As he pushed clear of the struggling horse and hit the ground his right foot landed on a large stone and twisted. In spite of the horse's snorting and the sound of rocks being rolled around by the horse's hooves, Doggett heard the distinct dry-twig snap of a bone in his lower leg and felt a burst of pain in the leg. He hit the ground on his side and smashed several ribs on the rocks.

Doggett rolled onto his back and lay for some time, aware of only the pain in his side and in his right leg. Finally he raised his head enough to see his right foot twisted at a strange angle from his leg. The pain in his ribs, however, made him lower his head and stare at the violet sky. He heard the horse drinking from the small pond. Damn fool beast would probably drink itself to death.

Thinking that he might be able to pull himself upright using a stirrup, Doggett called to the horse. However, he'd always treated the animal as a tool, and there was no relationship between the two. Doggett attempted to roll over somewhat to see whether the horse was near, but the pain in his side was excruciating. He had to admit that even if the horse came to him he likely wouldn't be able to pull himself up.

Well, Claude Doggett, he thought to himself, how the hell do you get out of this mess?

He'd fought all manner of men, and a few boys, in the war and as a lawman. His gun, his knife, his fists, or his mouth had always gotten him out of trouble. Although on consideration they'd also gotten him into some of that trouble. Now it looked like he'd die of thirst lying just a few feet from water.

Doggett lay with his eyes closed, lost in the agony of broken bones, the heat of the late afternoon sun and his maddening thirst. He could think of no solution to his situation. Well, there was one solution. He carried it on his hip, and it was still in its holster. His old Colt army revolver.

He tiptoed around the idea of killing himself. He was a hard man who had spent most of his adult life battling others, killing when he felt it necessary. He'd never considered any situation in which he would kill himself. Until now.

The Ranger was startled back into total consciousness by drops of water falling on his face. His hand forced the water into his mouth even before his eyes opened. The damned horse, its muzzle dripping water from the spring, had its head near Doggett's, apparently curious about its rider's immobility.

Doggett reached for the bridle, hoping he could at least pull himself to a sitting position. The horse snorted and dodged the man's reach. It walked placidly up the slope and disappeared from view.

Some time later Doggett awoke. The sun was below the rim of the ground around the spring, although the sky was rose-colored. Not quite sunset yet.

He was surprised to find the Colt in his hand.

God, his leg hurt. It felt like he would see a ball of fire at the end of his leg if he could raise his head. He closed his eyes again.

At some point he thought that he heard foot steps coming toward him. Doggett tried to raise his head again, but he felt pain in his side like someone had shoved a knife between his ribs. Dropping his head back to the rocky ground, panting for breath, he closed his eyes tightly, trying to ignore the pain.

In a couple of minutes he opened his eyes. Silhouetted against the darkening sky was a man looking down at him.

"Thank God," Doggett gasped.

The man emitted a small, humorless laugh. "Well, you may want to reconsider that comment shortly," the man said sarcastically.

Blinking his dry eyes, Doggett was able to focus on the speaker. The man wore tattered, once-fancy pants, an equally tattered vest under a coat with sleeves too short for the man's arms. On his head was a hat with a narrow brim and a rounded top. The man himself had a long, narrow face with a sharp nose and slightly protruding teeth behind an upper lip bearing a wispy, brown mustache.

"Don't I know you?" Doggett whispered.

"Well, hell. I should hope so. You killed me dead in Throckmorton last winter. Claimed I was cheating at cards. But maybe you've killed so many people that you've forgotten us all."

Dear mother of God, Doggett thought, closing his eyes, I'm imagining things. I must be dying.

There was the sound of more footsteps on the rocky ground, and there was suddenly an odor of decay. Doggett opened his eyes again. Standing around him were four other men, a couple of whom looked vaguely familiar. All were dressed in worn clothes, all looking like men who lived near the edge of civilization. All looking like the kind of men he'd tangled with in towns all over north Texas.

"What … what do you want?" he wheezed.

"What we want," one of the other men said, his voice a soft, deep-South drawl, "Is just to watch you die. Sort of like welcoming you over to our side."

"Y'all ain't real …"

"Kinda depends on what you mean by real. We're real enough for you in this situation. Let me show you."

With that the man kicked Doggett in the hip, not terribly hard, but hard enough to be real. And hard enough to cause the agony of his broken ribs to flash up. Doggett gasped and closed his eyes tightly.

"You've never been so terribly different from us," the man drawled. "No consideration for anyone else. Always looking for trouble in one form or another. But you got that damned badge. Somehow that's always made a difference. 'Til now. But now it ain't gonna help you any. In a little while you're gonna be as dead as us. But I don't think your dying is gonna to be as easy as ours was."

Doggett was frightened, but he still wasn't sure that he wasn't imagining all of this. Except for the kick, this had all been talk. And the kick could've simply been his broken ribs sending a jolt through him. The man's comment about Doggett dying on this rocky ground made him want it all to be his imagination. It couldn't be real.

But his heart was pounding. He lay amid the rocks and dry, sandy soil, panting slightly.

If it was real, there was nothing that he could do; he knew that. He couldn't shoot them all. He'd either take what was coming, whatever that might be, and die from it, or he'd just lay there and soon die from thirst. Or from coyotes and snakes.

Time passed, but Doggett hadn't the slightest idea how much. When he opened his eyes again the sky had turned slightly violet, however. So, essentially no time had passed. That couldn't be right, but then none of this could be right.

The five men that came to him earlier were standing to one side, barely in his limited field of vision when he turned his head slightly.

More footsteps approached, accompanied by the jingle of spurs. The smell of decomposition had lessened when the five had moved away. Now, it was back again, maybe worse.

A Mexican moved into view. Doggett knew this man right away. Diego Gomez, a Comanchero that Doggett had killed. Gomez was dressed as Doggett remembered: silver encrusted sweat-stained sombrero, gray shirt with flowing sleeves, tight-fitting dusty pants, mismatched gun belts crossed under his ample stomach with a pistol on each hip.

"Hola, Doggett. What a nice surprise to find you here."

"Go to hell, Gomez. You ain't really here. Go stand by those boys over there and let me get on with dying."

"Oh, you're going to keep dying, hombre. But my boys and me, we owe you. In case you forgot you shot all three of us after we'd given up. I knew I shouldn't have trusted you, but you and your compadres had us cold. I didn't think we had a choice. I should've gone down fighting. At least maybe we would've gotten some of you."

Doggett tried to clear his dry throat. "Hell, you damned Mex, why do you think we killed you all? Because I knew that as soon as any of us looked the other way you'd have tried to gun us. We knew you all had guns in your boots. We found them afterwards. We were just being safe."

Gomez spit tobacco onto Doggett's broken foot.

"Doggett, you're dying so why lie to yourself? If you knew we had those other guns why didn't you make us give them up? You shot us because we were what you call Mexes. Simple as that. You'd done it before when some poor Mexican pissed you off about something. Maybe you didn't kill them all, but you broke a bunch of heads with that big pistol of yours.

"Ah, here come my boys," Gomez said as Doggett heard more boots on the rocky ground. Looking down at Doggett with pure hate in his eyes, Gomez continued. "And they were my boys, you damned animal. Remember that if you wonder why this is so important to me."

Two young Mexicans walked into view. Doggett remembered Gomez because he'd chased the Comanchero off and on for several years. These other two meant nothing to him.

"Try to remember, Doggett, if you can," Gomez said after spitting tobacco onto the Ranger's chest. "These were really my boys, *mis hijos*, my sons, and I loved them."

Gomez suddenly lashed at Doggett with a quirt, slashing him across the face. The younger Mexicans began kicking him. The beating seemed to never end, Doggett's body flamed in a new spot with each blow.

Doggett tried to cry out, but his throat was too dry. Finally, as he felt himself on the verge of passing out, the torture ended.

Breathing rapidly, his body throbbing in pain, Doggett finally opened his eyes. Through his tears he saw the young Mexicans standing with the five no-goods from earlier. Gomez, however, still stood over him, smiling down at him.

"How was that, *bastardo*? I would like for it to have killed you. In fact, I wanted to kill you by myself, but … well, it's not time yet."

"Oh, God, Gomez," Doggett rasped. "Not more, please."

Laughing loudly, a laugh echoed by the seven men standing to the side, Gomez responded, "Oh, Doggett, that was just the beginning."

As the Ranger began to slow his breathing, he heard it again. The sound of feet coming toward him. But this sound was different—softer. And the sound was obviously made by several people. Again there was the overpowering smell of decay, obvious to Doggett even through the haze of his pain.

Appearing above Doggett were Indians, women and children. Doggett's muscles clinched in anticipation of what was to come. Gomez, he noticed, was still standing above him.

As if the old Comanchero could read his mind, and under the circumstances that didn't seem too unlikely, Gomez said, "They need someone to translate for them. You didn't mind killing them, but it was too much trouble to learn their language."

"But, Gomez," he gasped. "I never killed them."

"As one of those hombres over there said earlier, you don't even remember who you killed, do you?"

One of the women said something softly to Gomez, her dark eyes focused on Doggett. Gomez listened and then turned his head back down toward Doggett.

"She asked why you don't remember raiding her camp."

"Uh, what … "

Continuing to translate, Gomez said, "It was a Comanche camp on the Canadian River. Winter of six years ago."

The Ranger remembered a camp raid, but he didn't remember where or when it had occurred other than it was in the winter. Apparently his face reflected his confusion. The woman leaned down toward Doggett and hissed out a stream of words.

"She says," Gomez continued, "That you Rangers and the yellowlegs—what she calls cavalry troopers—rode through the camp three times, running down anyone in the way of the horses and shooting the men and anyone with a weapon. She and her two children were ridden down. These other women and children were either ridden down too or killed in some other way."

Doggett's fear bubbled up into his throat. In a panic he looked at the hatred in the face of the woman and then turned back to the Comanchero. He opened his mouth to speak but was suddenly pelted with rocks thrown by the smaller Indian children. As the stones hit him in the face he tried to turn away, but they were standing on both sides. And then the beating started, the older children lashing out at his prostrate body with sticks. He clenched his eyes, put his arms over his face, and tried to cry out, but his throat was dry and nearly clamped shut with fear.

At that point new pains burst out from his stomach and legs. He forced his eyes open and saw that the squaws had replaced the children. Each woman had a small camp knife and was stabbing him repeatedly.

With each blow Doggett grunted and gasped. At some point he passed out.

He regained consciousness and woke up sobbing, dry-eyed. Dear God, he thought, no more. No more.

After a few minutes he saw that the sky was now a little darker, but still not as dark as it should be given all that had happened. Swiveling his eyes he finally saw Gomez standing with the Indians and the other men off to one side. What could be next?

There was the soft sound of steps through rocks, coming slowly toward him. In a moment a short, stocky dark man appeared at his feet. Greasy long hair and high cheekbones. A Comanche.

The man pulled a knife from his belt and walked around Doggett's body to his head.

"Gomez!" Doggett gasped. "Please help. I'm sorry! Sorry!"

"No, hombre, I think that you are just sorry that your past has caught up with you. Now, this is going to very bad, Doggett. *Muy malo!* But it is the last thing. And then you die."

The Comanche squatted beside Doggett's head. With the last of his strength the Ranger brought up the heavy Colt and fired it repeatedly into the Indian's body. The Comanche just smiled as he reached for Doggett's hair, pulling it tight and lifting the Ranger's head. Then, he placed the edge of the knife against Doggett's skin. As the razor-sharp blade slipped under his scalp and grated against his skull, Doggett screamed and fired a final round into the savage's face.

The horse, which had been wandering around the edge of the depression looking for something to eat, jerked its head up when the gun fire began. As the shriek erupted from the spring the horse trotted away.

The next morning two riders arrived at the spring from the north leading two horses. One was a pack horse, the other was the Ranger's. The riders had an ample supply of water and had chosen to make an early camp the day before under the thin, lacey shade of a group of mesquite trees a couple of miles away from the spring.

As they neared the depression containing the spring there was a gust of hot wind from the south.

"Good god," one of the men said. "Something big's dead around here."

"Yep, and it must be down by the spring since I can't see anything around here. Hope it didn't foul the water."

As they reined up at the edge of the depression the two dismounted.

"Can't believe the smell is coming from that body. It looks pretty fresh."

"Actually, I think the smell's going away."

The two men walked slowly down the rocky slope to look at Doggett's body. The Ranger was still on his back, his spine arched. His left arm was bent at the elbow and the fingers of that hand clenched like a claw. His right arm rested on his chest, his hand loosely closed around a big pistol which was across his neck. His eyes, clouded now with dirt and small insects, bulged unnaturally, and his mouth, with dried blood down his cheeks, was frozen in a scream.

Pointing to the pistol in the corpse's hand, one of the men said, "That explains those shots we heard last night. But, sweet Jesus, what in hell was he shooting at with all those rounds? Don't look like he needed but one."

The body's head had a bullet hole just below the right cheek bone which was black with spent gun powder around the wound. The man's left temple was a shattered mess of bone and crusty blood and was covered in small insects. A fan of dried blood and brains coated the rocks beside the head.

The Nightmare Man
by James H Longmore

He awoke with a start, bathed in a cold, clammy sweat that clung uncomfortably to his skin, his heart pounding like a jackhammer deep in his chest, his breathing labored, his lungs heaving air like the panting of a rabid dog.

He clawed himself to bitter wakefulness, his mouth dry as graveyard dirt, head spinning with the vivid remnants of the cruel, vicious dreams that had so plagued his sleep.

Why am I having somebody else's nightmares?

And then he remembered.

This was to be expected because he, Charles McKeever Edwards, was the Nightmare Man.

There was always an excited buzz when Johnny Johnson's Carnival of the Spectacular rolled into town, and not one simply borne of the eager anticipation of the sights, sounds and smells of the big top and its myriad performers—both two legs and four—nor the delightfully ghoulish exhibits of the freakshow that accompanied the trapeze artists, lions and garishly painted clowns who delighted children of all ages, but also for the presence of Edwards and his renowned and remarkably singular abilities.

He reached out a hot, trembling hand from beneath the warm sanctuary of the stale air beneath the thick blankets upon his bed; he'd stacked them high the night before in the expectation of the morning's chill. The morning air was so frigid that Edwards could see his breath illustrated in small, strained wisps that he thought looked like tiny, tormented ghosts. His shaking fingers grasped the neck of the tall whiskey bottle that was never more than arm's length away, his parched tongue and throbbing head craving the amber relief that swished within the thick glass.

A couple of hearty swigs, and Edwards was halfway to feeling normal again—if one could ever describe the swirling echoes of so many terrible and entirely alien dreams that slithered about the ridges and recesses of his aching brain normal. The booze had the miraculous quality of banishing those dreams—and the memories of those dreams—long enough for his mind to secure them back into the tiny, mental boxes he so meticulously constructed for them.

It took a while for Edwards to remember where he was. The carnival moved so frequently from town to town that it was the Devil's own job to keep up; the best he could recall was that they'd set up the previous day in some quaint little town in South Texas, close enough to the great city of Houston to entice a reasonable level of moneyed clientele, yet enough of a distance to avoid the ire of the inevitable religious types who made it their job to oppose anything that may offend the dubious sensitivities of their Good Lord and savior.

The town, Edwards recalled, was called Peck. It had once been nothing more than a small farming community which had been populated largely by the European immigrants who journeyed across continents in the mid-1800's to take advantage of the seemingly infinite abundance of lumber and the richly fertile soil. Then, an opportunist entrepreneur who went by the name of Thomas Ball—folks that knew him just called him Tom—routed the railroad through the tiny town, along with building its picturesque station, which brought with it a whole new level of prosperity to the place.

It was Tom Ball himself who invited the carnival each year, allowing Johnson to set up his show for free on the town green, within easy walking distance of the modest station. Ball's only stipulation was a financial consideration of twenty-five percent of the week's takings and that Edwards be present—Ball was one canny businessman, that much was for certain; perhaps one day they'd name the whole damn town after him.

Edwards shook his head as if to dislodge the final, stubborn remnants of the jumbled nightmares that had joined his slumber, and dragged his weary body from his bed. The day was still young, the cold light of the fall sun only just daring its first peek over the horizon. He took another swig of his whiskey, alarmed at just how low the remainder settled at the bottom of the bottle— and hoped to his own god that it wasn't a Sunday. It was near on impossible to purchase hard liquor anywhere in Texas on the Lord's day.

Edwards stepped carefully around the crate that served as a low table in his tent and pulled on his breeches and thick, tweed jacket over his longjohns. He slipped a cold, stiff boot onto each foot, and ventured out of his spartan abode. His bladder badly needed relief, in spite of the chill air that clung to his moist body like a grim overcoat.

Eschewing the long walk to the public conveniences—Johnson had elected to position them at the opposite side of the Big Top from the ragtag collection of freakshow tents; it was no great secret that the semi-devout Christian owner of the carnival considered the sideshow inhabitants to be poor relations to the proper circus, even though the money they brought in was actually propping up the hugely expensive big top performers—Edwards elected to rid himself of the previous night's imbibition behind the Tattooed Monster's tent. The Tattooed Monster would definitely still be asleep, since he'd entertained the Siamese twins, Miss Trixie and Miss Constance, well into the small hours of the morning. Edwards wondered if there'd been anyone amongst the entire troupe who hadn't had the dubious pleasure of hearing their raucous cavortings.

A quick glance to ensure privacy and Edwards released his member, unleashing a steaming torrent of sour smelling piss into the calf-length grass behind the libidinous Tattooed Monster's tent, a long sigh of relief escaping his cracked, desiccated lips.

Not that the Monster was really a monster in any fashion; Terrance was in fact quite the accommodating type. The Monster was the sort of character who would do anything for anyone, and do it with a smile upon his elaborately inked face. His scary moniker was nothing more than clumsy showmanship on Johnny Johnson's part; but it certainly brought in the gawkers and the judgmental to gaze upon Terrence's near-nakcd, entirely tattooed body. Edwards had never inquired, but legend had it that the Tattooed Monster even had his member, scrotum and the circumference of his anus inked with the most incredibly meticulous, artistic depiction of geisha girls and lotus flowers. And the netherly placement of the carnal art was said to fetch two whole dollars per private showing.

It had been the same with the Elephant Man— Edwards had crossed paths with him when Johnson's carnival had visited the seamier side of London, England, and the two had gotten drunk together on disgustingly cheap gin on more than one occasion. There was one poor young soul who had been demonized merely to attract the crowds; yet he was a kind and decent man who suffered the physical and mental torments of his affliction his every waking hour. His real name was Joseph Carey Merrick, although he was often incorrectly called John. Edwards knew him simply as Joe.

Joe had died back in 1890, just five short years ago, his corpse placed on display in some stuffy museum or other, and Edwards often thought of him. He couldn't help but wonder just what hideous nightmares skulked within that cruelly deformed skull of his; if only he'd had the chance to find out. Just professional curiosity, of course.

"Edwards!"

A harsh, booming voice yanked Edwards from his reverie. He spun around to face his boss, limp member still in his hand, the last few dribbles of dark pee splashing on his boots. "Johnny!" Edwards exclaimed, as he hurriedly tucked himself away, grimacing at the feel of the warm wetness that spread along the thigh of his longjohns. "I didn't expect to see you this early in the morning," he continued, offering up a sheepish grin as fat snakes of steam from the pee-soaked grass arose behind him like some crazy illustration of guilt.

"This is Lord Castleford," Johnson announced, introducing the rather important-looking man who strode beside him, both men either choosing to ignore Edwards' common indiscretion, or not giving much of a damn.

"Pleased to meet you, sir," Edwards said, extending his shaking hand.

Lord Castleford stared down at the Nightmare Man's pee-splashed fingers with disdain, his own gloved hand clinging to the gold-topped cane he carried like his life depended upon it.

"Lord Castleford is in urgent need of your services," Johnson informed Edwards. "He's already paid his twenty-five dollars." Ever the businessman was the carnie owner, always straight to the point, never one for life's smaller niceties.

Edwards gave Castleford a wan smile, his head still throbbing a tad, although last night's whiskey was made more agreeable by the morn's reinforcements, and now mercifully loosened its grip on his aching brain. They were all the same, these moneyed folk; no respect nor empathy for private time—their money bought them what they wanted, whom they wanted, when they wanted. "If you'd care to step this way, Lord Castleford," Edwards chimed, turning on the old charm. Oftentimes a soupcon of flattery and kowtowing here and there would result in a hearty tip from his wealthy clientele. "I take it you have brought along a necessary item," he added as he led Castleford across the cold, damp grass to his humble quarters.

"Of course," Lord Castleford replied, his clipped English tone flat and abrupt.

It was then that Edwards noticed that the man's left ear was missing. There was a discreet bandage in its place, mostly hidden by the wide-brimmed gunslinger hat he wore. "Then we are all good, sir," Edwards said, more to break the silence between them than anything else. The short trek back to the tent was feeling inexorably longer than usual.

The whole ear.

It reflected poorly if Edwards didn't say so himself; unless, of course, Castleford was considering signing on with the carnival. The subtle humor of it amused him. The ear lobe, alone, would have been sufficient. A whole ear was drastic, he decided. And overly dramatic.

Edwards' tent was unremarkable amongst the carnival's host of similar dwellings, each one constructed from bland, beige canvas and held up by a spider's web of crisscrossed guy wires—each one a potential hazard to life and limb to the uninitiated—and each one sporting a short awning, above which hung a painted declaration of the freakish delights contained therein. Edwards' advertisement had once been loud and garish, but had faded over the twelve years and more he'd been travelling with Johnson's motley assemblage. The faded colors were now almost as insipid as the canvas upon which they'd been painted. They announced:

THE NIGHTMARE MAN!!!
He Will Cleanse Your
Most Terrifying Dreams!

Alongside this—certainly one of the more titillating carnival barks Johnny Johnson ever composed—was an expertly painted picture of a screaming woman, hands clasped on either side of her terrified but pretty face, her comely features contorted into a suitably horrified expression. As to precisely why Johnson had insisted upon the image being that of an attractive young lady, Edwards had no idea, but he assumed the largely male clientele that the freakshow tended to attract bore heavily upon the decision-making process. Oftentimes the showman, but always the businessman.

Edwards ushered Lord Castleford into his tent, lifting the flap aside to accommodate the man's stocky frame and expansive hat. They left the carnival owner standing outside in the cold, Edwards' pretext being that his unique ability only worked one-on-one. Truth was, it worked perfectly well in pretty much any circumstance, no matter how many people were in close proximity. It was simply the one tiny slice of power he got to hold over the man. Still, the great King of the Carnival, Johnny Johnson had all of his money to keep him warm.

Castleford took off his hat and sat himself down on Edwards' unmade bed. "Best we get this over and done with," he growled, and Edwards thought he caught just a hint of a Northern English accent hidden within the plumy one, but couldn't quite place it. "I have places to be."

"Of course, sir," Edwards replied, his voice hushed in mock reverence. The men who paid for his time and gift—for it was mostly the men, as if they somehow had garnered the monopoly on terrible dreams—were there only as a last resort, one last desperate attempt to rid themselves of the night terrors that so haunted them.

Often the next step would be suicide, that being the only way out for the poor folks who couldn't afford Edwards' cleansing.

"This is for you," Castleford handed over a small bundle. It was wrapped tightly in white muslin, a tiny pink stain of blood dried on one side, "I trust it is satisfactory to your requirements?"

Edwards unwrapped the cloth gingerly—he'd never quite got used to handling other people's severed body parts—and inspected the wrinkled ear that lay nestled within. "This will do perfectly," Edwards told the man who sat before him like some small, expectant child awaiting appraisal for untidy but lovingly created artwork.

It was an unfortunate symptom of his ethereal abilities that required Edwards to be in possession of a recently removed body part to work. Yet, while it nauseated him to have to deal with the plethora of hastily removed parts he was presented with day in, day out, Edwards' clientele had no such qualms. He'd seen rich, landed gentry snip off pinkie fingers and toes with cigar cutters and pocket knives right there in front of him. He'd had cattle barons slicing at their wrists for blood and hacking off chunks of flesh from their flabby flanks; and he'd been visited by sad, haunted old men who'd made their money in countless reprehensible ways yanking out their tired, yellowed teeth to present to The Nightmare Man as a cat presents a disemboweled mouse to its master. All of them, to a man, were desperate to have Edwards perform his miracle and rid them of the nightmares that plagued their sleep and haunted their waking hours; more often than not they would be nightmares borne from nefarious acts and guilt-ridden consciences.

"So, what happens now?" Lord Castleford asked, his timid voice somewhat out of place, coming as it was from such an imposing figure, his tone passive yet impatient. He remained seated, however, the look of nervous expectation etched upon his ruddy, rounded features.

"I guess we begin," Edwards said. He'd hoped the man would make his exit upon handing over his left ear; his sort usually did. There was really no need for them to be present during Edwards' ridding ritual, because once the Nightmare Man was in possession of a piece of his or her person, the process began.

Ah, the ritual.

This was something Edwards had fashioned deliberately in the early days of his illustrious career, his craft informed by his exposure to the great Johnny Johnson's philosophy of showmanship.

"They're paying us good money for you to do what you do," Johnson would say. "They want a show and it's your job to give 'em one, Charlie-boy!" Johnson had gone on to explain that, for the obscene chunk of hard-earned cash the carnie was charging for Edwards' services, the clientele expected to see something. It was not enough that Edwards assuaged them of their deepest, most terrifying nightmares. In order to feel as if they were really getting their money's worth, they wanted to watch him perform.

Edwards knelt down in the center of his tent, Lord Castleford's ear laid on the cold, uneven canvas before him. "I must ask you to remain silent throughout, sir," he whispered to the lord, who hung on his every word, eyes wide with wonder. This was all nonsense of course. as the noise level made absolutely no difference whatsoever. Edwards had performed his unearthly trickery amongst boisterous crowds before, in those long ago, heady days before he'd made the acquaintance of one Johnny Johnson. "Make yourself comfortable," he continued. "It may take me some time to summon the dream spirits."

Once again, pure unadulterated hokum. There were no spirits and no otherworldly beings to summon forth to rid Lord Castleford of his bad dreams. There was just one Charles McKeever Edwards plying the particularly unique ability his mother had long ago declared to be God-given. He often reflected, were she still alive, what she'd think of his "gift" now.

Playing to his audience's expectations, Edwards began to hum, a low, baritone noise that he created at the very back of his voice box, made all the more theatrical by his whiskey-parched throat. He turned and twisted and feigned a spasm.

Then, a scream.

Shrill, piercing, it echoed throughout the spacious Manor house like a banshee's wail, wrenching the man from his post-dinner slumber. Mind alert in an instant, heart pounding painfully in his chest, he staggered to the broad, sweeping staircase and mounted it two, three stairs at a time, the tall oil paintings of his ancestors glowering down upon him as if in earnest judgement.

The foul stink hit him before he'd reached the topmost stair. The thick, cloying stench of sickness and death lingered, and the man knew what awaited him in the nursery before he laid eyes upon it.

"He's dead!" his poor wife wailed. She clutched the small, lifeless body of their only child to her bosom, her clothes smeared with the reeking filth that had spilled out from both ends of the baby boy in his death throes. "Joseph is dead!" She slumped to the hard, wooden floor, her petite body shaking with great, wracking sobs. "You killed him!"

Gagging against the reek that burned deep into his nose and throat, the man knelt down at his wife's side. He reached out a hand to caress his dead son's icy scalp, as though he could resurrect the child by touch alone.

"Leave him be!" the man's wife screeched, yanking the infant away from her husband's reach.

The baby's head lolled back, and its stagnant, glassy eyes stared up at the man with a bone-chilling, accusatory glare. He saw in that instant what he had denied to himself all along—the giggling cherub had been considerably more unwell than he realized. And now the taut, paper-thin skin, the cracked, split and bleeding rosebud lips, and those eyes—those terrible, sunken eyes were burning themselves into his brain and would haunt him until he lay rotting in his own grave.

The child had been cranky of late, that much the man knew for certain, even as his temperature pushed the mercury high enough to alarm the nanny. But Lord Castleford had resisted calling the physician. All to save a few guineas that the man could well afford, in the firm but misguided belief that a mild infant fever would make strong stuff of his one and only son.

Castleford's wife had taken her own life not six months after they'd put their child's wasted, stinking corpse in the family mausoleum, her barren body unable to cope with a childless future, her mind sapped of all its anima. The man had discovered her hanging from the balustrade in the servant's quarters, along with a simple, beautifully calligraphed note on the family's crested paper. Her final sentiment was blunt: "You Killed Him."

That note, along with the indelible memory of his son's withered, sunken orbs, had followed Castleford into his nightmares every single night.

It was all over in an instant.

Edwards felt—lived—the memories as they gushed from Lord Castleford in one thick, painful jolt. But he remained still, eyes closed tight, his breathing deep and exaggerated, ensuring his client would feel he'd received his money's worth.

Edwards took that precious time to round up the Lord's nightmare in his mind, taking great care to capture each and every sight, sound and rank smell of Castleford's nefarious thoughts as they cavorted about his swirling brain like mischievous spirits. Once corralled, Edwards boxed them up neatly in one of the extra-special mental boxes he stored away in the farthest corner of his consciousness. Sure, a few escaped every now and then, the hellish memories somehow managing to find a way to creep into Edwards' own dreams; but that was simply the bitter price the Nightmare Man was fated to pay for his gift.

Edwards opened his eyes.

"All done?" Lord Castleford asked, his eyes dewy with hope.

"All done," Edwards replied, with an ashen smile.

"I…I don't know how to begin to thank you," Castleford stammered. "I can actually feel them...gone."

Unashamedly, Edwards glanced down toward the Lord's bulging pocket.

"But, of course," Castleford continued, letting out a nervous laugh and fumbling around in his pocket. He pulled out a thick wad of banknotes and placed it upon the low table, ignoring Edward's outstretched hand—as if to touch the grim receptor would be to run the risk of having his tortuous apparitions handed straight back to him.

"Thank you," Edwards said, scooping up the cash but resisting the urge to count it then and there. To have done so would have been terribly crass and, worse, bad business. "Are you sure?"

"You have relieved me of a heavy burden, sir," Castleford replied, as he struggled to his feet. "You can have no idea just how much you have changed my life."

Edwards had *every* idea of the relief he had afforded the poor, tormented man, but he remained tight-lipped, conferring a solemn nod to the Lord as he made his way out of the tent.

It was quite peculiar how Jeb Goedecke lost his pinkie finger.

"Are you sure you should be killing it now?" Jeb asked his wife, the delightfully homely Abigail. "Your family are not coming until tomorrow evening."

"You know me, my love." Abigail gave her husband a warm smile. "I always like to be prepared." She held the struggling hen tight against the wooden block, doing her level best to avoid its scrabbling claws and desperately snapping beak. "And besides which, it's always best to allow the bird to relax overnight."

Jeb clutched the cleaver tightly in his hand, his knuckles white, and studied the wretched creature that was pinned to the bloodstained wooden block by his wife's strong hands. Whilst he'd done nothing but support his good lady's attempts at self-sufficiency, he'd always balked when it came to the more base parts of her enthusiasm. It was all well and good for Abigail, she'd been brought up on a farm—bloodshed, death, spilled innards were pretty much the norm for the woman.

"Oh, give that to me," Abigail huffed, managing to remain good natured despite her husband's incessant dithering. It was always the same, Jeb would offer to do the unpleasant deed of separating a chicken from its head, but once the actual time came, his face would blanch, his hands tremble and he would stall until

Abigail took the lead. "You hold the bird down, my dear."

With a sickly smile dancing around the corners of his thin-lipped mouth, Jeb handed over the cleaver and pressed his hands on top of the chicken, amazed as always at just how warm its frantically wriggling body was—and afterward he would swear that he felt the poor thing's tiny heart hammering away beneath the thick layer of rust-red feathers.

"You might want to look away now, dear," Abigail whispered to her over-sensitive husband as she raised the cleaver. "It'll be all over in but a second or two."

Jeb twisted his head to one side and screwed his eyes tight shut just for good measure; he had no desire to witness the end of the poor thing that was destined to adorn their dinner table the next day, along with all of the usual sumptuous trimmings his wife would prepare. Beneath Jeb's trembling, sweating hands, the chicken made one last bid for freedom, just as Abigail brought the cleaver down.

Edwards felt the story of how Mr. Goedeke lost his finger was overlong and rather dull. In fact, he thought, it probably lasted longer than the ritual would. "You have the necessaries?" Edwards inquired, his face peering out from between the thick canvas flaps of his tent, his breath pluming in the chill, early evening air.

"Of course," the lady answered, sounding mildly offended. As proof, she popped off the lid of the tobacco tin she clutched in her gloved hands to reveal the wrinkled, bloodied finger nestled upon a crimson-stained bed of cotton.

"Then let us begin, Mrs. Goedeke," Edwards replied, adopting what he liked to call his bedside manner. His impatience was uncalled for, especially in light of what he assumed would be a short, frivolous turn. *How bad could the dreams of a man uncomfortable with dispatching yardbirds be?*

He pulled aside a canvas flap and ushered the woman inside, his eyes stealing a glance at her most formidable backside as she made her way into the warm interior of the tent.

"This isn't for me," Abigail explained as she made herself comfortable. "It's for my husband, Jeb. I feel like a monster," she sighed. "It's my fault, you see. He's been having the most terrible nightmares of late." The woman's words caught in her mouth, as if they struggled to make their way out. She coughed to clear her throat. "I do hope that this is acceptable."

"Perfectly," Edwards assured her, giving the woman his very best disarming smile. "As long as we have some part of him, then I can relieve him of his despicable burden."

"And you're sure his presence isn't required?"

"Absolutely."

Abigail placed the tobacco tin upon the low table, along with a bundle of money held together with a neatly tied piece of twine and a small bottle of good quality brandy.

Edwards smiled. It was not often that a client bestowed a tip in advance—Mrs. Goedeke was either cretinously susceptible to all manner of quackery or absurdly desperate to rescue her squeamish husband from the wily poultry that haunted his pillow. Edwards didn't understand. He was no charlatan, to be sure, but the fee and the tip seemed excessive, especially compared to the demonic slumbers he'd rid most of his recent other visitors of. "Thank you, Mrs. Goedeke," Edwards said, with a salacious glare at the amber-colored liquid that rested within the impressive decanter.

He anticipated many pronounced and lively nocturnal libations in the hours that would follow. Maybe he would even enlist the Tattooed Monster and conjoin his revelries with his Siamese friends.

"He is plagued by such terrible dreams, Mr. Edwards," Abigail reiterated. "Most nights he awakens screaming and drenched in the most dreadfully sour sweat." She snuffled back a tear or two. "I can't bear to share his bed any longer; Jeb and I have had separate rooms for several months now."

"I'm very sorry to hear that, Mrs. Goedeke."

"Abigail, please. Call me Abigail."

"Right you are, Abigail." Edwards made himself comfortable in the chair opposite the distressed woman. Just why these people felt compelled to relate their entire story escaped him. Did they not realize that he was going to get all the minutia anyway?

"The doctor suggested a course of mercury," Abigail explained. "But that only seemed to make matters worse, and it gave his skin a most unhealthy pallor. Personally, I put it all down to the books he's been reading."

"Books?" Edwards noted, sitting back up, actually intrigued. This was a new one to him.

"He started with that Mary Shelley book," Abigail confided. "He presupposed that—although it involved a monster constructed from stolen body parts—since it was written by a woman it would not offend his usually fragile sensibilities." Abigail was embarrassed.

"But then he read Mr. Poe's works," she continued. "And I saw a change in his countenance almost immediately." A solitary tear escaped one of Abigail's startlingly blue eyes. She wiped it away with the back of a gloved hand, huffing as if offended that the tear dared annoy her. "I told Jeb that I didn't want him reading any more of those blood and thunder books, that he really ought to stick to the Bronte sisters, or that nice Jane Austin."

"And did he?" Edwards prompted, guessing that he already knew the answer.

Abigail shook her head. "He did for a while, and then he bought himself a copy of Stoker's confounded vampire tale…"

Edwards was, of course, familiar with Dracula. A client had gifted it to him upon its release a year or so ago. He'd made several attempts at reading the weighty tome, but found the prose a tad too stodgy for his liking.

"The nightmares became ever more frequent, Mr. Edwards," Abigail added, her voice flat and strangely cold. "And more intense. I'm afraid that my poor husband will drive himself quite insane if this continues."

"Well, I am pleased you came to see me," Edwards replied, leaning forward and patting Abigail's gloved hand. "Mrs.—*Abigail*. I can take all of that away from him."

"I do hope so, Mr. Edwards," she said. "I've had to remortgage our home to afford to pay you." She glanced down at the bundle of notes on the table. "I'm ruined if what they say about the Nightmare Man isn't true."

"Oh, it's all entirely true," Edwards declared, puffing out his chest, his ego enjoying the attention. "There are no nightmares too horrifying for the Nightmare Man to steal away, no dreams too unpleasant to relieve you of." He gave the poor, distressed woman his very best spiel, figuring that if she was desperate enough to have remortgaged her home to pay him, then the very least she deserved was full value for her money.

"Thank you," Abigail said softly, her voice barely above a whisper.

Gingerly, Edwards picked the tobacco tin up from the table and eyed the contents that dwelled within. Visibly steeling himself for effect and drawing a hearty gulp of air (that almost made him cough), Edwards removed the withered pinkie from the tin, taking a little time to pluck off the fine wisps of cotton that clung to the dried blood along its underside, and noting just how neatly manicured the nail was. Then, adhering to his usual, carefully orchestrated ritual, Edwards took in one more deep breath, gave Mrs. Goedeke a reassuring smile and closed his eyes.

He commenced his humming, securing the illusion of slipping into a trance-like state, and almost immediately, the memories flooded into his mind.

The warm body writhed and struggled against the weight of his hands, and he felt the erratic thumping of a panicking heart. He glanced down and saw that, instead of a chicken, there was a young woman, pinned down by the full weight of strong hands and heavy knees, her tiny frame entirely naked and her pretty face distorted with pain as he pressed it hard into the damp dirt.

And then he was biting, chewing, gnawing at the soft flesh of her shoulder, moving his way inward toward her neck as one would nibble along a succulent corn cob. The young woman bucked her fragile body, as if to throw him from her, but he had the advantage of both strength and sheer weight – he had chosen his victim wisely.

She attempted to scream as his mouth located the yielding flesh of her delicate neck, and his lips closed in upon the wildly thrumming pulse of the thick artery that pumped there. Once more, she screamed, muffled by the thick, suffocating clay of the cold, clinging dirt, then she was silenced as his teeth bit down hard and tore away a goodly amount of the young woman's throat.

And then he drank from her.

Greedily he slurped up the spurting, liquid warmth that fled the young woman's ruined body, ignoring the sickly gurgling sounds his victim made as she slowly but surely drowned in her own life fluid. He rejoiced as to how powerfully her blood jetted into his eager mouth, spilling from between his quivering lips as he gulped the stuff down like a suckling and infinitely hellish infant.

And then came the violent wave of nausea, the crashing low as the realization of what he had done hit him hard, and along with it came the numbing terror of potential discovery; this was without a doubt something they would not hesitate to stretch his neck upon the gallows for.

A different woman this time, an ebony-skinned beauty with high cheek bones and dark brown pools for eyes that begged and pleaded for her very life. She lay facing him, her naked body trembling as she sobbed shallowly with his strong fingers clamped so resolutely over her mouth. Her blood tasted so delectably sweet, flowing into him, filling not only his stomach, but his empty soul, filling the void that his murderous actions had created within him; a void that no god could ever hope to fill. And it still tasted so beautifully sweet when his body ejected it, thick and congealing and bitter from the sharp tang of bile as it splashed across the slack, lifeless face of the dark-skinned girl.

The face changed once more, and there laid another woman, her throat torn asunder, a huge, ragged hole from which her blood leaked out, the pinkish-white nubs of her spine clearly visible through the gore. He spat out the thick clod of pale flesh that was crammed in his mouth—far too much to even contemplate swallowing—and he lowered his head toward the feast as the young woman's life abandoned her, resting his cheek against the warmth of her bare breast in order to lap at the scarlet liquid that he knew sustained his evil intent.

Another face, speckled with an array of gaudy freckles, her neckline and arms tanned in the way of land girls, her ruddy complexion rapidly waning as blood drained from her limp body. And even as she died and thoughts of his own wife cascaded through his fevered mind, he retched and heaved as his body repelled this most unnatural meal. And as he watched, her face changed again, morphing before his very eyes into that of another, and then another...

And another.

They all appeared to blend into one now, eyes staring, mouths flopping open and closed like that of some dumb, landed fish, corpulent bubbles of congealing blood forming at their corners, rising and popping with an audible noise that echoed through the nightmares that played out in his head.

How many now? Four, five? More?

This one was a feisty one, her long, flowing tresses of flaxen hair spread in the damp, flattened grass about her head like a golden halo around some heaven-sent goddess. She flailed her hands, slapping at his face, clawing his clothes, her lithe, buxom body bucking beneath him just like the wild broncos he'd seen when the Wild West shows came into town, her bare, bountiful breasts jiggling like pure liquid flesh beneath him. And yet, she too succumbed to his preternatural strength, his might too much for her womanly frame, the sheer ferocity of his vicious hunger unshakable, immovable. She made one final attempt to free herself, grasping at the tiny bandage on his right hand, squeezing down for all she was worth on the small, bloodied stump that protruded where his fifth and smallest finger should have been.

The pain was excruciating, it sent white hot flashes across his vision, an agony that shot all the way up along his arm and deep into his fevered brain.

Spurred on by the pain, he ravaged the young woman's throat, ripping and tearing until it was little more than a bloody, gore-soaked mess. And for once, he delighted in consuming the woman's flesh as she died, her eyes unable to tear themselves away from this wanton display of cannibalism as her murderer ate her alive.

Edwards opened his eyes and gasped.

He was drenched in the bitter sweat of pure terror, his chest heaving as if with the most arduous of exertions, the acrid, metallic taste of blood and rended flesh still fresh in his mouth, the dull throbbing sensation in his hand so real that he had to glance down to ensure that it was not his own severed finger he clasped so tightly in his palm.

"Mr. Edwards," Abigail said. "What is it, Mr. Edwards?"

Edwards dropped the finger back into the tin and dared to close his eyes once more.

The nightmare was still there, skulking around his mind in slick, wriggling slivers, resisting all of his best efforts to contain them. He'd no sooner corral some parts in the mental box, than they would slip out as he forced others inside. The insidious threads of Jeb Goedeke's sinister nightmares insinuated themselves deep into Edward's psyche, still tormenting him with vile imagery of torn, ruined bodies and spilled blood, along with the haunting lament of the dying.

And, of course, Edwards knew that what he had witnessed upon connecting with the severed finger Abigail Goedeke had presented to him were not nightmares at all.

They were memories. Nightmarish, yes, but hardly subconscious.

Repelling the scattered stragglers of Jeb Goedeke's murderous thoughts, Edwards snapped open his eyes and stared with deep intent, first at Abigail, and then the brandy decanter

"Are you alright, Mr. Edwards?"

"Mrs. Goedeke," Edwards spoke slowly, selecting his words with great care, and raising his gaze to meet hers. "You must listen to me, and listen well. You are in grave danger. Your husband is not what he has you believe him to be."

"Is this all part of the act, Mr. Edwards?" Abigail replied, making as if to stand up. "Because if it is, I have to say that I am not impressed. Did you, or did you not extricate my husband's nightmares, or have I removed his finger and saddled myself with interminable debt for no good reason?"

"I have done just that, Abigail," Edwards assured her, his voice softening. A look of the gravest concern spread across his pallid, clammy face. "But Jeb will go on to create more," he continued. "For within his human breast there beats the heart of a true monster."

Abigail sat herself back down, a nebulous plume of dust puffing up around her from the old chair. "What on earth are you talking about, Mr. Edwards?" she demanded, and there was just a soupcon of something in her tone that led Edwards to wonder if, deep down, the ostensibly naive Mrs. Goedeke suspected something amiss about her darling Jeb, something that she had suppressed for a very long time. "Well?" she prompted, lips pursed.

And so, taking a deep breath and a hearty swig of the expensive brandy the woman had kindly brought along for him, Edwards told her what he had gleaned about Jeb Goedeke from the man's vile waking nightmares.

Neither the allure of Miss Trixie and Miss Constance, nor the good company of the Tattoed Monster interested Edwards as the day's shadows grew long and the evening approached. And sleep, for the most part, evaded him for the duration, even as much as his brain was exhausted, his body weary. Edwards' brief, yet most brutally frank conversation with the Goedeke woman had drained what little of his energy had remained following his encounter with her husband's severed finger.

The poor woman had wept, of course. Who wouldn't upon being informed that their beloved spouse of fifteen years and more was nothing less than a cold-blooded maniac who found sadistic pleasure in the torture, murder and consumption of innocent young women? And, when Edwards was finished wrecking Abigail with what he knew—what he'd seen—she had gracefully dabbed her eyes dry, thanked him most politely for his time, and been on her way, leaving behind her husband's dreadful digit.

Edwards lay awake wondering just what she would do with the dark knowledge of her husband's grim secrets; would she simply not return home, or would there be a fearful confrontation? Or, would she simply push everything Edwards had told her to the back of her mind and continue along with a life of denial, as often a good wife will do in the face of her husband and provider's indiscretions.

Tossing and turning in the narrow bed, his nightshirt stuck with rank sweat to his aching body, Edwards chased around the final few and incredibly elusive fragments of Goedeke's madness, desperate to enclose them within their designated containers and shove the whole malevolent affair as deep down in the inky crevasses of his fevered brain as was humanly possible. But, for as hard as he tried, they skillfully evaded him, jeering at his conscious mind with recollections of the noises of a rattling, blood-choked throat, the sickly coppery taste of freshly liberated blood, and the cooling touch of recently dead flesh.

"Are you in there?" a voice barked suddenly, Edwards at first unsure of which side of sleep it emanated. "Charles?" Johnny Johnson fought his way through the heavy canvas and barged into Edwards' tent.

"What the –?" Edwards managed, sitting bolt upright in his bed, surprised at just how damp his perspiration had made the sheets.

"I know it's late, Charlie-boy," Johnson said, glancing down at the bulging leather purse in his hands as if it excused his rudeness.

"Good evening," a second, unfamiliar voice added, splitting the awkwardness between Johnson and Edwards. The imposing figure behind the second voice stepped out from the gloom, his tall frame accentuated by a most impressive top hat. "I am so sorry to disturb your sleep," he offered. "Perhaps we should do this another—"

"Nonsense!" Johnson interjected with his usual ebullience. "The Nightmare Man is always open for business, isn't that right, Charlie?"

Edwards grunted his displeasure, but he was actually grateful of the distraction. "Of course," he said. "Please, make yourself at home," he continued, greeting his new client as he clambered from his bed.

The tall man made his way across Edwards' tent, eyeing the grimy surroundings with disdain, his hands jammed resolutely in the pockets of his no doubt ridiculously expensive pants.

Edwards held out a courteous hand for the shaking, only to be surprised when his impromptu client offered his opposite.

"A left-hander, I see." Edwards teased, with the friendliest smile he could muster. He groggily noted that the tall man kept his right hand firmly entrenched in his coat pocket.

The client sat down, casting a curious glance toward the half-open tobacco tin that remained on the makeshift table.

"So," Johnson said, his duty as facilitator work done. "I'll leave you to it. Charlie will have you fixed up in no time." He stretched out a hand to administer a hearty slap on the shoulder of the tall man's luxurious, long coat, but a withering glance had him reconsider. "Right then," Johnson murmured. "I'll be gone."

Clutching the clinking bag of money, Johnson made his way toward the opening in Edwards' tent. "Oh yeah," he growled, stopping dead in his tracks. "I assume you'll be needing this." Turning on his heels, Johnson tossed a small, neatly tied brown paper package across the gloomy tent to Edwards, who plucked it deftly from mid-air.

And with that, the carnie was gone.

"I trust that will suffice?" the tall man ventured, his manner a step beyond abrupt. "It's my wife, you see, she is in much need of your—expertise."

Edwards plucked at the tiny bow atop the package, slipped off the coarse twine, and unfolded the crisp, brown paper. "I'm sure it will do just f…" Edwards' voice trailed off.

There, nestled amongst layers of red-tinged tissue and wax paper, lay what was quite unmistakably a human tongue.

"What is this?" Edwards jumped up, the offending body part clutched in one hand. "I don't want any part of this…"

But it was too late.

The tongue slipped from its flimsy paper confines and lay in Edwards' sweat-slicked palm. The instant it touched his clammy skin, the nightmare began.

He just wouldn't stop biting.

His teeth chewed through the delicate flesh of her cheek, and she could taste the sour flavor of her own blood as it poured through the hole he'd made and into her mouth. She slapped at him, scratched and kicked and pushed, but all to no avail; he was far bigger than her, and outweighed her by a goodly hundred pounds or so.

He bit lower, the sound of his teeth grinding against one another as he masticated the exposed, vulnerable tissues of her throat, strangely mechanical, as if he were no longer the man she had married a lifetime ago, but some gruesome, blood-enraged automaton.

Against all odds, she somehow managed to push him away, her blood-streaked arms finding a strength she never knew she possessed.

And there he stood, towering over her petite frame, his face awash and dripping with her scarlet blood, a ragged chunk of gristle protruding from his mouth. And from his throat, there came a low, primordial growl, akin to that of some obscene creature that had dragged itself up from the very lowest pits of hell itself.

"No," she managed to utter, although her throat was clogged with thick, gobbets of congealing blood and much of her tongue was gone. "Please, Jebediah—"

Edwards yanked himself out of the trance, heart pounding, breath coming in short, painful gasps, the solid pressure around his throat choking the very life from him.

Of course.

How could he have not known?

He looked up into the pitch black, murderous eyes of Jeb Goedeke and understood—one does not see one's own face in a dream.

Edwards fought in vain against the unrelenting grip of the massive hand that encircled his throat; his chest screaming with white hot pain as the breath it so craved was denied. He couldn't cry out, he hadn't a prayer of fighting off the monster whose nightmares he'd so willingly accepted, and now Charles McKeever Edwards was caught in a living nightmare all his own.

"You just had to tell the interfering old sow, didn't you?" Goedeke's deep, resounding voice rumbled. "You made me do it—and this," he spat, knocking the severed stump of his wife's tongue out of Edwards' hand with an ugly grimace as the bloodied, bandaged nub of his absent pinkie finger knocked hard against the sideshow freak's wrist.

Dark, creeping shadows closed in on Edwards' consciousness, the searing pain in his air-starved lungs began to fade, as if into a dim, distant horizon. Edwards accepted that he was dying even as he flailed weakly against the unrelenting grip of his killer, his strength failing him.

Then, as life made ready to leave the Nightmare Man, the mental boxes that he had so meticulously tucked away amongst the dark, shadowy corners of his mind flew open, each and every one breaking free and leaving him. The fiend who was murdering him was also setting him free, and, as Edwards stared up into Goedeke's burning, rage-filled eyes through the greying fog of his own diminishing existence, he realized the nightmarish fugitives were fleeing into his executioner's mind.

And so, death embraced the Nightmare Man, bringing to him a benevolent peace that he had never known in life, and a welcome respite from the raging torments of the nightmares he had stolen and the pain he had stored for countless others.

Goedeke released his grip on the freak's throat, experience bringing him the satisfaction that the man was well and truly dead. Edwards' body was lowered onto its dingy pallet, and soon he was slumbering as deeply and soundly as he ever had. Goedeke's mind reeled, suddenly wracked by a heaving riot of screaming, terrified voices, and a hellish daguerreotype montage of horrors, most of which were entirely alien to him. They crawled and slunk across and into the soft, fleshy folds and ridges of his manic brain, intertwining with the murderous lunacy that resided there already, driving Goedeke ever more insane, and threatening to fuel his perverted lust for death and fresh blood to altogether new heights.

Stooping down, Goedeke plucked the tobacco tin his wife had brought along to her visit with the Nightmare Man earlier that day. "I do believe that this belongs to me," he said, as he stepped toward the exit of the Nightmare Man's tent, making his way back into the cool of the night.

And with that, he was gone.

Private Sale
by Bryce Wilson

In the back of his car Anthony kept items that would link him to no less than five hundred murders and three dozen serial killers. There was dirt from the grave of Ed Gein, greasepaint from the collection of John Wayne Gacy and a length of rope from the BTK killer's work shed. There were glossy glamour shots of Richard Ramirez with his "autograph" scrawled across them and a battered Beach Boy's LP that had been owned by Charles Manson.

Anthony didn't know if any of this stuff was real; the certificates of authenticity which he had printed en masse at Kinko's didn't do much to convince him. He doubted most of it was, (all except the grave dirt—he had collected that himself). But he made a good show of being a true believer when rubes came around to his battered card table.

Another thing that Anthony had in his car was the ghost of a nineteen-year-old girl. He was pretty sure the ghost wasn't real either, but like the crap in his trunk, that didn't mean it wasn't there.

The girl was waifish with long hair that flowed down to the middle of her back. She was translucent, except for her eyes which looked like someone had scrawled across them with black magic marker. Anthony could see fast food wrappers and empty coffee cups through her legs. Occasionally he would reach through her lap to get CDs. Most people would have been too scared to do that to a ghost and too embarrassed to do that to a girl. But they had been riding together for a while now and Anthony was past the point of skittishness or awe.

Whenever he would reach through her for something by the Zac Brown Band or to crack the window on the passenger side, she would glare at him, or at least he thought she did. She certainly looked in his direction for a long time while furrowing her otherwise unlined brow. But he didn't care. He hadn't asked her to hitch a ride so if she wanted to haunt his car then she could keep her opinion of his manners to herself.

Anthony hadn't done hard drugs in ten years. If he was having a psychotic break he was a few decades overdue, and though he drank a fair amount he was never hallucinating-dead-girls drunk. He knew that a psychologist would probably say that the girl was a manifestation of guilt over what he did for a living. He supposed stranger things could be true; but the girl mostly just nagged him over his line of work.

"It took me three days to die all told," she said in a sing-song monotone. "He lost interest after two. Just kind of left me in the corner to bleed out...but that's not what did it in the end. I had a punctured lung and it filled with blood. I ended up drowning in it." She said it all so matter-of-factly.

"That part wasn't that bad," she continued. "Truth to tell, slow, but it could have been worse. I was only half conscious and I was pretty much nuts by then and at least he'd stopped raping me. Still, wasn't a patch on what I had planned for the evening. I was going to go see the new Marvel movie with some friends. Instead I got tortured and raped for two days before drowning in my own blood on the third."

He'd heard all this before of course. That was the problem with the dead, they never got new stories.

"My Momma didn't give up hope until they pulled me out of his crawl space." She paused and when she spoke again her voice dropped to a whisper, "She's still crying now."

"You're not the only one to make money off my death," she continued. "My Momma paid this one lady two hundred dollars to have her tell that I had run off with a cute boy to Luxembourg, just so she could believe it for a while, and then one of those true crime shows did an episode of him and I was in it, just in a montage. But there's just something about you that I find so fucking galling."

When he didn't answer, and he never did, she sighed and looked back out the windshield. "Never did get to see that movie...Sometimes, when you're playing the radio, it'll just go silent on me, dead air, not even static. I'll look over and see you beating out a rhythm and realize that you can still hear whatever is playing. Happens on the TV too, suddenly the picture will go dead and I'll just watch you stare at it. It's like anything that was made out of my timeline is just inaccessible to me."

Anthony seemed to learn new and disappointing things about the afterlife every day. But, despite her monologues, he never really learned who she was or what piece of merchandise she was connected to. She never offered any real clues to her identity. Anthony had tried to figure out, but googling "murdered girls" led down some severely depressing paths.

He pulled in to the hotel where the convention was being held. Nothing fancy, just an Embassy Suites on the outskirts of Fort Worth, rented out exactly six months after Texas Frightmare. A few conference rooms for panels, and one for a dealer hall. The girl disappeared when he got out of the car. She always tended to be scarce during business hours. He supposed she didn't care for the company.

He smoked a last cigarette out in the parking lot, taking the final drag with a vicious zeal before grinding out the butt, then started bringing in his boxes. Table space had been provided, along with a metal folding chair, he found his spot fairly quickly. A piece of paper with his name scrawled in scented magic marker had been scotch taped to his space.

He started hauling in his boxes and made a display. The Ted Bundy T-shirts, the bootleg copies of *Faces Of Death* and the Charles Manson cigarette cases. The higher ticket stuff he left in the trunk of his car. He'd be able to sniff out the people who'd be interested in them pretty quickly. Besides keeping the merchandise in his car gave it that extra whiff of the forbidden, which was what his customers really craved anyway.

This convention probably wouldn't have much high dollar interest anyway. It was a horror show, not a true crime con. Here, he was something like the freakshow barker at a carnival midway; his job was to put something a little darker and dangerous on display and offer a little genuine edge to the shiver. The fans would cruise by and gawk, maybe buy a few mementos. It'd be enough to cover his dealer fees and his gas to the next town but probably not much more. The true crime conventions tended to be more serious. That was where people came to buy.

He'd started out here on the horror circuit. Going to swap meets and conventions, selling Michael Meyers action figures, Captain Spaulding T-shirts, autographed one sheets, (these, unlike his serial killer headshots, he tried to keep authentic) and bootleg DVDs. The job wasn't that different, except for the fact that he didn't make any money at it. He'd clung on to the circuit for two years until one especially dispiriting day, when he had left deep in the red. It nearly broke his spirit. As he was packing up his boxes and wondering if McDonald's was taking applications, he was approached by a heavyset, mouth-breathing guy wearing a shirt that read, "Just Dahmer It". Anthony had been dealing with his kind all day and was tired of them. They'd come, stare at his table and then shuffle on with a monosyllabic, "nice." Feeling utterly defeated, he sighed and glared at the guy, on the verge of lashing out.

The guy pointed to a pair of overalls that were draped over the table next to him. "What are those?" he asked. To this day Anthony, still wasn't sure where those overalls had come from.

"Albert Fish's overall's," Anthony said glumly, choosing to inject a little sarcasm. And it paid off. The guy dug into his wallet and pulled out five hundred dollars before Anthony even understood what was happening.

You met some credulous folk in this business.

Little by little, the Murderabelia collection edged out the horror movie stuff. Anthony hadn't wanted it to, but the demands of the market insisted. The profit margin was just so much better.

He didn't understand it. He'd grown up loving horror movies as a kid and his interest in the macabre was a real passion. But it was a passion for make-believe, no matter how grim it got. Knowing that someone had actually died to give a keepsake or souvenir entertainment value took most of the fun out of things for Anthony. You couldn't really describe an actual mother-daughter sexual assault and double-murder as "spooky." But most of crowds he worked didn't seem to be able to differentiate between Ted Bundy and Jason Voorhees. It was all fun for them.

It wasn't just mouth-breathers, geeks and white trash either. The straight people that wandered into the true crime conventions never ceased to amaze him. Men in suits that cost more than his car. Women who looked like the mousiest soccer Mom in the pack. It was bizarre, but also, occasionally, quite lucrative. Anthony was good at his job. He had a knack for finding plausibly creepy-looking shit in swap meets, the capacity to read people and the ability to know a good deal when he saw one. It was an effective triumvirate.

But Anthony didn't like the work much. It's not that he felt overly guilty about it. Hosing suckers was practically the American Way. It wasn't his fault that people were Morlocks. He didn't invent what they wanted; he just kept their appetites sated.

The convention passed in a blur. He watched the people shuffle back and forth from the panel room to the dealer hall. As predicted no one gave any sign that they wanted anything big ticket. But he did sell a pair of his and her Helter-Skelter chain wallets to a fearsome-looking fellow with a shaved head and gauged ears. Charlie's mug graced one side of the outside cover of one wallet and Squeaky Fromme grinned absently from one side of the other. The skinhead was almost shy when he explained it was for his anniversary. It was nice to see that love wasn't dead.

"Sharon Tate was pregnant when she was murdered," Anthony's stowaway apparition observed.

He groaned internally as he handed the man his change. She usually stuck to the car because she didn't care for the company of the freaks (as she called them) at the events, but sure enough she was standing behind the table, staring at him with her scrawled out scowl.

"Just sayin'," she added.

The rest of the day and night passed a little slower under her judgmental stare, but he was able to grind out a couple hundred dollars and was glad to have it. While he was in the state, he also planned to drive down to Austin and visit the Gas Station, where one of the shooting locations of The Texas Chainsaw Massacre had been transformed into a memorabilia store. It was the kind of place that would have made Anthony's head explode when he was a child, and the owners didn't mind him peddling his "artifacts" there, especially since his little card table in the parking lot attracted attention. He usually did pretty good business, and they gave him a break on BBQ.

"Hey, kid." It was Gary.

Anthony looked up and gave him a nod. Balding and sporting a sparse mustache, horn-rimmed glasses and a blazer and tie that he thought made him look dapper, Gary resembled an accountant or municipal bureaucrat who had gone to seed and was probably hitting the bottle on his lunch breaks. Nothing about Gary suggested he was one of the most unsavory people Anthony knew, but Anthony wasn't a hypocrite. It took all kinds and Anthony, himself, had profited off people's interest in the unsavory.

Gary sold pornography, which was something you could still apparently do in the age of the internet. Most of what he brought to the conventions was pretty harmless stuff. Old school cheesecake, vintage pin ups and their modern day descendants. Selling to men whose erotic true north forever pointed to Barbara Steele and Betty Page and women who needed inspiration for their new tattoos.

What most people didn't know was that Gary, like Anthony, kept the rare stuff in his car. But Gary traded in films that could pass as snuff, and snuff that could pass as film, should anyone want to take too close a look. A lot of ugly things had leaked across the border in the last decade and a half and Gary had come into possession of a fair amount of it. He'd turned himself into a living red room.

Anthony wondered if Gary had any ghosts in his car. He had certainly seen enough dead girls. Anthony carefully weighed whether or not it was within the bounds of professional courtesy to ask.

Gary wasn't one to loiter. He got down on his haunches next to Anthony.

"I have a proposition for you," Gary said, the overhead lights giving the flop sweat across his face a disturbing sheen. "More like an invitation, really," he corrected, trying to turn the favor he was asking into a favor he was offering. Too late. "There's a private sale tonight," he continued "A group of exclusive collectors, our kind of thing."

Anthony bristled at being lumped in with Gary, but decided that he didn't really have the ammunition or the inclination to argue.

"They're into the transgressive, kid," Gary persisted. "I figure you can provide some of it for them."

The needle on Anthony's Too-Good-To-Be-True-O-Meter had buried itself firmly in the red. He decided to cut to the chase. "And what would incline you to offer your competition a piece of the action?"

Gary somehow blushed from the crown of his bald head down. "We don't go toe-to-toe," he said. "You zig, I zag. Like I said, these clients, what they're looking for, it's novelty. They need new material every month. Just so happens that this month I've been short on first runs. If you were some other dealer I'd buy a boxful of your junk and just hope for the best. But these cats have discriminating taste. You always have the goods, I figured grab a nice array of ghoulish shit out of your collection, put it on display and show these folks a good time."

"How much are we talking about?"

Gary gave a five figure answer that Anthony was fairly sure he had misheard, but before he could seek clarification Gary was talking again. "And that's just what you get for putting it on display. It's like a retainer. They consider our time valuable. And if any of these perverted fucks actually decide to buy from your collection, it's all gravy. I usually manage about a three hundred percent markup myself."

Those kind of numbers went a long way toward disassembling Anthony's natural, healthy skepticism. "Where is this place?" Anthony asked.

"A ranch house, overlooking the Colorado. About fifteen miles outside of Bend."

Anthony deliberated.

Even if the whole thing was too good to be true, it wouldn't take him very far out of his way to Austin. The cost benefit analysis on the detour definitely favored

Gary's proposition. Something was still nagging Anthony, though. And he couldn't quite put his finger on it until he did.

"You're scared to go alone," Anthony observed. "You're afraid to go back out there by yourself."

Impossibly, Gary managed to get even redder and Anthony could hardly believe it. Gary's trade brought him into contact with the lowest of the low, the base, the vile and the incorrigibly twisted...people so unconcerned with murder that one contingent had even decided to publish a little Vlog about it. What had the characters near the Colorado done to get under his skin?

"Who are these people," Anthony pressed. "Manson wannabes? Satanists? You could find a half-dozen of either out on the convention floor right now."

"I think they'd find Satan jejune." Gary muttered, before allowing his indignation to override his embarrassment. "*Look*—these Mammie-rammers are just a bunch of rich assholes with lots of money and fucked up taste. A century ago they'd be dancing in graveyards naked and pretending to know what Aleister Crowley was talking about. These days it takes a little more effort to convince themselves they're bad and they have enough green that they can pay for folks like you and me to come to their house and give them the experience in private. They're a bit spooky, but in the final analysis they're about as exotic as a coven of sorority girls looking to pick up matching yoga pants."

Anthony made up his mind. "Fine," he said. "We'll go." He needed the money and Gary had apparently dealt with them before, which meant that he had made it out alive, and, more intriguingly, meant that Anthony had an opportunity for repeat business, which he was always keen on establishing. A steady paying customer was something to be prized, and there wasn't anything at risk here besides a couple gallons of gas.

But Anthony was a little unnerved by the relief that seemed to wash over Gary's face when he accepted.

Three hours later and they were almost there. The meeting was set for midnight, and they'd make it unless Anthony's car broke down. He needed a new timing belt, and if this sale was as profitable as he'd been promised, he might even be able to afford a new ride.

He had followed Gary's car—a midsized sedan in better condition than his, but just barely—down the interstate, out onto farm roads and then down a series of two-lane back roads so remote that they showed up on his GPS only grudgingly. His stowaway wraith had positioned herself in his front passenger seat, glaring at him behind her scratched out eyes. But she remained silent and statue-still. She didn't spend the drive sharing details from her previous life or providing any unsolicited, guilt-inducing commentary. It was mildly disquieting for an Anthony. If she was a delusion—and he could only hope she was—this kind of prolonged hallucination did not bode well in terms of his mental health.

"Well...*what is it?*" he finally snapped, all too aware that talking back to one's hallucinations and expecting them to reply didn't exactly bode well for his sanity either.

For the first time since the ghost had begun haunting him, she looked reluctant, tucking her chin down and hesitating before she spoke. "You should turn back," she said.

He snuck a glance at her, but kept his eyes on the twisting road.

"Why?"

"There's something here," she answered, twirling a lock of hair with her index finger. "I could smell it on your friend and all the time you're driving you've been getting closer to it."

"*It?*"

"The smell."

Was she warning him? The notion was just sinking in when Gary's turn signal came on. He abruptly pulled off the two-lane blacktop and onto a dirt road. The girl froze.

When she moved again, it was in a stutter-stop motion. "This is a bad place," she said. "This-is-a-bad-place."

"I heard you," Anthony responded, watching the dirt road.

"This—is—a—bad—place," she repeated again, her speech pattern stop-starting and the words hitched, like a cellphone signal fighting through an overpowering jammer.

Anthony glanced over, disconcerted. His stowaway flickered, for just a moment, and then was gone. Anthony hit the brakes and stared wide-eyed at the spot she had occupied. This was not good. How do you scare away an imaginary wraith?

If the girl was just a manifestation of his guilt, anxiety and lack of health coverage, wasn't her presence a mechanism to help him cope?

And if she wasn't?

If the girl had always been real, trying for whatever reason to force him to give up his loathsome vocation, then that meant that whoever or whatever was ahead at their destination was packing enough supernatural or psychic interference to drive away his stowaway. Just what the fuck would that kind of thing be?

Anthony did not like entertaining this possibility. If his stowaway wasn't real, he was just insane or headed that way. If she was real, ghosts and specters and spirits were real, and he was being haunted for his callousness. Well, that might be significantly worse news, right? And it could lead him to some significantly worse conclusions. Specifically in regards to where his own spirit might spend the rest of eternity.

Maybe even a dark place like the one he found himself approaching now.

His metaphysical quandary was interrupted by an impatient honk. Gary had noticed that Anthony had stopped, and actually backed up to make sure everything was okay. He was about fifty yards ahead, his left arm out his driver-side window, waving Anthony to follow.

Still reeling from the apprehension that continued to unsettle him, Anthony took his foot off the brake and rolled forward. They drove down the dirt road for another half mile before they came to a wrought iron gate with a pair of Gothic initials molded between the bars. The gates were fronted by a modern electronic panel. He watched Gary's arm flick out and swipe a key card in front of the sensor.

It occurred to Anthony that he had no key himself, that there was no guarantee that they would let him out as easily and eagerly as they were now admitting him. Hazards of the trade, to be sure, but legitimate concerns. He checked the back seat in his rearview mirror. *Where was she?*

Another mile or so and a ranch house came into view, though really ranch house was far too humble. This place was more like a villa, splayed wide and tall. Nothing like the McMansions around Austin and Dallas, but the genuine article with a sense of age, history and almost of inevitability. It was fronted by a circular drive way that wouldn't have been out of place in front of a five-star hotel. Gary stopped his car near the front entrance, got out and waved for Anthony to do the same. Anthony pulled up behind him and cut his engine.

The house was on a bluff, overlooking the Colorado River a couple hundred yards away. The night air was cool and it carried the scent of the cedar that grew along riverbank. Anthony was no big nature lover but it was a beautiful sight, the silver moonlight cast on slow, wide river, framed by dark trees, which the wind whickered through. He imagined all sorts of things coming out of the woods, making their way down to drink.

Anthony was so lost in his thoughts, he hadn't noticed that a man had appeared at his side, his hand out for the car keys. He was a thick-bodied man with a neckless, shaved head, and it protruded from his nicely tailored suit like an imposing thumb. He looked more like a bodyguard than a valet, and Anthony guessed that's exactly what he was. The man held out his hand, not with the ingratiating air of servant, but with a cool authority that would brook no argument. He looked over at Gary who was turning over his keys to another man who had been assembled from the same kit.

"I have my things in the trunk," Anthony called out, "I thought we'd get some time to set up."

Gary glanced down at his phone, "No time, just grab some high-ticket items and let's get in there."

Anthony shrugged at the bulky shape, walked around to the trunk and unlocked it. He looked down at his cardboard boxes and consider his options. If these people were as perverse as Gary had indicated, they'd want the most authentic things in his collection. He dug around for some crayoned, Disney portraits that Gacy had supposedly done in prison. They weren't guaranteed to be real, but the chain of ownership on them was better than most. He also retrieved a few knives with convincing blood stains on them and vetted stories attached. Then, a nametag that one of The Grim Sleeper's victims had been wearing at the time of her death. And, finally, a diary filled with psychotic ramblings and disturbing diagrams of for planned performance art installation by the Detroit Monster. That one was always good for silencing even the most jaded of critics.

He gathered the artifacts into his arms, handed the silent valet his keys and followed Gary and his keeper to the large crimson double doors that led the way into house.

The man who answered the door also wore a nicely tailored suit and a doll's mask of black porcelain with bronze stag horns emerging from the temples. He made no sign of welcome but instead puffed his chest out with an imperious air. "Hello," Gary said, his tone nervous and already wheedling, "We've brought some things, er...relics."

The baby-faced stag made no reply but stepped so his back was to the door, granting them admittance.

"You might have mentioned some details," Anthony muttered, as they proceeded their way down a dark hallway, with white walls and a Spanish tile floor. But he kept his cool.

People paid for eccentricity, paid to be allowed to think of their fetishes as pageantry. They emerged from the hall, not into a torture chamber or gothic, demonic cathedral, but into a neat, upscale kitchen that didn't offer any more signs of the overt occult than the average William Sonoma catalogue. The counters were high black marble, the furniture dark wood, the floor warm, cirrus tile and the walls tastefully blank and restrained.

But Williams Sonoma might have gone with different models. There were three; that Anthony could see anyway. One a paunchy, broad man, dressed in similar finery to the man at the door, though his mask was that of a great brass bull, the lips parted in a snarl. The second a woman in a little black dress and a mask of silver, polished to a mirror shine. The mask hurt Anthony's eyes to look at. It had a liquid quality as if the mask were made from mercury instead of silver. The final participant, presumably the host, stood with his back to them and wore no mask.

Anthony was not unduly disturbed by this. He had, after all, just spent his day in the company of intricate cosplayers; why shouldn't he spend his evenings that way as well? Was someone dressing up as an affluent bull any more ludicrous or menacing than someone less affluent spending countless evenings of effort putting together a Leatherface costume? If they wanted to dress up like Anton LaVey's wet dream rather than movie slashers, who was he to judge?

Heavy footfalls told Anthony that the stag and the two valets had joined the party, at which point the unmasked man turned around. His shoulders were so thin that they seemed absent. He was bald on top and the fringe of dull brown hair around his crown was greasy. His expression was a kind of loathsome smirk which caused his lips to pucker. "You were almost late," he said to Gary, in a playful, chiding tone that made no effort to disguise the threat underneath. He weaved and bobbed as he spoke, reminiscent of a snake. Anthony half-expected the man's tongue to flicker out to taste the air. But he sensed Gary tense up beside him and was wary.

Gary gave a shrug that failed spectacularly at being nonchalant. "I think we have some things you'll be happy with," he began. The bald man interrupted him before he could get into his spiel.

"I should hope so," the man said, his voice reedy and rounded. "I must admit that as of late your offerings have lacked variety. They've been a bit unsubtle. Eventually, you must understand, they bore the palate."

While Gary was getting dressed down Anthony noticed, for the first time, the one odd detail about the kitchen. Beneath the track lighting and beside the enormous, stainless steel appliances there was a perfect circle of dark, plank wood in the midst of the floor tile. As though someone had decided to drill a well in the middle of their kitchen, changed their mind and boarded it up. Or maybe it was wine cellar. Or a sophisticated safe room in the basement.

The rise in pitch told Anthony that the host's sermon on the mediocrity of Gary's product was nearly done. Gary had accepted his humiliation with eager grace. "I know you haven't been happy," he said, "That's why I brought my friend."

"Oh, we both know that's not the only reason you brought your friend," the smiling host said.

"Just let us show you what we've got," Gary countered, shooting Anthony a desperate glance. "Come on kid."

The bald host gestured to a long, dark walnut dining table and, after taking a moment to tamp out his mild case of stage fright, Anthony began to lay down his products one by one, giving each a space to display its own malevolent shine.

It only took a moment for him to fall into the instinctual rhythm of his patter. Anthony was a good salesman and a good salesman could sell to anyone, be they pimply kids looking for the twentieth century version of a geek show or high-class ladies in little black dresses and fucked up liquid metal masks. He modulated his tone between insincere solemnity and venal exploitation with a huckster's practice. He relayed the dark history and psychic stain of each item as he laid it out on the table, allowing each item to breathe before moving onto the next one with the air of a good sommelier. He built a dark atmosphere out of words and inference, even though he knew his items were possibly, probably, bunk. He simulated the deep conviction of a street preacher so effectively that most customers never suspected that he might have doubts. Faith was more about commitment than truth, and Anthony was very convincing. He slowly drew them all under his spell.

When he had finished all four of the principles had drawn near and were staring at the items arrayed before them. The woman was the first to move. She reached down and touched one of the blades and a shudder ran up her arm, exiting her mouth in a satisfied, orgasmic coo. The bull-headed man reached for the notebook and began to flip through it, taking in the gothic illustrations. He was breathing heavily from beneath the mask, and Anthony could hear it echoing back at him. He imagined the smell of the man's hot breath re-entering his nostrils.

The host broke the silence. "All very well," he said. "This is a most promising crop, indeed. But you must understand that before we can discuss price we will have to authenticate."

"Of course," Anthony said smoothly. "I have documentation."

The bald man smiled and held up his hand. "We have our own methods, thank you."

He gestured to the valets who quickly crossed the distance from the hallway they had been guarding to the center of the kitchen and the hole covered in wood.

Anthony was now fairly certain that whatever was down there was not a wine cellar.

One of the valets bent down and ran his hand along one of the smooth planks. His fingers found a hidden notch and he pulled it back revealing a trap door.

On the back side of the door was an iron hoop, to which was fastened two chains that led down to the darkness below. The only thing visible was an old flight of wooden stairs. The valet took hold of one of the chains, and his partner took the other. After a second, the valet found a hidden hinge on the hoop and released it, freeing the chain. Then, they both wrapped the chain around their hands and began to pull.

The thing that was on the other end of the chains resisted at first, but then gave in and began to come up the stairs with a scuffling sound. Anthony looked over at Gary who looked like he was about to shit his pants, but also exhibited a distinct lack of surprise.

What came shambling up the stairs were two of the saddest looking creatures that Anthony had ever seen before. They were both about four feet tall, or was it long, and whippet thin. They were human-shaped in a general way but it only took one look to see that they had never been anything approaching human. Their skin drew close to the ribs and allowed the sinew and tendons to stick out like a relief map. Their skin was translucent and Anthony could see the blue veins running from their foreheads to the soles of their feet. Their hands, feet and faces were elongated, so much so that what was at the end of their limbs looked like something between paws and hands. They had no eyes, only shelves of bone, one dark snuffling hole where their noses should have been and one dark hole only a bit larger that was identifiable as mouths only because Anthony could see their teeth.

Encountering these quasi-human wretches—they could only be described as creatures, really— immediately threatened Anthony's tenuous grasp of reality. What struck him most of all was how miserable they looked. They looked so weak, so ill-used and spent. The only attire they had were iron collars around their necks and Anthony could see where the thin skin had rubbed and chafed against the metal. The duo made no sounds aside from the snuffling and the scratch of their feet as they made their tottering way up the stairs. They frightened and saddened him at the same time. It was like seeing a miracle and wanting to vomit. But Anthony was too shocked to do anything but take a few tottering steps back. He glanced at Gary, whose face had gone pale but who was still relatively serene. The handlers led the creatures from the pit over to the table, guiding them with tugs of the chain, but always carefully maintaining a wide buffer between themselves and the pitiful beings. Anthony realized that they were heading right for him and quickly removed himself to the other side of the table, joining his prospective customers.

It didn't take the creatures long to reach Anthony's display and when they did they propped themselves up on their hind legs and bent over, taking deep, wet, snuffling breaths with the gaping hole in the center of their faces. Anthony was too stunned to worry what it might mean. They both gurgled and snorted and then wheezed, sighing in unison and then throwing back their heads in unison and speaking in English that was hideously articulate.

"COUNTERFEIT!" One howled in hideously articulate English.

"INAUTHENTIC!" hissed the other.

Then, the two snuffling appraisers exchanged their cries and began harmonizing in unison: "*Fraud...Fraud...Fraud...Fraud...*

Anthony heard Gary let out a low moan beside him and turned to see that the man who had led them here had a dark splotch of something across the front of his pants.

Urine.

Next to him the woman drew her hand back from the knife she had been caressing as though it was suddenly scalding. The bull-headed man threw down the book with a grunt of disgust. The man with the stag horns simply seized Anthony by the arms, and pinioned them to his sides with surprising strength. He was turned roughly to face the bald host who gave him a smile that was surprisingly conciliatory. "I'm sorry sir," he said. "We trusted you to bring your best wares and we regret to inform you that your best is not nearly good enough for our standards. Now we must seek our sustenance from other sources."

The stag man pushed Anthony forward and bent him over the display table before he could even protest. He watched one of the valets pass the leash of the creature he was handling to his partner and approach Anthony with a zip tie to secure his hands behind his back, then moving once more out of Anthony's field of vision.

The feel of the cool wood of the table against his hot flesh reminded Anthony that this was actually happening. He started to thrash, but it was useless. The stag had him firmly pinned. Even in his growing panic, Anthony could appreciate the irony.

"I'm sorry kid," Gary said, also out of sight, and he really sounded like he meant it. "I thought you were the real deal, I really did."

The valet re-entered to Anthony's line of sight and what he had with him wasn't comforting. It was a dark cloth hood. It hung oddly as though it was weighted, and only then did he notice what the valet was now wearing to handle it. Heavy, canvas gloves; but he still held the covering very gingerly. For Anthony's benefit, the valet flipped the hood conspicuously, so Anthony could see the inside.

It took him a while to understand.

The hood gleamed back at him. It was lined with shards of glass and razor blades.

A tremor of stark, profound terror shook through Anthony at the sight of it. He heard everyone in the room inhale, in that unconscious way people did when they walked into a kitchen where something delectable was cooking, even the creatures, even Gary. They all let out a breath in a shuddering gasp. Anthony felt the stag actually grow hard behind him.

"Wait!" Anthony cried, "I have more, in my car... just let me get them!"

"More trinkets undoubtedly," the bald host said in a tone of unmistakable boredom.

"No," Anthony screamed. "I have real trophies, I have something so real in there that a real ghost fucking follows me around for it!"

The host arched his eyebrow. "Interesting," he said. "We'll have to examine your collection more thoroughly than I thought. Unfortunately, now—in spite of the fact that you were our guest—you've whetted everyone's appetite, so a substitute won't do.

Before Anthony could reply the bag was over his head.

He shut his eyes, knowing it was useless, already feeling the blades against the skin of his face.

The last thing Anthony heard before a rope was cinched tightly around his neck and powerful hands began massaging the hood into his face in a way that was almost gentle, was the wet, sucking sounds that the twin creatures made.

Sounds of satisfaction, of an appetite sated.

2908 Porch Swing Lane
by Jacklyn Baker

Eliza Miller had worked in home-building for twelve years and in all those years she had never seen a starts package as thick as the one she held in her hands.

The home at 2908 Porch Swing Lane was nothing more than a pre-marked lot of land right now. Construction was scheduled to this coming Tuesday. It was Friday now and Eliza had printed out next week's work to review over the weekend. Though she had an Apple iPad, she preferred to have physical files as well. Call her old-school. As she clipped them together, her hands paused on 2908. Starts packages were composed of all the paperwork required to start building a house: the lot checklist, the plot plan, the options summary, three different reports, and, in San Antonio, the CAD files for the foundation plans. Most packets were around thirty pages. This one was nearly as thick as her thumb.

Eliza set the stack down on her desk and began flipping through it to see where so much paper was coming from. The option selections were short; the home was to be the Welcome Center for the neighborhood and was therefore marked with standard brick color, countertops and the like. The checklist and plot plan, like always, were only one page each. The reports looked pretty standard. That left the foundation plans provided by an engineer over at SDPI.

Aha, she thought. There was the excess paper. The designs proved to be twice as long as usual. Curious as to why exactly, Eliza began skimming the pages.

While she looked over the expected elongations and required wall bracings, she frowned. When she reached the soil report, she actually grimaced. She'd never seen a soil report like it before. Everything fell within the acceptable ranges, but the amount of recommended precautions listed were extensive.

That the soil in most of Texas was expansive and shifted with even the most miniscule of dry and wet weather was nothing new. But for whatever reason the ground that 2908 Porch Swing Lane sat on posed a particular risk.

Construction on 2908 Porch Swing began without any problems. It was September and it was hot, but everyone who lived in Texas already knew that and had learned to suck it up a long time ago. Many of the workers from south of the border had experienced even hotter conditions back home, so the soupy, sweltering heat did not bother them.

Eliza watched over the proceedings with a careful eye. The onsite foreman, George, reported that everything was going smoothly.

That lasted for all of four days.

George told her as soon as she set foot onto the lot just an hour before noon.

"Some of the tendons snapped."

Eliza closed her eyes for a few seconds, then shook her head. When she opened her eyes, they pinned the foreman in place. "George. Tendons don't snap. They buckle and rupture, sure, but that's only after extended wear and tear. They don't just 'snap.' I'll tell you what does snap though, and that's construction managers who don't have time for this."

"I'm sorry, boss," George said. "I know how it sounds. But these tendons snapped."

Eliza took in a deep breath and then released it slowly. "Show me."

He led her to the rear of the site.

Construction tendons, much like their anatomical counterparts, were strong cords that allowed for flex. They were installed in a house's foundation to prevent concrete from cracking and were particularly necessary in an area where there was expansive soil.

The neighboring frame boards contained neat grids of tendons laid in perpendicular lines just as they should be. The one George indicated did not.

The plastic sheathing was shredded, grease bleeding from it and forming black puddles. Within, the steel cables were exposed and very clearly snapped in half. Eliza did a quick count. Six tendons were in this mangled state.

She was quiet a long moment, before asking, "What else can you tell me, George?"

George shook his head. "Nothing. Damnedest thing I've ever seen. We anchored them last night. Same as all the others. I don't know what happened."

Eliza stepped into the frame and crouched to get a closer look at the boards where the anchors should have been. Cracks ran up the sides of the wood in several places. A quick inspection of the other side revealed the same.

She stood and leveled a look at George. "I'm going to put the blame on faulty frame boards. The wood was...rotten or something, I don't know. Get this reframed and get new tendons reinstalled. I'll make sure you have enough materials."

"Yes, ma'am."

Eliza walked back toward the street, pulling up the digital file for 2908 on her tablet. Her eyes scanned over the materials orders, but her mind was still back in that frame.

Subpar boards were reasonable enough. But that still didn't explain how steel cables were snapped in half. If anything, the cables would have punched through the weakened wood.

Eliza shook her head to clear it. She didn't have time to ponder over the physics of it. She just needed to make sure they got the mess fixed so they could move on.

Later in the week, Eliza came out to the homesite again to evaluate the new framing job. Everything checked out and she was pleased to see that it had merely been a fluke. But something else caught her attention. Her head turned and she peered at an odd, dark declension in the ground. When she realized what it was, she was furious.

Eliza stomped over to the corner of the future backyard. "Are you kidding me with this? George!"

The foreman came running over.

"Why isn't this hole filled in?" she demanded.

George floundered. "It—It was, boss. I know it was. We did all of our pocket work on day one."

Eliza's brow remained pinched. "Well, it doesn't look like it to me. This is an enormous hole, I don't see how you could miss it." The hole in question, or "soft pocket" as the industry called it, was three feet across one way and about five the other way, making for an oblong drop-off in the grade. It was deep enough that it would reach at least mid-calf on both Eliza and George's legs if they stood in it.

Eliza glanced behind her at the block of foundation, pulling up the plans in her mind. "This is right next to where the patio will be. Fill this in immediately and don't let me find any other holes you missed."

"Yes, ma'am, you got it. I will get someone on it right this second."

"Good." Eliza turned away and left to go inspect her next site.

The following day the hole was twice as deep.

George called Eliza's cell phone at 7:00 am to report it to her.

"I don't know, boss. I don't know what's causing it. We filled it in yesterday, I swear."

"I believe you," she said, because she did. Even if they hadn't that wouldn't have accounted for the hole getting deeper. "Have you noticed anything else being tampered with? Anything missing?"

"No, ma'am. You think some kids did this?"

"It's a possibility. It's an odd prank, for sure, but there are some odd kids out there. But before we go running to the police with a potentially false report, let's get a soil engineer out there to take a look first. I'll call SDPI."

"Okay. Sounds like a plan."

Eliza hung up and then tapped the phone against her chin, while she mulled over this new development. 2908 Porch Swing Lane was proving to be a pain in her ass.

The soil engineer, a middle-aged man named Rick who had done the initial survey for the project, declared the soil to be just the same as the rest of the lot.

"Don't know what to tell you, Miss Eliza."

"No, that's all right, Rick. I don't think there's anything for you to tell. I know what to tell the police though."

After sending Rick on his way, Eliza filed a formal report with the police. George filled the hole up again and that night a cruiser staked out the lot from across the street.

When, the next morning, the hole was sunken in yet again and the two officers on duty had reported seeing absolutely no one and nothing go in or out of the lot that night, Eliza thanked them for their time and said she'd try the next theory.

The next theory was no theory, because 2908 Porch Swing was behind schedule and they were only losing more time. Without the hole filled they couldn't work anywhere in back of the house for safety reasons. Not to mention if they hauled in one more load of dirt the cost was going to be too high to justify to her superiors any longer. Plus, she wanted the damn vendor to be paid in full and off her back.

Eliza stared at the form boards that marked off the patio area and tapped her phone on her chin. It felt like it was mocking her, the area perfectly cordoned off to prevent any mishaps and at its center, staring at her with a smug eye, the hole.

Eliza tapped her phone to her chin three more times in quick succession, tap tap tap, and made her decision.

Three days later, Eliza and George reviewed the new plans for a deck.

Construction continued. For a while Eliza thought that her problems with 2908 Porch Swing Lane were over. But then came October, and with it, the rain.

Her cell phone rang at 9:00 am on October 9th. It was George, and Eliza frowned upon seeing the name on her screen. She was at another homesite in a different community and waved away the foreman she had been speaking with before answering briskly. "George."

"Boss," the man's voice crackled through the phone. "We've got a problem over here at 2908."

Eliza sighed. "Don't tell me. Another hole?"

"Sort of."

"Spit it out, George."

"Well, with all the rain yesterday the drainage trench filled up with water. And then some."

"Okay. Is there too much water to work on the site today?"

"No, not quite."

"Then what is it?"

"Right, well. The water level was high enough to submerge our safety grading in the back of the house. And, well, it looks like it took the ground right with it when it receded."

Eliza's tone was flat. "What?"

"The grading's completely gone, boss. I've never seen anything like it."

"Yeah…" Eliza was silent a moment, letting that information filter through her brain.

George spoke up again. "We've got to get that grading fixed before we continue construction."

"I know, I know. I'll get more dirt ordered in." She wanted to pull her hair out at the thought of having to call up that vendor one more time.

Eliza began the trek back to the neighborhood's trailer so she could pull the files for 2908 Porch Swing and rework the timeline and the budget while she was at it. It looked like a call to her boss would be in order soon.

"Is there anything at all you can do today?" she asked George.

"Not really. Even if we figured we'd be all right with any run-off today, we can't really work around that drop-off. It's not safe."

Eliza stopped in her tracks, mouth dropping open briefly. "Drop-off?"

"I meant it when I said it took the ground with it, Eliza. It's just gone."

She could hardly believe what she was hearing. "Where the hell did that much dirt go?"

"Can't rightly say." George must have turned his head, because the sudden sound of a steady wind picked up over the receiver. "I guess it might've run off into the neighborhood behind us. Got under the fences."

"Yeah. That's probably it. Whatever. Send everyone to other sites if you can. I'll let you know when the dirt will be delivered."

"Sure thing, boss."

The day went on.

Eliza performed her regular duties, but 2908 niggled in the back of her head all day. She still couldn't fully wrap her mind around what George had been saying about a drop-off, and so she decided to see it for herself.

The drive to the Balcones neighborhood, which had not been on her circulation schedule for the day, took nearly forty minutes. She parked directly in front of the house itself instead of the foreman's trailer.

Wooden framing stuck out of the concrete slab, the beginnings of the actual house. In the waning light of dusk it cast sickly-thin shadows across the lot, long fingers that looked ready to grab hold of trespassers.

Eliza was not a trespasser, and she charged straight ahead and rounded the work-in-progress structure to get to the backyard area. She pulled up short when she nearly plummeted over an abrupt ledge.

She stumbled, but caught herself and then stared with wide eyes at what George had not done any justice in describing. The "drop-off" was nothing short of one side of a pit. Long and narrow, it ran almost the entire length of the back of the house. It wasn't very deep where Eliza stood, maybe five inches give or take. But peering past the shadows it looked like it got deeper and deeper. It had to be at least a foot deep at some parts. The whole thing looked like the beginnings of a mass grave.

The hollow was, as George had said and Eliza had unknowingly agreed, like nothing either of them had ever seen.

Eliza looked to her right out at the fences of the houses that would one day be part of the border of Porch Swing's backyards. Curious, Eliza crossed the length of the yard to get a closer look. The fences didn't look to be particularly muddy, but the rain would have washed away any dirty water that had splashed up during the onslaught of mud. She chalked it up to nature doing what it so often does, namely, erasing humanity's consistent efforts to mold or define it.

As she reappraised the lot again, she took a longer look at its neighbors. Neither plot of land had been processed for construction yet, and the two patches stood as empty as could be. Eliza paused and looked from side to side. Their landscapes appeared to be completely untouched by the torrent that had ripped out a chunk of the yard between them.

What kind of weird rainstorm did they get last night?

Again, Eliza shook her head and dismissed it. It was Texas. If there was one thing that was unpredictable in this state, it was the weather.

That's just what she told her boss when she got a call from him the following day.

"I don't know what else to tell you, Kurt. This house has been giving us all kinds of problems and the rain isn't helping. The soil seems to be particularly sensitive."

"You're more than two weeks behind on it."

"I know, Kurt. George and I are doing our best to get them to catch up."

"That's the Welcome Center, it has to be done so we can start showing the neighborhood. I can't have a bunch of empty houses on that street just sitting around unable to be sold."

"I know. I will get it done in time."

"Be sure that you do, Eliza. If you can't handle this, we'll find someone who can."

Kurt's last comment infuriated Eliza, but she wasn't going to let it rattle her. She would get the damn house built and make him eat his words.

The lot for 2910 Porch Swing officially got the green light three days later. Over the following month Eliza found herself in the Balcones community with increasing frequency. It was on such a visit in the second week of November that she arrived to find George with a grimace on his face.

"I don't like that look, George."

He winced. "I don't like making it."

"What happened now?"

"You're not going to like it."

"Tell me anyway."

"It's 2908 again."

Eliza bared her teeth in a snarl. "Again? What is it this time?"

George rubbed the back of his head, a nervous habit the man had had as long as she'd known him. "Well...the, uh..."

"George."

He rushed out his answer. "The rain got in last night."

"What do you mean 'got in'?"

"I mean, we have an entire room that flooded in here."

"What?" Eliza snapped. "What the hell do you mean it flooded?"

"I mean it looks to have gotten about two inches of water last night judging by the water line."

"Water line? How much freaking water could have possibly gotten in? Why didn't it drain away from the house?"

George didn't answer, but his face said enough.

"No. No, do not." Eliza took a deep breath. "Don't tell me the grading is gone again."

George shrugged for lack of a better response.

Eliza released a growl of frustration. "What about 2910?"

"It's fine."

"And the rest of the street?"

"All fine."

Eliza's hands curled into fists. She stomped her foot and shrieked, "What the hell is going on at 2908?"

George remained calm. "I don't know. I'm sorry, boss."

Eliza clenched and unclenched her fists a few times. "George, I've worked at this job for twelve years. I've worked with you for five of them. And neither you nor I have ever, ever experienced anything like this. Really, George, what is wrong with this lot?"

George was quiet another moment and then said, "I really don't know. I've never even heard of something like this. The ground here is just...unstable."

Eliza frowned sharply. "SDPI has told us multiple times that nothing is wrong with it and it's perfectly fine to build here. There's no explanation for this."

"I know. Nothing makes sense. It's almost like it's..."

George trailed off, but Eliza was having none of it. "Like what?"

That nervous habit reared its head again and he scratched the back of his neck, avoiding eye contact. "Like it's cursed, or something."

Eliza was silent for a long moment. "Do you really believe in that sort of thing?" she asked in complete seriousness.

George gave a shrug. "I didn't before, but I don't have another explanation. Do you?"

She considered this carefully, though she already knew the answer. "No. No, I don't."

George gave one more shrug, hand falling from his neck. "Well, then..."

Supernatural forces, Eliza thought. If only it were that simple. "There's no such thing as curses," she said. "It's just unstable soil that's still somehow within safe construction parameters. That's all."

"If you say so, boss."

"I do. I'll order more dirt—again—and you'll get this fixed."

"Yes, ma'am. You got it."

George did as instructed and they moved on.

When the walls of 2908 finally started going up, Eliza almost breathed a sigh of relief. They were finally getting somewhere. But then the entire first floor flooded with mud.

A layer of thick, black gunk covered the entire slab, from exterior wall to exterior wall. And it smelled.

Inside the construction trailer down the street Eliza tore into George..

"How in the hell could this happen? The walls are up. The walls are up, George! Even if the rain was getting in how in the ever-loving hell could all that mud get in?"

"Boss, I wish I had an explanation for you. But I really don't. We installed everything by the book, followed the plans to the letter. I don't know how it got in."

Eliza leaned over the desk, fire in her eyes. "How can you not know how something this disastrous happened?"

"I—I have a theory, but it's…"

Eliza slapped her hands down. "What, George? It's what?"

George scratched the back of his head and avoided her gaze. "It's kind of crazy."

She snarled, "This better not be about curses again, George."

"No! No, nothing like that."

"Fine. Tell me."

"I think the house…*I think it sunk.*"

Eliza blinked several times. "George. *That. Is. Impossible.* "

"I know that!" George railed. *"You think I don't know that?* But, goddammit, I don't know what else it could be. You said it yourself, the ground has been unstable since day one no matter what we do and I swear that if we went out there and measured we would find out that the whole damn thing had sunk a couple of inches. And that's how the mud got in. The grading was doing its job in reverse, leading the water right toward the house. The mud probably came in right through the front door!"

"Enough! I don't want to hear it. I can't tolerate another mess on this goddamn lot. I don't care what the hell caused it. Clean it up and make sure it doesn't happen again."

"How the hell am I supposed to do that?"

Eliza exhaled very slowly through her nose, hands squeezing into fists just as slowly and completely negating the effect of measured breathing. *"I suggest. That you get more dirt.* And actually get the goddamn grading right. Now, get out!"

George stormed from the trailer and Eliza sank into the chair behind the desk. She covered her eyes with a hand and sat there for a long time.

Over the next week the mud was cleared and more dirt was ordered and 2908's grading was redone under the instructions of Rick, the SDPI engineer. Eliza made sure he was onsite to oversee the installation.

When the work was nearly done, she called him into the trailer.

"Rick, what is wrong with this soil? Why are we having so many problems with this lot?"

Rick leaned back in his chair and laced his hands over his belly. "Nothing's wrong with it, Miss Eliza. I told you that."

"You did. But I have to disagree. There must be something wrong. There's been too many problems to be even near the range of normal, much less actually within it."

"It's just unusual circumstances, I suppose."

"Costly circumstances," Eliza informed him. "I'm beginning to think SDPI is off their game, especially since we've had to call them out here so many times." She carefully didn't use the word 'you.'

Rick scrunched up his chin and nodded. "You know, I think you might be right, Miss Eliza. Not that we're not doing our jobs, mind you, but that it has been rather costly for y'all. Considering the unusual circumstances of the situation, I think I might just be able to make a phone call or two and get a discounted rate for you and your special little project here. How's that sound?"

There was only one way to respond to that. "That sounds great, Rick. Thank you."

"It's no trouble, Miss Eliza."

She nodded, tapped her hand on the desk a few times. "You're sure there's nothing wrong though?"

Rick smiled, wide and full of teeth. "I promise you, everything out there is going according to plan."

Rick called the next day with a renegotiated rate for their services. He even offered to come check the soil again next month to see that nothing had changed, pro-bono. Eliza accepted and the work on 2908 continued with slow caution.

Beside it, 2910 Porch Swing surpassed its progress.

Kurt wasn't happy about that to say the least.

"What the hell is going on out there?"

Eliza closed her eyes and pinched the bridge of her nose. "I couldn't even begin to explain, sir. Might I make a suggestion that 2910 be assigned as the new Welcome Center? The specifications are similar enough and we can upgrade it as needed. I just don't think that 2908 is going to—"

"No. We decided it would be 2908 because it's at the center of the neighborhood. For Chrissake it's the first house you see when you come down the cross street."

"Kurt, I really think—"

"I don't care. Get your shit together and get that house finished."

The line clicked.

Eliza leaned back in her chair and screamed into her hands.

The final straw for Eliza happened on a Tuesday.

The first floor was nearly complete and the second floor was underway. Eliza prayed that nothing else went wrong.

Her prayers were not answered.

She was onsite when it happened. Two pieces of wall bracing slid clean out of place.

The wall wavered and the ceiling above it bowed. A worker on the second floor stumbled back several steps and went plummeting over the side. He landed on the deck with a sick thwack and the sound of half a dozen metal tools banging into the wood.

Everyone rushed to the site of the accident. Eliza's pulse pounded in her throat as she pushed through the crowd. Her heart stopped when she saw the man lying there, unmoving, limbs sprawled awkwardly across the deck. It was George. For a brief moment she was sure he was dead.

"Everyone back!" she ordered. There was a mad flutter of activity as she took control of the situation.

Eliza knelt and took George's face in her hands. "George. George, speak to me, please, say something."

A pained moan escaped him. It wasn't words, but she would take it. Her heart kicked into double-time as she realized she had an injured man and not a dead one on her hands, and that meant that action needed to be taken, and quick.

Once the ambulance was on its way, Eliza inspected him. There was no blood, no bones protruding from skin. It didn't look too bad. But Eliza could tell that his right arm was broken and possibly something in his back. He almost certainly had a concussion.

She stayed beside him and kept his head still until the ambulance came and then she sent another worker to the hospital with him. Once the ambulance was out of sight, her thoughts immediately turned to the wall bracings.

The remaining workers milled about apprehensively, watching her as she knelt to inspect the felled beams. Her hands ran over the length of them, searching for cracks. Then she examined the ends where the braces had met wall and concrete. It was here she found her answer, but not on the braces themselves. The concrete where the anchor had been was chipped and brittle. It had lost integrity. She raked her fingers through the clumps, picked up a handful, and then let them fall back to the ground.

She stood and faced the nervous crowd. She shouted at every worker she could find asking who in the hell put those anchors in. Eventually, a worker came forward and Eliza fired him on the spot.

She sent everyone else home for the day, with pay, and then stood alone in the trailer. Tears burst forth without warning. She was completely shaken and, for the first time, scared. Something really was wrong with 2908. But she had been too stubborn to acknowledge it. Unstable soil or a curse or whatever it was, it was dangerous, too dangerous to build on, and she had been too blind to see it until it was too late.

She wept until she ran out of tears and then wiped her face clean. She still had one thing left to do.

She had to call Kurt.

The conversation with her boss did not go well.

"You're overreacting, Eliza."

"I am not."

"Nobody died."

"Somebody nearly did!"

"Look, the guy's got a couple of broken bones and a bump on the head, but he'll be fine. We fired the person responsible for it, everything will be fine now."

"I am telling you, Kurt, there is something wrong with that lot. We need to abandon the project."

"Eliza—"

She cut him off. "Kurt. I cannot in good conscious allow construction on that house to continue."

Kurt was silent a moment and then sighed on the other end of the line. "Well. I guess it's not your problem anymore then."

Eliza blinked. "Sir?"

"You're officially off the job, Eliza. Off all jobs. We've been reviewing your file and your past work just doesn't outweigh the lack of progress you've made with Porch Swing."

"Sir, you can't—" She gritted her teeth. "You don't understand. That house is dangerous. That lot is dangerous. You have to stop building there."

"It's not your call anymore. Consider yourself relieved of your duties, Miss Miller."

The line clicked and Eliza sat in stunned silence for what felt like a very long time.

When she finally came back to reality, it was to see the ever-changing stack of homesite folders sitting on her desk.

2908 Porch Swing Lane sat on top.

The image of George's body prone on the deck flashed through her mind. She made a decision.

The moon was high in the sky, midnight approaching. Eliza crept through the shadows cast by 2908 Porch Swing Lane. She reached the rear of the house and went to the deck, setting a sloshing, red container down on the planks.

Eliza was going to put an end to 2908 Porch Swing Lane. And she could burn it down just as easily from the outside as the inside. In fact, she would do it from the wooden deck she designed herself.

She unscrewed the cap on the gas can and splashed it on the deck and the nearest walls. As she took a step, the plank under her foot cracked in half.

She yelped, falling through the wood up to the knee. The gas can escaped her grip and landed on its side. Gas started pouring out again with a steady glugglugglug.

Once the initial shock passed and pain began to seep in, Eliza bent over to plant her hands on the floor and haul her leg out of the hole.

A loud *creeeak* and the noise of something sliding across the deck stopped her before she could.

She looked up to see the gas can, still leaking, moving across the planks, which were suddenly angled sharply downward. They formed a black pit at the middle of the deck that swallowed the gas can up before Eliza could even begin to try making sense of what she was seeing.

The boards bent and splintered and disappeared into an impenetrable darkness beneath. Then the wood beneath her own foot did the same. She had been too mesmerized by the unnatural sight to notice that the lip of the expanding maw had reached her. Her hands were still planted and with quick reflexes she managed to catch herself before she went the way of the gas can. She scrambled up until she reached a piece of the deck that was stable. And then that fell out from under her too.

She screamed as her hands latched onto the balustrade of the deck. Barely an inch of the jagged wooden floor remained on each of the four sides.

A massive groan from below drew her attention. She looked down to see the earth buckle and collapse. More groaning and the soil began rapidly slipping into unknown depths.

Panicking now, Eliza attempted to pull herself up by the spindles of the balustrade, feet struggling to find purchase on the slick siding. The earth quaked and nearly shook her off once, twice.

She screamed again, louder. "Help me, please!"

Everything grew still and Eliza limited her movement. Then she looked down and choked back her shock.

Beneath her was a hole. The Hole. The one that had burdened them so much in the beginning, the one that she had built a deck over to hide because she couldn't seem to get rid of it, The Hole—it was enormous now. It must have been the entire size of the deck, stopping just at the edges of the barrier, roughly rounded at the corners. Eliza looked into it and saw only blackness.

That's where all the dirt went.

She finally knew.

A great belch of fire rose from the depths of the earth, hissing and shrieking. Eliza's own scream was drowned out as the smoke hit her first and then the flames.

It burned hot on her shoes, scorched her ankles and blistered her skin. And then it grabbed hold with what could only be the fingers of a hand.

Eliza screamed again, her nails scraping against the wood of the hand rail as she desperately tried to hold on. Then she heard a voice.

"Now, now. No need for such fuss, Miss Eliza."

She looked up and saw Rick standing there, hands in his pockets, head tilted to one side. His calm demeanor was a wild counterpoint to her terror.

"Rick! Pull me up. *Pull me up. Please!*"

His mouth twisted to one side. "I'm afraid I can't do that."

Tears streamed down Eliza's cheeks. Sweat rolled down her temples, her neck. The skin on her legs began to peel away. "Please," she croaked. "Please just pull me up."

He shook his head.

"Why? What the hell is wrong with you?" she shouted at him. Her arms were growing tired from holding her up, her grip getting weaker and weaker.

Rick looked down at her. Firelight and shadow fractured his blank expression. "Sorry, Miss Eliza," Rick replied. "But you're right about Hell being involved. See, when the pit gets hungry, you gotta' feed it. And I'm certainly not going back in." His mouth split wide in a smile, teeth a little sharper than they should be, eyes black where there should be white. "Now don't keep 'em waiting, okay."

The hand on her ankle gave one swift yank and her fingernails splintered before she lost her grip completely. She had just enough time for one last scream before she plunged into the fire.

The earth gave a final bellow as it closed up, followed by the sound of wooden planks slapping into place.

And then, the lot was silent.

The Man from Plan(e)t X
by Michael H. Price

I 'm a businessman, see? No time for shenanigans or tomfoolery. Run this company like it was a piece of machinery, keep it oiled and cleaned, ride herd on the crew just as though they needed ridin' herd on. Most of 'em don't, and all the better for that. Just ask Mr. Cowan, the founder, or his partner, the late Mr. Clowe.

Well, that is, you could've asked Mr. Clowe, if he weren't long since croaked and planted.

Planted. Plant.

Have to make sure I spell those right. This account is something of a mental exorcise.

Mr. Clowe would've told you the same as Mr. Cowan: Jonathan Andrew Prescott is a businessman. Takes care of business, all right.

I usually went by just-plain Andrew, but the full-length, bright lights moniker had a professional ring, wouldn't you say?

No patience with distractions, back then, especially not the weird kind. This shouldn't have been the type of business that would attract weird stuff, to begin with—construction materials, excavation machinery and irrigation pumps, land the like—but every once in a while...

Like that time in 1947, when I got a call from our branch in Roswell. In New Mexico, y'know. Some Air Force bigwig at the military base out yonder had called Clowe & Cowan, Inc.'s N.M. outpost with a summons for some corporate expert who knew metals and could come out and give 'em an expert opinion on some wreckage that had come crashing out of the sky. "Better call ol' Jonathan Andrew Prescott, over at H.K., in Amarillo," our branch manager told the U.S.A.F. brass.

"What's an H.K.?" asked the Air Force honcho.

"Why, head kwarters, of course," replied Beauregard Mann, Clowe & Cowan's chief of operations in Roswell. We called him "Bogardus" or "Bogie" for short.

"Then shouldn't you say, 'H.Q.,' if you mean 'headquarters'?" corrected the officer.

"Well, I reckon that depends on how you spell kwarters," said Mann. Ol' Bogey got away with such tomfoolery on my watch because he knew better than to pester me with it, personal-like. Took care of business, too, which at the moment involved placing a long-distance 'phone call to my office at corporate H.Q., or H.K. A long-distance call was a bigger deal in those days than it is now, back when we had honest-to-gosh switchboard operators in charge of who called whom from where, and when.

So anyhow, no sooner had Bogey Mann relayed the Air Force brass's request, than I was hightailin' it down the old two-lane for Eastern New Mexico. Now, I knew metals and alloy better than anybody else in the racket, if I do say so, my ownself, and the U.S.A.F. was aware, likewise, of my service during World War Twice as an Industrial Rationing Warden, so they knew I was an ol' boy who could distinguish sheet metal from Shinola. Except what the Powers That Did Be wanted that I should examine was unlike anything the Air Force, or I, had ever come face to base metallurgy with. A cut-and-dried case of Military–Industrial Complexity.

Whatever airborne object it was that had come to ground near Roswell, the thing left traces. Any flesh-and-cartilage casualties must have been dispatched to Parts Unknown or, I daresay, per hearsay, Parts Off Limits. But some of the more casually retrieved fragments of a—a what? A whatsit? A what's what and what not. They wound up at Clowe & Cowan's Roswell plant. I examined these in search of some source of manufacture, serial number or manner of fabrication tell. I concluded that not only were they not like any metal I had ever held nor heard tell of, they displayed properties I wasn't even aware existed. And I pocketed a few shards, whether for further comparative analysis or merely as a memento. That's what a machine man does. That's what metal men do. We take a swing at it later. We have business to attend to.

The substance of the shard metals embodied certain contradictory traits—like rigidity seeming to coexist with malleability—along with a syncretistic, engraved surface a luminous aspect in dimmed lighting. Weirdness seeks out those of us who would prefer to avoid it.

We just decided to let the mystery be, then, and I parted ways with the Air Force people on a handshake and a "nice talkin' to yuh," like that. Nothing nefarious or untoward toward them or from me. I had forgotten about the scraps I'd pocketed until, back home in Texas, I was hanging up my suit coat and sensed noticed a glow coming through the fabric in the dimly lighted clothes closet. I tossed those fragments into a shoebox and shoved the box way back on a high closet shelf, thinking I'd subject them to further scrutiny at a later date, again, like metal men do. Didn't mention it to my wife, except to say that whatever had happened at Roswell was a sure-enough mystery and just let it go at that. She was expecting our first sprout, anyhow, and she probably didn't need the specifics of my general befuddlement nor aware-abouts of the fragments I'd brought home with me.

Never really thought on it much afterwards, except on those occasions when I did.

I'd get bored when trapped on the 'phone with a tedious caller—aren't they all?—or when waiting for service at some restaurant, and I'd grab me a scratchpad or a placemat and start doodling out shapes like unto what I'd seen on that metal from Roswell. Runic-looking symbols, mostly triangles and kind of swastickle-like pictographs. But not the Nazi kind. More like the Plains Indian type, which points in an opposite direction. Maybe like some hieroglyphic images. No telling.

Well, anyway, I think I must've begun to get leery of the Yew Ess Military's maybe taking an interest in my comings and goings, just in case somebody might've noticed shard fragments missing from their scrap pile at Roswell. No uniformed agents ever came calling, but all the same I finally retrieved that shoebox from high up in the clothes closet, drove out one night to the mud flats alongside of Wild Horse Lake, and dumped the works, box and all, into the murk. My decrepit old Uncle Ed, black sheep of the Prescott family (and proud of it), operated him a junkyard and bootleg-whiskey trade out there alongside of Wild Horse Lake, which he had told me was a fine place to dispose of contraband if it got too hot to handle through the accustomed channels. So there you go—or went.

Our first kid was born right around then, cigars all around for the Clowe & Cowan men. The company was doing right well in the industrial-supplies market, and things were about as good as good gets, overall. You get busy with life and living or making a living, guilty as charged. But, I must admit, I got a little fretful a couple of years on, when the local newspaper published a report about a mess of deformed fish and pallid mutant-looking amphibians getting snagged out of Wild Horse Lake. Thin skins and thinner blood, and the occasional third eye; and one even had wings, like something out of Roy Chapman Andrews's books about prehistoric life. But I 'scoped out our little ol' boy, then, and I didn't see any webbed fingers or extra eyeballs, so I figured the only effect that Roswell stuff had on the household was to make me its patriarch a trifle paranoid. Thinking on the unthinkable wears on a man, even a metal man. Even machine men.

I enjoyed a mystery in theory or in fiction, but soon mysteries started settling in too close to home. 'Roundabout 1951, my brother–in–law invited me and my kid, Mickey, to come out to the picture-show theatre he operated, downtown, and watch us a preview of this new movie called *The Man from Planet X*, the day before it opened up to the customers. Sounded about half–silly to me, but I figured what the hell, my boy's comin' up on four years old, and a movie might be a treat for him, anyhow, 'specially as it came with a Popeye cartoon or some such.

Turned out to be a pretty fair little ol' movie, too, about this traveler from space, landing out in some godforsaken wilderness where some scientist and his daughter and his assistant (a real stinker, as things turned out) had staked out the territory in the hope of communicating with the spaceman. Oh, and also, a newspaperman who had known the good-guy scientist from college days. They (whoever they are) call these movies "escapism," like an escape from reality, but for my money it felt more like I was almost watching a documentary account of what might have happened with that Roswell crash. That is, if anybody had known or revealed any details of what had happened at Roswell or made the Parts Off Limits public knowledge.

Creepy little picture, it was, and that so-called "Man from Planet X" looked about as otherworldly as I could imagine—like a shriveled-up real guy, lost on unfamiliar turf and none too happy to be there, 'specially when that crooked lab assistant started roughin' him up to make him spill his spaceman secrets. No fair giving away the outcome in case you might want to take a squint at that now antiquated stretch of Celluloid one of these days, but suffice to say things turned out okay for those who deserved for things to turn out okay. And my kid liked it okay, too, and that was more than okay. He didn't seem the least little bit scared. That was his Poppa's lot.

It left an impression, I mean to tell you, that "Man from Planet X." But I tried not to show it. I'm a businessman, a metal man, a machine man. Things have to get done and I have responsibilities that don't allow for dwelling on such outlandish nonsense. But I'd be lying if I said I wasn't about halfway creeped out. Not constantly, mind you, but in a kind of a recurring way that could be triggered by the damnedest chance reminders. Like when they declared Wild Horse Lake deadsville and rolled out dozers and filled in what was left of it.

Was it Jonathan Andrew Prescott's fault?

Businessmen with full-length, bright lights monikers didn't make those kinds of mistakes. Weren't allowed to.

Except in their own noggins. Which probably made me susceptible to what became my own personal "Man from Planet X" story, coming a couple of years after we'd gone to see that movie. I was in my office at Clowe & Cowan's H.K., or Head Kwarters, as ol' Bogardus would say, and Billie Sue Lovelady, the switchboard operator, hollered over as to how she was about to put through a long-distance call to my desk. Except she called it "a long distant call," without trying to be clever. Well, sir, this one was mighty distant, but it didn't last very long.

"This is Jonathan Andrew Prescott, speaking," I answered.

"This is Mr. So-and-So," said the caller, "from Planet X."

He didn't really say, "So-and-So," but I was too taken aback by the "Planet X" part to catch his right name.

Thought for a second that it might be my brother–in–law, on account of he had noticed that that movie had kind of unnerved me at the time, but I'd have recognized that emphatic Foghorn Leghorn voice of his, and he wouldn't be calling long-distance, anyhow. Besides, he knew better than to pull any shenanigans or tomfoolery around me.

So I said, right back into the telephone: "I beg your pardon?"

The caller answered, in a kind of a lazy drawl: "I said, 'This is Mr. So-and-So, from Planet X.'"

"Okay," I said back at him, "so where are you calling from?"

"I'm from Planet X. I'm calling from Earth!"

Enough was enough was too much. So I hung up on the jerk.

Moments later, Billie Sue shot through a second "long-distant" call. It was a return engagement, except now the caller sounded mighty honked off. He said, in mechanical, deliberate tones: "This is Mr. So–and–So. I work for Southwestern Gas & Electric Co.'s Plant X, P–L–A–N–T–X, in the town of Earth, Texas."

"Well," I said right back at him, "how come you didn't say so, to begin with?"

"I did say so," he barked, but before he could call me a dense knucklehead or any other derisive some such, like I figured he was about to do, I just reassured him that, sure, I knew all about the power company's Plant X branch and the Plains-area town of Earth, Texas, and of course SWG&E was a good established customer of ours, and so on and so forth. Which he knew, already, naturally, but anything to dissuade him from calling me stupid or rude or whatever he was about to call me. We wound up transacting some business on behalf of Plant X—P–L–A–N–T, that is—because, like I said, that is what I did on account of I am a businessman, first and foremostly.

I'll still swear to it that the guy had said, "Planet X," on that first call, but there's always the off–chance that I was just feeling some delayed paranoid reaction from all those peculiarities left over from Roswell and *The Man from Planet X* screening.

Or then again, maybe the caller's natural-born drawl had just inserted an extra syllillillable into the word "Plant." Go figure. Anyhow, weirder things have happened, but not lately—until the other day.

Wild Horse Lake, now long gone, re-emerged as a grassless lawn, an empty patch on an otherwise limitless grassy plain. Nothing would grow there. Highfalutin city planners zoned it commercial, then industrial, then commercial again, the sequel, but with nary a taker or staker. No one would touch it. Then, a group of businessmen and metal men and machine men said enough shenanigans, and enough tomfoolery. We will build what the people from our world call a mega-mall there, with mega-mechanized stairways and meg-mechanized shopping. Everything under the sun.

They're not even going to closed on Sundays.

melinda pouncey (signature)

An Ill Wind Blows Good
by Melinda Pouncey

The day was hot and humid, just like most days in southeast Texas, too miserable to cut the grass or attend a graveside service. Bill fired up the John Deere in the sweltering midmorning to take his mind off the funeral he dared not attend. Two hours later, forced indoors, he grabbed a beer from the fridge before dropping down onto the couch in the den and snapping on the television.

He had thought keeping busy today would help him forget but, from the flower boxes abutting the patio to the ridiculous little throw pillows on the chairs in the den, every part of the house displayed her touch. Even the football highlight reels on TV brought painful memories flooding in. Tears misted his eyes and he brushed them away, taking another swallow from the bottle. Hard to believe how quickly life could change.

Just ten days ago they stood out by the drive, necking like teenagers before she pulled away and gave him a smile.

"Come back inside, Junebug," he said. "You still have a couple of hours."

"I truly don't. I have to stop by Dora's and see the grandkids, then I have to run by the store. I still have the books to do this month."

"Another half hour?" he wheedled, kissing her and nuzzling her neck. Damn, she smelled good.

"Not another minute now, Billy," she asserted, giving him a peck on the lips and running a hand over his chest. She stepped away and his arms instantly felt empty. "Don't worry, hon, I'll come over again next weekend," she said, in response to his crestfallen look.

"How about I fire up the smoker and we can have a barbeque?"

"That sounds nice. I'll make dessert." There was a brief pause as they stood looking at each other, both reluctant to say goodbye. He seized the opportunity to pull her in for one last hug before releasing her.

She moved away, then turned and gave a playful wiggle of her white capri-clad hips and blew him a kiss before hopping in her pickup.

"Don't miss me too much, hon," she teased, her blue eyes twinkling with mischief and affection.

Her bottle-blonde bouffant gave a little bounce as she turned her head to back out of the drive. He gave her a last wave he knew she couldn't see, then headed into the house wearing the smile she always put on his face. He was already making plans for the following weekend.

The harsh jangle of the phone startled him from his thoughts.

He picked up the handset from the end table, sighing when he saw the caller ID. He didn't want to answer but that wasn't an option. If he didn't, she'd be on his doorstep with a casserole in no time and he'd never get rid of her.

"Hello, Linda."

"How you doin', Bubba?"

"How do you think?" he snapped. "The funeral was today."

"I know that."

Linda sounded peevish. His fault for getting angry but he was grieving and here she was playing mother hen, as usual. There was a brief pause and he could feel the weight of her unspoken affront slam against his temple through the receiver.

"What I meant," she continued, softening her tone, "is how are you holding up? Would you like me to come over tonight?"

Her interest in his well-being came yoked to an intrinsically superior air that reminded him of their mother, always mistimed and nigh impossible to escape once bestowed. Still, he accepted the olive branch. He didn't want an argument, not now.

"I'm doin' all right," he lied. "Just got in from the yard. The grass needed cutting and edging. Got a few other little chores yet to keep busy. I think what I need is just to be alone right now."

"I understand," she said. Her tone suggested she was put out that he didn't jump at her offer. Not his problem. "If you change your mind," she added, "give me a call. Don't you wallow now, and don't drink too much."

His voice rose. "What is that supposed to mean? If I want to get drunk I think I'm entitled." He took a deep breath. "Look, Linda, I appreciate your concern but it will be all right. I just... I just..." Bill's voice cracked and he clutched the phone tighter, covered his eyes with one hand. The whole conversation was taking on a sense of unreality. His head was beginning to ache. "I have to go. I promise to call if I need anything," he said, hanging up before she could protest.

He turned the TV off and finished his beer in two gulps then went into the kitchen and brought back a bottle of whisky. Despite his sister's advice, or maybe to spite her, he proceeded to get drunk while flipping through pictures of his beloved June on his cell. It was all the little moments he found himself remembering now that she was gone: her cheeks flushed with excitement when she watched the Texans play, her uninhibited, but never vulgar, dancing to the honkytonk music she loved, the determined way she hoisted her rifle to her shoulder to take aim at a ten point buck.

She had that elusive something he was certain only southern women possessed, an effortless genteel veneer over a core of indomitable strength. She was funny, sassy, smart, just a little wicked, and he loved her more than he had ever loved anyone. He didn't know how he was going to live without her, or live with the knowledge he had killed her.

"Oh, Junebug, I'm so sorry," he muttered, his voice thick with tears and drink.

He didn't know what time he finally passed out, but he was awakened in the small hours of the morning to the muffled sound of Willie Nelson's 'Always on my Mind'. It was their song and his ringtone for her.

Disoriented, Bill groped around for the phone, digging it out of the couch cushions just as the music stopped. The screen flashed a missed call from June's number.

Now wide awake and beginning to sweat, he struggled to his feet and stumbled to the bathroom, to make an abrupt offering of whisky and bile to the porcelain god. Carl, June's husband, must have found his number in her phone.

Panicked, Bill splashed cold water on his face and went into the living room where he peered through the blinds, half expecting to see June's husband charging up the drive, gun in hand. He checked his phone again but there was no trace of a missed call. No alert, no voicemail message, nothing in the call log. He had heard grief could do strange things to a person's mind but had never expected anything like this.

Bill went outside and the smell of early morning mist and fresh cut grass cleared his head a bit. It had to have been a dream, right?

Had to be.

He went back inside, showered and dressed for work. It was too early to clock in but maybe he'd stop by the Waffle House for breakfast.

He fired up his truck and headed out, turning his thoughts to eggs and black coffee. Still not feeling fully awake he pulled onto the wrong highway and sped along without conscious thought. His phone lay on the passenger seat with the ringer turned to mute. An occasional glance almost convinced him it had all been a figment of his troubled mind.

His aimless driving soon found him on a lonely stretch of two lane highway, a gauntlet of pines standing tall along both sides. The early morning fog was just dense enough to necessitate the use of low beams and to obscure familiar signs and landmarks. Even though the sun was rising rapidly the trees were thick enough to keep the highway in relative shadow, so he didn't realize where he was until he saw the tire tracks. Then the sick realization struck him. This was it, the location of the accident.

Slowing down, Bill noted the mile marker and the set of deep tracks zigzagged into the ditch halfway to the tree line. The news report said the truck had flipped, killing the driver instantly—single vehicle, one fatality. Police thought she had swerved to avoid a deer, mistaken the accelerator for the brakes, and lost control. But Bill knew what the police didn't and what he hoped they'd never find out. June couldn't have braked if she'd tried. The brakes on that truck didn't work.

Why cutting those brakes had been any kind of solution in his mind Bill didn't know now, but at the time it had seemed the only way. June had expressed her unhappiness on numerous occasions. Marrying Carl had been a mistake, she said. He was a mechanic and he had a classic Chevy pickup he had spent his life refurbishing and maintaining. June said he used to joke when they were dating that it was the only thing he loved as much as her. She was amused by the notion at first, regarding his love for the truck as nothing more than a hobby. But when she looked back over her marriage, she came to the inescapable conclusion that the truck was more obsession than hobby, and it robbed her and the children of his time and affection. The more their marriage cooled, the more June found herself bored and increasingly jealous of Carl's "mistress."

"I'll tell you something naughty," she had said to Bill a couple of weeks ago when they were lounging in bed enjoying a steamy afterglow. "I think about scratching a key down the side of that Chevy sometimes or taking out the headlights with a baseball bat. You know he told me a couple of months ago he wants to be buried in the thing. Can you imagine?" June's head was on his chest and he was toying with a strand of her hair. "I don't think he's joking."

"Can you imagine the irony if the truck buries him first?" Bill grinned at the thought.

"What do you mean, hon?"

"I don't know, like an accident or something."

"Don't even joke about that, Billy," she said. She propped up on one arm and slapped him on the chest with the other in mock outrage. "Besides," she said settling in again, "he never lets anyone drive it. Hell, he barely drives it himself, only to car shows and cruise nights."

"When is the next show? Are you going with him this time?"

"Nah, I'm not invited. It's September, in Georgia. He'll be gone for a whole week. But he's taking it to Houston soon for a test run and to buy some parts."

That was when the idea first began to form. If Carl had an accident June would get his insurance and they would both be free. The kids were grown now, no reason for her to stay with him except she was afraid of what he might do if she left. Carl was not normally violent, but he had struck and threatened her once when he thought she was being too friendly to a customer at the garage. He told her then, in a drunken rage, she had better never even think about leaving him or they would be sharing a grave.

It didn't take much for the initial brainstorm to become a tempest. Bill began searching online for the things he would need: how to make a key impression, how to circumvent security cameras, where to find the brake line on a '65 Chevy C10. He felt like a fool that night, sneaking around dressed in black like some sort of redneck ninja, but he had managed to complete his mission undetected.

'Things are going to change for the better now,' he thought.

Well, change they had—but not for the better.

Bill would never know why she had been driving a truck she wasn't allowed near and he didn't really want to. It couldn't possibly matter at this point. "I hope you know I would change places with you in a heartbeat if I could, Junebug," he whispered.

He turned around and headed back the right direction, so lost in thought he almost didn't see the deer that darted out in front of him. He applied the brakes vigorously, leaving skid marks on the highway. It was early morning and seeing a deer wasn't unusual, but coming on the heels of all the rest, it was a grim omen.

Bill spent the day in a state of gloom and agitation. The events of the morning stuck with him well into the afternoon, along with a lingering hangover. As if that wasn't bad enough he made so many mistakes at work his supervisor started asking if he was okay. All he wanted to do was go home and fall into bed and forget the nightmare his world had become.

On the way home, he stopped to put gas in his SUV and the screen on the pump popped up the news. A Category 4 hurricane that had formed in the Gulf a few days ago was bearing down on Corpus Christi. Bill mumbled a quick prayer for the people down there and slotted his credit card in the pump. A woman entering the convenience store caught his eye—blonde hair, petite figure, white capris. Just before she disappeared inside she gave her hips a little wiggle and glanced over her shoulder. The awning over the door threw her face into shadow, obscuring her features.

The familiarity made Bill's heart race. The world bobbed and weaved for a moment as he stood stunned. Then he bolted into the store and strode up and down the aisles trying to find her. The kid behind the counter took notice.

"Can I help you?"

Bill ignored him at first, but when his search turned up nothing, he responded. "Did you see a woman come in here? White pants, blue top, blonde?"

"No sir."

"Come on, are you sure? Maybe she went to the bathroom?"

As if in answer, a black woman came through the door marked 'Restrooms'. She frowned at the two men looking at her.

"What? Bathroom's still free isn't it?"

"Yes ma'am," the kid said. Both men dropped their gaze. The kid stared at the register, Bill picked up a candy bar from the shelf he was standing next to then put it back.

The black woman left the store and Bill scanned the parking lot. Then, he went back to the restrooms. The women's and men's bathrooms were both empty.

Bill realized he had forgotten to remove his credit card from the slot when he went chasing after the mystery woman. When he went back out to the pump, it was gone.

Cursing, Bill dug his cash stash out of the hidden pocket in his visor and paid for the gas. Next, he called the company to cancel the card. He was almost home by the time he got the account frozen. When he hung up, there was a text message from June's number. He opened it with trembling hands.

We still on for next weekend, hon?

Bill he threw the phone on the seat and ran into the house.

For an hour he paced the floor unsure of what to do next.

Dammit, why was he getting so upset? Someone was playing cat and mouse with him that was all. Someone who knew his secret.

He thought he had been so careful, so clever. But he must have been seen. Now this person was tormenting him, trying to get him to confess.

"Nice try, whoever you are," he growled to the empty air. "You don't know who you're messin' with if you think you can make Bill Wooten crack so easily."

The phone rang then and he nearly jumped out of his skin.

No, he thought. It couldn't be. He picked up.

"Thank goodness you're home," Linda chirped.

Bill's stomach sank into his shoes. "What's up?"

"It's all over the news," she continued. "Carl has been arrested. The police think June's accident wasn't an accident. The truck's brakes were tampered with. Oh, Bill, I'm so sorry. I knew he was a shitheel, but I never thought he'd do anything like that."

Bill grasped the end table for support and lowered himself onto the couch.

"He did what?"

"Carl killed her, Bubba. I'm so so sorry," she was practically weeping now.

Bill felt he should console her but he didn't know what to say. She really knew nothing at all about Carl, just what he had told her that June had told him. Now, he regretted it. This was all turning into grist for the town gossip mill. He wondered if Linda would be his undoing. How many of her friends knew about his affair? Linda told him she hadn't told a soul, but wasn't that what busybodies always said?

"Terrible news, Linda." His brain was on autopilot. "What makes them think Carl did it?

"It's just common sense isn't it? Carl's a mechanic, it was a problem with the truck."

"But she was driving his truck."

"Exactly. Just how fiendish is that? You said he never let her drive it. He must have messed with the brakes then sent her out on that highway in it, hoping something like that would happen. Plausible deniability, Bubba. But it's come back to bite him now. I hope he fries for it."

"Me too," Bill said. "Thanks for letting me know. I'm going to check the news report."

Linda was sniffling now. "You take care of yourself, Bubba. You have had too much grief lately. I'm going to come over tomorrow with a casserole. I know you like to think you're strong but you're going to need help with this. I won't take no for an answer, hear?"

"Sure, sure, that will be fine." He didn't want this conversation to go on any longer.

He hung up and turned on the television. It was too late for the six o'clock news, so he'd have to wait until ten. He went out to his SUV and got his phone, almost afraid to look—but there was nothing there.

Disturbing, but not unexpected. Especially in light of the morning's events.

Bill did a phone search and found the article on the local news channel. No video, just text: 'Local Man Arrested for Wife's Murder', and a few lines about the suspicion of foul play. Under the headline and before the story were side by side pictures of June and the wrecked truck.

Foul play.

Bill slumped back against the couch and scrubbed at his face with one hand. This was turning into a shitshow of epic proportions. He thought of the call and text from June's number. Maybe it was the police stringing him along, trying to see how much he knew. This kind of thing was just the sort of trick he occasionally saw on CSI or Law and Order. Drawing the killer out, getting them to make a mistake that would implicate them.

Nope. He wouldn't be falling for that old chestnut.

The next time he got one of those calls he was going to answer and maybe get some answers of his own. Play it like he had nothing to hide. That was the way to handle it. They couldn't prove anything, he had been too careful. In a way, the thought of police involvement settled his jangled nerves. A sound, logical explanation was what he needed.

For the next several hours he fiddled with the phone, checking for texts and calls, fiddling with the apps. The phone record of his conversations would suggest that he and June were having an affair, but that was all the more reason for Carl to have killed her. Jealous husband and all that. Bill had been devastated by June's death. Linda could attest to that. But would she attest to it in court?

The top story on the TV was the hurricane hitting Corpus Christi. The destruction was heartbreaking and there was talk of the storm turning and heading north. Jesus! He didn't want to have to worry about hurricane preparations on top of everything else. Just before the news switched to weather an anchorwoman mentioned that the accident that had been reported last week was now a suspected homicide. The police investigation had revealed that the brake line was cut. The husband would be arraigned Friday.

Bill turned off the TV and got ready for bed. But just as he was settling in, the clock radio came on and Bill and June's song filled the room. He knocked the clock off the nightstand in his haste to turn it off. He sat on the edge of the bed staring at the radio like it might jump up and bite him. It was going to be a rough night.

He pulled himself wearily out of bed in the morning after only dozing intermittently through the night. The unplugged radio sat quietly on the nightstand. It wasn't like he expected it to start playing again after he turned it off, but...yeah, well, maybe he did. He was so tired he wouldn't be worth shooting at work.

Fortunately, the hurricane was such a major topic of conversation there was not much work getting done anyway. There was talk of shutting down over the next couple of days if the situation warranted, and if that happened he would have to work double shifts next week. Nobody was planning to evacuate just yet, but guys with families were considering it. Everyone was keeping an eye on the situation. Bill just missed June. If she was still alive, he knew they would be trying to figure out some way to hole up together and weather the storm side by side.

Bill knew he had to stock up before he went home because there would be nothing on the store shelves tomorrow. He stayed prepared for the most part this time of year but he did need batteries and extra water. There was also the possibility the windows would have to be boarded up if the storm looked like it was coming toward Houston; but he wasn't in a hurry to mount that kind of work effort unless he had to. The community had seen this kind of thing before. After hurricane Rita in '05 Emergency Management had gotten their shit together. Some of his coworkers were even talking about hosting hurricane parties.

When Bill got home that evening, he found a detective waiting for him.

"Mr. Wooten, I'm detective Malone. I'd like to ask you a few questions."

This was it, the visit he'd been dreading. And sooner than he expected.

His palms were so sweaty he almost dropped the case of water he was carrying. "Sure, won't you come in?"

The detective followed him through the mudroom and kitchen, where Bill stopped to put the water on the counter, and on into the den.

"Do you know why I'm here, Mr. Wooten?"

"No, not really."

"You haven't been watching the news?"

"I caught it last night. There's a storm coming in. Have a seat."

The detective moved a throw pillow and seated himself on a chair while Bill took his usual place on the couch.

"Nothing about June Windham?"

"Oh, yes. There was something about the accident."

"Her husband has been arrested."

"So I heard."

"But you were having an affair with her."

Bill swallowed and looked the detective in the eye. "I was."

"Well that was easy. I thought you might not want to admit it."

"I didn't want to but it's the truth. We tried to be discreet but I'm sure you saw the texts on her phone."

"No, she was definitely discreet. Your number was written on a piece of paper we found in her purse."

"Then why did you think she was having an affair?"

"There had to be some motive for her death and that usually tops the list."

"So you just showed up here on a hunch?"

"One that seems to have paid off." The detective took out a notebook. "What did you know about their relationship?"

"Just that she said it wasn't a happy one. She indicated that he had been abusive in the past."

"And you believed her?"

"I did."

"Did you ever meet her husband?"

"He worked on my car sometimes. He wasn't a friend or acquaintance."

"You don't consider a mechanic an acquaintance?"

"More of a service person I'd say."

"Interesting distinction. Would you be willing to come down to the station Wednesday and answer a few more questions? Nothing formal, you're not in trouble. We just need all the information we can get on this case."

"I have a shift that day. With the hurricane I might be working doubles for a while. I can give you my schedule."

"That will be fine." He handed Bill his card. "Give me a call Monday and let me know what days you're available."

"Will do."

"Thanks for your time, Mr. Wooten."

He got up to leave, picking up the throw pillow and putting it back on the chair. He smiled at Bill. "A woman's touch."

Bill laughed. "Yes, those were not my idea."

"All right, Mr. Wooten. Thank you for your time. Have a nice weekend."

"You too, Mr... ." he looked at the card. "Mr. Malone."

Bill showed the detective out and after a few minutes went out to the patio on the pretext of watering the flowers to make sure the guy was gone. He had no more than gotten back in the house than his cell started playing the familiar ringtone. By the time he got to it, the call was ended.

There had been no indication from the detective that he was a suspect. They weren't playing him. But wouldn't they make it appear that way if they were?

No. He was reading too much into all this. He wasn't going to lose his shit like some character from a cheap pulp novel just because of a few odd incidents.

Thankfully, there were no calls over the weekend. And nothing strange or out of the ordinary happened. However, the threat of the hurricane increased by the day. Now the prediction was for it to slow churn and dump enormous quantities of water over the Houston area. He was called in to work a double shift on Sunday and Monday. His schedule was changed to give him Wednesday off but he didn't call detective Malone. The investigation would have to wait.

Then the rains came and they were unlike anything the area had ever seen. There was a gray, apocalyptic feel to the deluge that almost seemed permanent. Rainfall totals were skyrocketing and Bill worried that his house might not make it. He got his boat prepared and had supplies packed in the event his place started to take on water and he had to flee. He called Linda to check on her, but she and her husband had their preparations in order and were doing well. As night began to fall, Bill heated up the last of Linda's casserole for supper and topped it off with a pint of Blue Bell ice cream, in case the power went out (or so he told himself).

The brief respite from the rain broke and he could hear it coming down so loud it threatened to drown out the TV. He peered out the window, alarmed to see the water rising. Why did the worst of the storms always happen at night with these hurricanes?

Around midnight the local power grid crashed. For a long time the only sound was the sequestered rain pouring through gutters and downspouts too overwhelmed to keep up with the massive flow. Then, Bill heard another sound.

Thump.

Thump.

Thump.

Bill shined his flashlight out the back door to see the water had now risen to the edge of the patio. As alarming as this was, it was nothing compared to the sight of the object thumping against his shed.

A casket.

Bill blinked to make sure his mind hadn't taken a dive off the deep end, but it was really there. A blue and gold casket was floating on the floodwater like a macabre boat, bumping over and over into his shed as the rain thundered down from the black sky.

It was impossible. But there, before his terrified eyes, the lid of the casket opened and a shape rose from inside. The beam of his flashlight caught the glint of a wisp of honey-gold hair that disappeared in the torrent of rain. The thing tried to pull itself up and out of the casket but because it was floating free it swayed and tipped, causing the body to fall into the dark water.

Bill was frozen to the spot, the flashlight dancing in his shaking hand. The body began to crawl toward the patio until it was on solid footing. It then stood and shambled toward him. She wore her blue Sunday dress but she was barefoot. A string of faux pearls adorned her neck but it was already beginning to sag with the weight of the water, and Bill was transfixed as the string gave way, sending the beads into the rising water.

The decomposition process had begun despite embalming, no surprise in the Texas heat. Her sagging face showed red beneath her eyes and there were black blotches where the skin had already begun to fall away.

Her hair was plastered to her cheeks and neck, some of it literally falling off her shoulders in the downpour.

This shape, this thing, this former love of his life was alternately revealed and cast into darkness by the wild movement of the light Bill held. He gripped the flashlight with both hands to steady it, watching in helpless horror as she came nearer, nearer...

"Damned bastard didn't even have them put my shoes on," she rasped, through jaws filled with cotton.

Bill fainted.

The flooding was immense, whole neighborhoods, whole communities, drowned out, but Bill was one of the lucky ones. Not only did his house weather the storm, the water never reached his door, though his shed and its contents were a loss. The insurance would take care of that. As for the rest, the investigation, Carl's trial, all that would take care of itself in time too, he was sure. The hurricane had been nothing but a blessing for him. It was the night he got June back.

He came in through the mudroom and grabbed a beer on his way through the kitchen.

"You want a beer, baby?" he called.

"Sure thing, hon. Did you wipe your feet before you came in?"

Bill went back out and did just that, then snagged a beer for her too. He opened it for her—she still had some motor skill issues—and plopped down on the couch, putting an arm around her shoulders.

"I'm so glad you're back, Junebug," he said, nuzzling her ear. "When I saw you out there I was afraid you came back because you were mad at me."

"Never," she said, patting him on the thigh. "I'm just glad you have that smoker. It would have taken forever for me to dry out otherwise."

"Anything for you, angel," he said. He couldn't remember the last time he'd been this content.

"Now give me that remote, Billy boy," she said with a twinkle in her milky blue eyes. "I think the Texans are playing today."

About your Texas Authors

SAMANTHA ANDRASKO

A resident of North Texas, Samantha Andrasko is a student of Southern Methodist University's The Writer's Path. She is currently working on her first novel and can be found online @SamAndrasko on Twitter.

JACKLYN BAKER

Jacklyn Baker is a native Texan currently living in the Dallas area. She is a member of the SMU Writers Path and spends much of her time with her writing group, "the Hive." When not writing she relaxes with her two cats, drinking tea and wondering if today will be the day something finally drags her into the crawl space beneath her house. Her short story "Southern Hospitality" appeared in the second volume of *Road Kill: Texas Horror by Texas Writers*.

E. R. BILLS

E. R. Bills is an author, journalist and screenwriter born and raised in Texas. A co-creator of *Road Kill: Texas Horror by Texas Writers*, Texas' first horror anthology, Bills has been an editor and contributor to the annual collection since its inception in 2016. His nonfiction titles include *Texas Obscurities: Stories of the Peculiar, Exceptional and Nefarious* (History Press, 2013), *The 1910 Slocum Massacre: An Act of Genocide in East Texas* (History Press, 2014), *Black Holocaust: The Paris Horror and a Legacy of Texas Terror* (Eakin Press, 2015), *Texas Far & Wide: The Tornado With Eyes, Gettysburg's Last Casualty, The Celestial Skipping Stone and Other Tales* (History Press, 2017), and *100 Things to Do in Texas Before You Die* (Reedy Press, 2018). Bills also writes for publications around the state, including *Texas Highways*, *Texas Co-Op Power* and *Fort Worth Weekly*. He received an honors degree in Journalism from Texas State University in 1990 and currently lives in North Texas with his wife, Stacie.

SHAWNA BORMAN
Shawna Borman graduated magna cum laude from Southern Methodist University in 2012 with a BA in English specializing in Creative Writing. During her time at SMU, Shawna won second place in the school's annual fiction contest, as well as the Margaret Terry Crooks Award for Most Outstanding Creative Writing Student. She also earned an MFA in Creative Writing from the University of Southern Maine's Stonecoast program in January 2015. Shawna is currently focused on her novel-in-progress, *Garnets and Guardians*, and, though she dabbles in all genres, her true love is horror. She resides in Texas with her father.

MADISON ESTES
Madison Estes lives in Magnolia, Texas with her family and three dogs. She grew up near Houston and graduated from Lonestar College with an Associate of Arts degree. She has had work featured in *Inkling Magazine*, *One Sentence Poems*, *Enter the Aftermath* by TANSTAAFL Press and *A Wink and a Smile* by Smoking Pen Press. Her work will also be appearing in *Transcendent* by Transmundane Press and in the non-fiction anthology *The Daily Abuse*. In her spare time, she enjoys reading, drawing, sculpting, swimming, and volunteering with children who have special needs. You can find her on Twitter @madisonestes or Instagram @madisonpaigeestes

JEREMY HEPLER

Native to the Texas Panhandle, Jeremy Hepler is a Bram Stoker nominated author who lives in the heart of Texas with his wife Tricia and son Noah. He has had twenty-four short stories published in various professional markets, placed second in the Panhandle Professional Writers short story contest in 2014, and his debut novel, *The Boulevard Monster*, was published by Bloodshot Books in April 2017. For more information hit him up on Twitter (@JeremyHepler), Facebook, or Instagram.

JAMES H. LONGMORE
James hails originally from Yorkshire, England having relocated with his family to Houston, Texas in 2010. He has an honors degree in Zoology and a background in sales, marketing and business. His writing style and storytelling has already been compared to James Herbert, Richard Laymon, Stephen King, Dan Brown and Robert Ludlum. An Affiliate Member of the Horror Writer's Association, and founder of HellBound Books Publishing LLC, James has to date five novels published, plus his definitive short story collection, all in addition to three novellas and a whole bunch of short stories dotted about in myriad anthologies.

www.jameslongmore.com
www.hellboundbookspublishing.com

BRET McCORMICK
A native Texan, Bret McCormick has been writing fantastic fiction since the early 1970s. From 1984 to 1996 he wrote, produced and directed indie films for worldwide distribution. His 1986 gorefest, The Abomination, has a rabid cult following. His recent *Texas Schlock* is a popular nonfiction book which examines B-Movie sci-fi and horror produced in the

Lone Star state. Bret lives with his partner, Patrice, four dogs and four birds in Bedford, Texas.

AARON MILSTEAD

A novelist and short story writer, Aaron Milstead is a lecturer at Stephen F. Austin University and the author of the 2015 horror title *They Don't Check Out*. His next offering, *Ear Worm*, will be published by Blood Bound Books. He lives in the Piney Woods of East Texas with his wife and three children.

DENNIS PITTS

Dennis Pitts is a Texas author who primarily pens short stories, one of which was featured in *Road Kill: Texas Horror by Texas Writers, Vol. 2*. He also writes science fiction and is currently working a short story collection that revolves around a post-World War II detective in Fort Worth.

MELINDA POUNCEY

A psychologist by training, Melinda Pouncey has a particular interest in the psychological element of fiction. An avid reader of horror, science fiction, and fantasy from an early age, she recently decided to pursue writing in these genres. Preferring the succinct punchiness of short stories to novels, Melinda enjoys infusing her work with humor and twist (or twisted) endings.

MICHAEL H. PRICE

Michael H. Price is lead author of the long-running *Forgotten Horrors* series of film-history books and a prolific author-illustrator of such graphic novels and horror-comics anthologies as *Fishhead & Other Carney Gothic Horrors* (with Joe R. Lansdale and Mark Evan

Walker), *Leo Kragg: Prowler* (with Timothy Truman), *Ghosts & Girls of Fiction House*, and *Deep in the Horrors of Texas* (with Frank Thorne and Jack "Jaxon" Jackson). Price's original artwork is represented by Heritage Galleries of London and New York.

BRYCE WILSON
Bryce Wilson is an author and critic living in Austin, Texas. His stories have been featured in *Road Kill: Texas Horror by Texas Writers, Vol. 2*, *The Edge: Infinite Darkness*, *This Book Is Cursed* and *Switchblade Magazine*. His books *Son Of Danse Macabre* and *The Unquiet Dead* are available for purchase online. He can be reached at bryced021@gmail.com.

ALSO AVAILABLE on AMAZON.COM

Road Kill: Texas Horror by Texas Writers: Vol 1

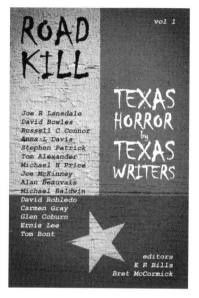

An ancient demon plays cowboy and *takes on* the Texas Rangers. Three teenage girls sneak into a "body farm." An aging African American couple defies the Grim Reaper. An FBI agent discovers an entire city that's gone to the "dogs." A handyman learns that the fixer-upper he's working on has a doorway to the past that's way out of square. And a pack of possums burrow into the body politic. Join seventeen Texas authors for a harrowing spin on the twisting freeways and dark back roads that wind through the Lone Star State. Includes works from Joe R. Lansdale, David Bowles, Anna L. Davis, Stephen Patrick, Carmen Gray, Russell C. Connor, Michael H. Price, Tom Bont, Ernie Lee, David Robledo, Alan Beauvais, Michael Baldwin, Glen Coburn, Joe McKinney, Tom Alexander, Bret McCormick and E. R. Bills.

Road Kill: Texas Horror by Texas Writers: Vol 2

A hanging tree takes the law into its own limbs in "The Tree Servant." A mother's love is tested by the walking, crawling and thumb-sucking dead in "Mama's Babies." A famous author lays his process bare in "A Writer's Lot." Not for the faint of heart, this terrifying batch of Texas horror fiction delivers a host of literary demons who will be hard to shake once they get comfortable.

The second volume of the critically acclaimed *Road Kill Series* from Eakin Press, featuring seventeen Texas writers. Some of the writers are established and have been published in a variety of mediums, while others are upcoming writers who bring a wealth of talent and imagination. Edited by E. R. Bills and Bret McCormick, this collection of horror stories is sure to bring chills and make the imagination run wild. Writers include Jacklyn Baker, Andrew Kozma, Ralph Robert Moore, Jeremy Hepler, R. J. Joseph, James H. Longmore, Mario E. Martinez, E. R. Bills, Summer Baker, Dennis Pitts, Keith West, S. Kay Nash, Bryce Wilson, Bonnie Jo Stufflebeam, Stephen Patrick, Crystal Brinkerhoff and Hayden Gilbert.

<u>Other HellBound Books Titles</u>
<u>Available at: www.hellboundbookspublishing.com</u>

<u>Graveyard Girls</u>

Female authors + Horror = something spectacularly terrifying! A delicious collection of horrific tales and darkest poetry from the cream of the crop, all lovingly compiled by the incomparable Gerri R Gray! Nestling between the covers of this formidable tome are twenty-five of the very best lady authors writing on the horror scene today!

These tales of terror are guaranteed to chill your very soul and awaken you in the dead of the night with fear-sweat clinging to your every pore and your heart pounding hard and heavy in your labored breast…

Featuring superlative horror from: Xtina Marie, M. W. Brown, Rebecca Kolodziej, Anya Lee, Barbara Jacobson, Gerri R. Gray, Christina Bergling, Julia Benally, Olga Werby, Kelly Glover, Lee Franklin, Linda M. Crate, Vanessa Hawkins, P. Alanna Roethle, J Snow, Evelyn Eve, Serena Daniels, S. E. Davis, Sam Hill, J. C. Raye, Donna J. W. Munro, R. J. Murray, C. Bailey-Bacchus, Varonica Chaney, Marian Finch (Lady Marian).

Schlock! Horror!

An anthology of short stories based upon/inspired by and in loving homage to all of those great gorefest movies and books of the 1980's (not necessarily base in that era, although some do ride that wave of nostalgia!), the golden age when horror well and truly came kicking, screaming and spraying blood, gore & body parts out from the shadows...

This exemplary 80's themed/inspired tales of terror has been adjudicated and compiled by one Mr Bret McCormick, himself a writer, producer and director of many a schlock classic, including *Bio-Tech Warrior*, *Time Tracers*, *The Abomination*, *Ozone: The Attack of the Redneck Mutants* and the inimitable *Repligator*.

Featuring stories from: Todd Sullivan, Timothy C Hobbs, Mark Thomas, Andrew Post, James B. Pepe, Thomas Vaughn, Edward Karpp, Jaap Boekestein, Lisa Alfano, L. C. Holt, John Adam Gosham, Brandon Cracraft, M. Earl Smith, Sarah Cannavo, James Gardner, Bret McCormick, and James H. Longmore.

Demons, Devils & Denizens of Hell: Vol, 2

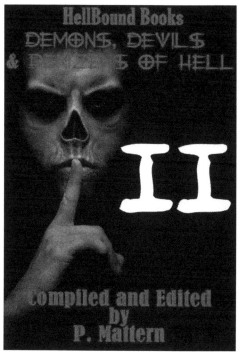

The second volume in HellBound Books' outstanding horror anthology fair teems with tales of Hades' finest citizens – both resident and vacationing in our earthly realm…

Compiled by the inimitable P. Mattern and featuring: Savannah Morgan, Andrew MacKay, Jaap Boekestein, James H. Longmore, Stephanie Kelley, Ryan Woods, James Nichols, P. Mattern, Marcus Mattern, Gerri R Gray, and legion more…

Shopping List 2: Another Horror Anthology

Once again, HellBound Books brings you an outstanding collection of horror, dark, slippery things, and supernatural terror - all from the very best up and coming minds in the genre.

We have given each and every one of our authors the opportunity to have their shopping lists read by you, the most wonderful reading public, and have the darkest corners of their creative psyche laid bare for all to see...

In all, 21 stories to chill the soul, tingle the spine and keep you awake in the cold, murky hours of the night from: Erin Lee, The Truth Artist, John Barackman, Serena Daniels, M. R. Wallace, Isobel Blackthorn, Alex Laybourne, Jason J. Nugent, Josh Darling, Jovan Jones, Nick Swain, Douglas Ford, Craig Bullock, Craig Bullock, Jeff C. Stevenson, PC3, David F. Gray, Sergio Palumbo, Donna Maria McCarthy, David Clark & Megan E. Morales

**A HellBound Books LLC
Publication**

http://www.hellboundbookspublishing.com

Printed in the United States of America

Made in the USA
San Bernardino, CA
23 September 2018